ROMANCE RULES FOR WEREWOLVES

LINSEY HALL

CHAPTER
ONE

ISOBEL

MY NERVES FLUTTERED as I walked up to the reception desk in the chic hotel lobby. I didn't belong in a place like this, one of the most luxurious hotels in London. But to my complete shock, my boyfriend had invited me here for dinner. Tommy didn't usually plan such outings, and I couldn't believe my luck. Date nights were generally a takeaway curry while he watched darts on the telly.

The scent of the fresh roses filled the air, and I turned back to survey my sleek surroundings. A woman with glossy, highlighted hair marched toward the door. On her way, she shot me a brief, disdainful look.

I looked down at myself. Did my boots look wrong with my dress? If only my witchy skills included the ability to divine how to dress for a fancy human part of town like Mayfair.

I turned back to the registration desk, and the woman behind it smiled at me. "Welcome to the Regent. How may I help you?"

I smiled back and tried to sound like I did this kind of thing all the time. "I'm here for a dinner. On the roof."

Surprise flashed on her face, but she covered it quickly. Crap, I was definitely dressed wrong.

"Oh, of course," she said. "We've been waiting for you. If you'll please follow me."

She stepped out from behind the counter and led me across the lobby, past a bank of elevators with gold doors. As she walked, she turned back and said, "I'm afraid you'll have to take a service elevator, since the roof isn't open to all guests."

A wave of giddiness washed over me. This was far more elaborate than I'd been expecting. Tommy was pulling out all the stops. She led me toward a small corridor tucked around the back of the lobby and into an elevator that, though much smaller than the others I'd seen, was still beautifully decorated with marble floors and wood paneled walls.

"Wow. This is quite nice," I said.

"Only the best at the Regent." She smiled. "And special guests use this elevator occasionally. A few parts of the hotel that are reserved for our VIPs, and the roof is one of those."

"Wow." I stepped into the elevator, buzzing with excitement.

She leaned inside to press the button that would take me to the top, then smiled at me. "Enjoy your evening."

"Thank you." I leaned against the wall as the door whooshed shut, my mind spinning.

I couldn't quite believe Tommy had planned all this. Honestly, I'd been starting to think he didn't appreciate me. Maybe he'd finally realized he needed to step up his game.

The elevator stopped a few floors later, and a man pushed a room service cart inside. He wore a perfectly pressed uniform, and his brows twitched slightly when he saw me. I thought I saw surprise flash across his face, but he said nothing.

I couldn't help but notice the champagne on the cart, sitting next to two small plates covered with polished silver cloches.

When the man didn't push a button for any other floor, I realized he must be going to the roof. A little smile tugged at the corners of my mouth.

Champagne.

That was a rare treat and definitely meant that something big was going to happen tonight. We'd lived together for eight years, and we *never* drank champagne. I usually picked up something just labelled *FRENCH WHITE* because it was the cheapest. Tommy did like to splurge on whiskey, but never champagne.

As the elevator rose, the man kept shooting me glances. I smiled back, unsure whether I should say anything, so I didn't. Finally, the elevator doors opened, revealing a little foyer. The man nodded to the door opposite us. "That leads to the roof. Let me get it for you."

He pushed the cart out, then left it sitting by the wall as he opened the door. A gentle breeze blew my hair back as I stepped onto the roof, marveling at how the weather had cooperated. In London, we were more likely to get a drizzle than a lovely night for al fresco dining, especially at the beginning of autumn.

Ahead of me, a large pergola had been constructed to protect a single dining table. The pergola, built of gleaming wood, was decorated with fairy lights that perfectly illuminated the scene—

I stopped dead in my tracks, staring at Tommy and the woman who sat opposite him. She wore a stunning red dress and had a mane of golden hair that looked like she'd just stepped out of a salon. She leaned toward Tommy, her scarlet lips parting in a smile.

My stomach dropped.

The note wasn't intended for me.

I'd thought it was strange, the way it had been scrawled on the paper left on our counter instead of addressed to me. Clearly, it was a reminder for himself that he'd forgot to throw out. Somehow, Tommy's laziness in keeping his affair secret was almost more offensive than the affair itself.

I drew in a shuddery breath, pain and anger clashing inside me.

Idiot. I'm an idiot.

And the worst thing was, a big part of me wanted to slink away before they saw me. But they turned, and I stilled like a deer in headlights.

"Isobel." Surprise colored Tommy's voice. "What are you doing here?"

"I—" I drew in a shuddery breath. "What are *you* doing here?" I looked at her. "And who are you?"

She folded her arms, glaring at Tommy. "This is why you

needed to tell her sooner. Not being funny, but you're mugging her off, and it's pathetic."

I laughed, a weak sound. "We've been together for almost ten years, Tommy. How could you?"

He offered a little shrug. "I didn't think you would mind this much, honestly."

Cold shock flashed through me. "Wouldn't *mind*?"

"You're so easygoing," he said. "So accommodating."

Accommodating.

It sounded worse than if he'd called me a stone-cold bitch.

"Not being funny or anything," the beautiful woman said, and I quickly understood this was her favorite phrase, and that in all likelihood, she was probably never genuinely funny. "But Tommy told me about you. Don't take this the wrong way, love, but at the end of the day, you're a doormat. A mug." She wrinkled her little nose. "Sorry."

I stared at her, blinking. I probably had my mouth open, too, just like a fish. Here I was, thinking I was about to be proposed to, and my boyfriend's mistress was telling me that I was a doormat.

Then something wet and gloopy landed on my forehead. I looked up, spotting a pigeon flying overhead.

Perfection.

My head buzzed as I wiped the pigeon poo away, and the waiter who'd ridden in the elevator with me hurried forward with a cloth napkin. I wiped my hand off, feeling the silence in the air like an oppressive weight.

I looked back at the table. Pity flashed in the other

woman's eyes, and something snapped inside me. It lit me up like an inferno, and it felt *good*.

Deep in my belly, my magic unfurled, the dormant power awoken by anger. What the heck was I doing here?

As if he could sense the oncoming storm, Tommy said, "Come on, Isobel. Be reasonable."

"Reasonable?" I felt my brows rise, and something hysterical bubbled up inside me. "I've *been* reasonable." I looked at the other woman. "And if she's to be believed, I've been a doormat." I hated to think it about myself, but I was pretty sure she was right.

"Not a doormat," Tommy said. "Just sweet. Accommodating. That's what I like about you."

I laughed, and it sounded as mad as I felt. But this wasn't a madness driven by the loss of Tommy. It was the loss of *me*. Seeing this beautiful scene that he'd created for another woman made it so clear how I'd become a facilitator in someone else's life.

"You can have him," I said to the other woman. "You're apparently getting a better version than I ever did." I turned, intending to stalk away.

But suddenly, it didn't seem like enough.

I spun back to them, eyeing the remains of the dinner on their plates. I squinted, focusing all of my unused magic on them, and conjured a blast of wind. It appeared from seemingly out of nowhere, creating a tiny explosion of food that splattered all over their stunned faces.

Tommy glared at me, thunder in his eyes. Satisfaction surged through me. I was pretty sure that his date was human, so she had no idea what had just happened.

Tommy did, though, and as the ketchup dripped off his chin, he looked like the idiot that he was.

"Enjoy each other," I said, giving them a little wave.

As I stalked past the food service cart, I grabbed the bottle of champagne and took it with me.

CHAPTER
TWO

Isobel

I stepped into the elevator, the champagne bottle hanging from my hand. The waiter had already uncorked it. Perfect. I raised it to my mouth and took a sip. The bubbles exploded over my tongue, delicious until they took on a sour taste.

I glared at the bottle, then turned my glare to the mirrored wall. It wasn't the champagne's fault. It was Tommy's fault. *My* fault, for letting him pull one over on me like this. I rubbed at my forehead with the back of my sleeve, removing the last bit of bird poo. Mascara streaked under my eyes, and I looked a state.

I hadn't realized I'd been crying. How embarrassing. Maybe I could have convinced the birds to attack in a chaos of wings and poo.

How had I let this happen to me?

The elevator stopped on the twenty-second floor, and the

doors whooshed open to reveal a fabulously dressed woman in her sixties. She stepped in, grace personified. She was everything I could have hoped to be—polished, sophisticated, *confident.*

She looked from my tear-streaked face to the champagne bottle in my hands, then raised a brow.

I lifted the bottle to her. "Want a sip?"

"I'll pass, thank you." She smiled, and it was kinder than I'd expected it to be. "But whoever did this to you, they're not worth it."

I gave her a weak smile.

"Truly," she said as the elevator continued its trip. "Grieve tonight, but tomorrow is a new day. Wake up and say, "Screw him." She smiled. "Or her. Either way, you're better than them. And life will be better without them."

When the doors opened, she gave me one last nod, then stepped out and swanned across the lobby, leaving a trail of elegance in her wake.

I blew out a breath. "Wow."

Pretty amazing, huh?

The voice came from near my feet, and I looked down to see a chubby calico cat at my side. It was my familiar, whom I hadn't seen in months. Probably a year. "Poa? What are you doing here?"

I felt a change. Like you grew a pair of ovaries and got your head out of your butt.

Poa had never liked Tommy, which should have been my first clue he was no good. She also didn't like the fact that he'd discouraged me from using my magic.

"I should have listened to you," I said.

Well, listen to me now and get out of this elevator before it takes you back up there and another bird shits on you.

I nodded, gripping the neck of the champagne bottle tightly. "That's good advice."

I'm full of it, honey, trust me. And my next suggestion is to get into the loo and clean yourself up.

I sighed and headed out of the elevator. "Good point."

I found the ladies' lavatory near the elevators and did the best I could to remove the mascara from under my eyes. I washed my face—twice for the forehead—then applied a fresh coat of lipstick.

Good work. You look almost normal.

"Ha, ha." I grabbed the champagne, which I'd set on the counter, and tested it. After the woman's pep talk and the fresh lipstick, it tasted better. But could I walk around London with an open champagne bottle in my hand? Did it make a difference that it was expensive? Wealthy people rarely got in trouble with the police, and I wasn't one of them, but with this champagne, I might be able to pass.

Where will you go now? Poa asked as we walked out into the lobby.

I glanced around to see if anyone noticed the cat at my side. It wasn't like she was a teacup poodle or Frenchie, both common to see out and about. Cats, on the other hand... But if anyone noticed, they didn't say anything. Maybe it was because we were in a fancy hotel and they thought I was one of the eccentric guests.

I liked that idea and tried straightening my shoulders and adopting the walk of the fabulous woman who'd encouraged me in the elevator. No one ever bothered people who looked that fabulous and confident.

I felt Poa's gaze on me and looked down. She shook her head. *You're not pulling it off.*

I glared. "Mean."

Truthful. Don't be so stiff.

"I can't believe I'm taking advice from a cat."

Honey, if you'd taken my advice sooner, you wouldn't be in this position.

"Fair enough." I sighed. "What do you suggest?"

To start, go over to that bar and ask for a champagne glass. Then you won't look like a wino.

"I'm not sure that's true, but okay." I veered toward the hotel bar and took a seat on one of the emerald velvet stools. Poa jumped up onto a stool next to me, and I hissed, "It's not normal to have a cat in a bar." I lowered my voice. "Not in human London, at least."

The humans can't see me.

I raised my brows. "Really?"

She nodded. *There's a lot you don't know about me. You would, if you hadn't abandoned your magic.*

Embarrassment flushed through me. She was right. I'd abandoned my gifts for a man. A worthless man. It had happened so slowly, with Tommy subtly suggesting that I didn't need to use my power so much, that I almost hadn't noticed. It had happened all the same.

Incoming. Poa nodded toward the other end of the bar, and I turned to see a bartender approaching. He was young, no more than twenty-five to my thirty, and had a friendly smile. "May I get you a glass for that, Miss?"

"Thank you."

He nodded and turned to retrieve a glass, then presented it to me. I took the flute, looking between the bottle of wine and him. "You don't mind that I brought my own wine to your bar?"

"It's from the hotel, so it's fine."

"How can you tell? Is this your signature variety for cheating boyfriends and their mistresses?" I clapped a hand to my mouth, shocked by the words that had escaped. Next to me, Poa crowed her delight.

The bartender gave an awkward laugh, his gaze flicking toward the elevators. "Something like that."

I sighed. "Whatever. I don't care."

He picked up the bottle and poured it into my glass in a graceful stream.

I don't suppose you could ask him for a saucer? Poa asked.

"No."

The bartender frowned. "You don't want the wine?"

I pulled the full glass toward myself. "Oh, I do."

"Then I'll get you a glacette." He left to complete the job, and I looked at Poa.

She could clearly see my confusion, because she said, *it's an ice bucket for champagne, you plebeian.*

"Hmm." I downed half my glass before looking down at her again. She stared at me with irritation. "I'll get you some wine when we're not in the hotel, all right? It would look weird if I put a saucer of champagne on the bar next to me."

Fine.

"Are you sure cats can have wine?"

This cat can.

12

I rolled my eyes and slumped into the cushy back of the barstool. It was a bold move to drink at the hotel bar where Tommy and his mistress might walk by at any moment, but I didn't care. I was going to drink his expensive champagne while I sorted out my life, and I couldn't exactly do that on the street.

So, what next?

"You're back with me now?"

If you stay this cool, yes.

"I will." There was a note of determination to my voice that I liked. "I let Tommy make too many choices for too long. I need to make my own."

I hope they'll have something to do with your magic.

It was a good first start. Tommy and I had grown up in a magical neighborhood in London, one that humans hadn't known about. We'd coupled off young. He'd been a sorcerer without much power, but I hadn't minded.

Looking back on things, it was clear that *he'd* minded. He'd said he didn't care about his limited magic, and I'd believed him because I'd been an idiot in love. I'd agreed when he suggested I not use magic around the house because we lived so close to human London. He'd wanted to move there after school, and I'd gone with him.

Why wouldn't I? My parents had moved to Australia as soon as the commencement ceremony was over. They hadn't been bad parents, but they'd been more obsessed with each other than anything else. Tommy had been obsessed with *me*.

"I didn't notice it happen," I said, absently sipping at the champagne.

Notice what?

"Losing myself."

Poa sighed loudly, which was a strange noise from a cat. *I noticed.*

"It's why you left."

I tried to warn you.

"I remember." But I hadn't been willing to listen to her. She'd appeared shortly before my eighteenth birthday. Not all witches had familiars—only powerful ones—but I'd been too wrapped up in Tommy to care. He'd made me feel like the center of the world, and I'd needed that. I'd lapped it up. When Poa hadn't been able to get me to focus on my magic, she'd eventually disappeared.

I sipped the champagne.

Where will you go?

"I have no idea." Last I'd heard, my parents were in Tokyo. I couldn't exactly show up on their doorstep and ask for a place to stay. Not that I wanted to. And the temp jobs that I held didn't pay enough for me to get my own place in London. Tommy had wanted me to focus on making a home for us, and I'd spent most of my time doing that. The temp jobs were my own little rebellion, and in hindsight, they'd been pathetic.

Now that I thought about it, that was another way that Tommy had bound me.

"Why did he put so much effort in tying me to him if he was just going to cheat?" I asked.

Because he's a bastard. And who wouldn't want someone to take care of them like you took care of him?

"Good point." What an idiot I'd been.

I thought of what the woman in the elevator had said. I didn't want to wait until the morning to push him from my mind. "I need a plan."

Who else can you go to?

"I don't suppose you have a flat in a nice part of London?" I laughed low. "Doesn't even need to be nice, actually. I'll settle for anything."

No. I'm a cat.

"Okay, then, that's out." I sipped the wine, going over my list of friends and family in my head. Unfortunately, there was just about no one I could count on. All my friends were acquaintances from temp jobs, and the only family I had besides my parents was a grandmother I hadn't seen in years.

What about your gran?

"Can you read my mind?"

No. But she's the only one you've got.

I sighed. "I guess we should head to the train station."

Don't you want to stop by your place to pick up some things?

I thought about the home I'd created for Tony and myself, and suddenly, I never wanted to see the place again. "No."

Clothes?

I looked down at the floral dress I was wearing. It was muted shades of mauve, with long sleeves and buttons to the waist. I'd chosen it, but if I were honest with myself, I didn't like it. Tommy had spent the first years of our relationship being very vocal about what clothes he liked, and I'd listened. The praise had been worth the compromise on my outfits, but in the end, everything in my closet made me blend with the world around me.

"He wanted me to disappear into the background, didn't he?"

As long as you did the cooking and cleaning, yes. I think that was the case.

"What an idiot."

Poa patted a paw on my thigh. *There, there. With my help, you won't be so boring anymore.*

"Boring." A cat had just called me boring. "I'm not going back to the flat. There's nothing for me there except for some ugly clothes." I was wearing my favorite boots, which were the only thing I'd chosen for myself, and always wore the gold necklace that Tommy had given me. I could sell it if I needed some money to keep me afloat. It had once been so special to me, and now I liked the idea of using it to escape him. But for now, I had enough in my purse to get us to St. Ives, where my grandmother lived. From there, I'd figure it out.

CHAPTER

THREE

ISOBEL

IN THE END, we took a bus. By the time I'd checked on the trains, it was too late to catch one to St. Ives. Buses were cheaper, anyway. Poa had complained, of course, but we arrived in St. Ives by morning all the same.

What do you mean, we're walking? she asked as we set off toward my grandmother's house.

"It's not that far from the bus station, and we need to save our money."

She sniffed. *At least you're calling it our money.*

"We're a team, right?"

You're singing a different song than you used to, and I like it.

I smiled. I should have listened to her earlier, and I wasn't going to make the same mistake twice.

My grandmother lived in a large house on the outskirts of

the coastal town of St. Ives in northern Cornwall. I'd only visited a couple times, but since she'd been even less interested in me than my parents had been, I hadn't had much incentive to return.

Was I really that hard to love?

I shook the thought away. I needed to keep my spirits up, keep moving forward. And now that I had literally nothing, I had no other choice than to ask if my grandmother could help me.

Hopefully, she wouldn't be annoyed to see me. I just needed a place to stay for a short time while I figured out who I was and where my life was going.

When we arrived at the house, the state of the garden made me stop dead. Weeds tangled around the iron fence that bordered the grass, and the interior looked like a jungle. Clearly, no one had tended it in months, and my grandmother had always been fanatical about her garden.

This isn't good.

"I know." Dread unfurled inside me as I pushed open the creaky gate and started up the weed-choked path. The house was a two-story stone building with a dark blue door that swung open before I reached it.

An older man stood there, wearing a perfectly pressed suit that matched his impeccable hair. Not a strand of the iron gray was out of place. His gaze moved between Poa and me, and I knew that he must have magic if he could see her. A frown flattened his lips. "Isobel Whitwell?"

"Yes. How did you know it was me?"

"I've been sending you letters for a month."

"I haven't received any letters."

"Well, be that as it may, I sent them. I also had confirmation that they were delivered to 13B Rollington Road in London."

That was my address, and if he had confirmation they'd been delivered, that must mean that Tommy had got them and not given them to me.

Anger bubbled inside me, far greater than what I'd felt when I'd found him cheating on me.

I drew in a deep, calming breath. This wasn't about Tommy. "Is this about my grandmother?"

"Yes. You'd better come in."

"Just tell me." Anxiety pricked my skin, and I couldn't wait for the news. It wouldn't matter if I were sitting.

He frowned. "Are you sure?"

"Tell me."

He sighed heavily. "She's passed."

I blinked at him. That was what I'd been expecting, but hearing it was somehow still shocking. I swallowed hard, suddenly full of regret. I should have visited her sooner. Not for her help, but to know her. True, she'd been disinterested in me when I'd visited as a child, but things could have changed. I should have tried harder.

Quit with that line of thought, and let's find out what's going on.

I looked down at Poa. "I thought you couldn't read my mind."

Your face is scrunched up like an old sock. You're clearly thinking bad thoughts.

I rolled my eyes, then looked at the man.

"Are you ready to come in now?" he asked.

I nodded. It had been a long night, and the champagne had left me feeling a bit crap.

"I'll put the kettle on," he said. "Why don't you take a seat in the living room?"

"I'll come to the kitchen," I replied, not wanting to be left alone in her house.

He just nodded and led the way down the narrow hall and past two rooms. The place was covered in a light film of dust, as if he weren't here often or were a terrible house-keeper. Given the impeccable state of his suit and hair, I had to think it was the former.

When we reached the tidy little kitchen, I asked, "Are you my grandmother's...?"

Actually, I had no idea how to finish that. As far as I knew, she wasn't married. But it would be ridiculous to call this man a boyfriend.

"Her solicitor, yes." He filled the kettle with water. "Malcolm Ludlow. You may call me Malcolm."

Thank Hecate I hadn't called him her boyfriend. Of course he was her solicitor.

"How did you know I would arrive today? I assume your office is somewhere else."

He nodded. "My assistant put a ward on the town that would alert me to your arrival. I didn't want to miss you if you happened to show up. This matter has been left hanging for far too long."

I blew out a breath and sat. The kettle clicked off, and he

poured two cups of tea, then brought them to the table. "No milk, I'm afraid."

I didn't bother asking about sugar. It wouldn't have expired in the last few weeks since my grandmother's death, but he didn't seem like the sort to acknowledge the existence of sugar.

Poa hopped up on the chair next to me and looked at my teacup. I pushed it toward her in offer, and she turned up her nose. *Pass.*

The solicitor ignored his cup and folded his hands on the table. "Now, on to the matter of the will."

"The will?"

"Yes. You were the primary beneficiary, so that leaves the estate to you."

I blinked, dumbfounded, then looked around at the house. "This house, you mean?"

He shook his head. "No. This house has been sold. A family from New Zealand will move in at the end of the month."

Crap. I really could have used a place to live.

I winced. I shouldn't be so mercenary in the face of my grandmother's death. I pasted a bland smile on my face and tried to look appropriate, whatever that was.

"It's a bit of an unusual situation, you see." He leaned down and pulled some papers out of a briefcase that sat on the floor near his chair. "Your grandmother owned a home in Cornwall, outside of the town of Charming Cove. Lavender House, it's called. It's in fairly poor shape, but I believe she was hoping you'd fix it up. There's a good bit of land with it, along with a building on the water that I believe she called the boathouse."

I blew out a breath. That sounded like a fun challenge, but... "I have no money. I can't afford to fix anything up."

He gestured to the house around us. "The sale of this house has been put into an account for you. It's more than enough to cover the cost of repairing Lavender House."

"Oh, wow." I smiled and sat back. My luck was really turning around.

"There are some conditions, however. And challenges."

I grimaced and leaned forward. "Go on..."

"Your grandmother tried for years to get the main house fixed up, but none of the contractors in town will work on it. Something about the house being inhospitable to guests."

Okay, that wasn't ideal.

"So it will be primarily up to you to do the labor. The will stipulates that you have a month from your arrival in Charming Cove to complete the job. I will come by on the thirtieth day and see if you've finished. If you have, then Lavender House and the money are yours. If you fail, it all goes to your cousin Albert."

"Albert? But isn't he already wealthy?" And also a jerk, I was pretty sure.

"Indeed. Your grandmother wasn't fond of him. I believe she wanted to incentivize you to fix Lavender House. She loved that place, though she was never able to live there."

I drew in a breath. I could do this. I liked a challenge. I *needed* a challenge. Something to get my mind off of Tommy and help me reinvent my life.

"It's unlikely that you can live in the house in its current state," he said. "But there is a renovated apartment in the boathouse. It's small, but your grandmother said it's nice enough. She used to live there when she would visit Charming Cove."

Excellent. That solved my biggest problem. Now I just had to fix up Lavender House.

CHAPTER
FOUR

ISOBEL

FORTUNATELY, my grandmother had also left me a car. The little Vauxhall was old but in good condition, and Poa reported that the passenger seat was sufficiently comfortable. She made sure I knew it wasn't perfect, but that it would do for now—until I could get something better, as she'd put it.

She'd be waiting a while.

Since the meeting with the solicitor hadn't lasted long and I had nowhere else to stay, we'd departed St. Ives in the midafternoon after getting the car jump-started. Fortunately, it was full of petrol. I didn't have the cash to fill it up, and the solicitor had said I wouldn't have access to my new accounts until tomorrow.

"It's time for a new life," I said to Poa as we drove down the country lanes to the southern coast of Cornwall. I'd lowered the windows, and the cool autumn breeze blew my hair back from my face.

Poa also had her face turned up, the wind blowing through her whiskers. *Good, because your life was really sad.*

"Harsh." I shrugged. "But true."

But now I had a chance to reinvent myself. The thought of Tommy made me sad, but not in the way I'd expected. I'd miss the idea of him, but if I were honest with myself, our relationship hadn't been good in a long time. I was sadder for the years that I'd wasted on him.

But no more.

Charming Cove awaited me, along with the challenge of a lifetime.

By the time we arrived, the sun had set, and a chill nipped the air. It was too dark to really see Lavender House, which sat on top of a rocky hill overlooking the sea, but I could see the shadows of it. The building was bigger than I'd expected, and worry tugged at me. A month wasn't a long time, especially if it would be difficult to get help.

I shook the thought away. Nope! I was going to be positive. The ability to see the good side of things had always been one of my strengths, and I would lean into that.

The lane led down to the sea, where a large rectangular stone building sat on a rocky ledge just a stone's throw from the water. The solicitor had called it a boathouse, and I could see why. A wide path led from a huge door on the seaward side of the house to a ramp down into the water.

Do you think there will be boats inside?

I looked over at Poa, who peered out the window with skepticism. "Maybe. Do you not like boats?"

I'm not too fond of water, so no, I don't like boats.

"I'll be sure to get rid of them for you."

Liar.

I laughed. "Yep. But you don't have to ride in them."

I pulled the car into the gravel parking area near the back of the boathouse and climbed out. It was actually a pretty big building, with several large windows and a heavy wooden door that would hopefully open with the key the solicitor had given me. The peaked roof was tiled in rough slate, and there was a little window right at the top. Fading roses climbed the walls of the house, and with the sea crashing on the rocks in the background, the place would probably be beautiful in the summer.

I caught sight of the light that shone through the window to the far right. Had someone stopped by to turn it on for me? That was kind, but who had it been?

Unlock the door. I'm ready for a nap by a fire.

"Hold your horses, I'm getting there." I pulled the key from my pocket and went to the door.

It slipped easily into the lock and gave a satisfying click when I turned it. The heavy door swung open on well-oiled hinges, and the scent of freshly cut wood washed over me as I stepped inside. The light that I'd seen shining from the corner of the building illuminated two large shapes covered by tarps.

Boats? They had to be.

Large electrical tools sat against the walls, hulking machines that must have cost a fortune. Nothing looked dusty or out of use like I'd expected in my grandmother's abandoned boathouse. Had someone been working here until her death?

Poa sniffed disdainfully. *We must remove those. Replace them with cushy couches.*

"We're staying upstairs," I said. "And whoever is working will be gone now that I own the place. We'll talk to them about getting the machinery out later." Or maybe I could rent the boathouse to them once Lavender House was fixed up. I wouldn't turn down any extra income, especially the kind I didn't have to work for.

Poa stalked past the tarp-covered boats and found a set of stairs that led to the upper floor. I followed her, my footsteps creaking on the wood, then entered the tiny flat and flipped on the light switch. The golden glow illuminated a cluttered interior. It took me a minute to see that there was a method to the madness. The room wasn't actually messy—my grandmother had just been intensely committed to knickknacks. They littered every surface, tiny figurines and vases and shells. The faint smell of dust filled the air, and closer inspection revealed that it covered everything in sight. Whoever was keeping the downstairs tidy wasn't worried about the flat above.

I blew out a breath. This, in itself, would be a job.

Now this is what I'm talking about. Poa strolled toward one of the cushy couches and jumped up. A cloud of dust poofed around her, and she gave a delicate sneeze, then began to knead the cushion.

"This is your style?" I asked.

What's not to like? She looked around. *The dust is a bit much, but everything else is perfection.* Right next to her, the

27

porcelain figurine of a milkmaid with freakishly angelic features smiled at me with an expression that looked more like a grimace. Poa stared at it approvingly.

Fantastic. My cat has the style of a ninety-year-old woman who collected haunted bric-a-brac. She wasn't going to be pleased when I cleaned the place out, but I didn't mention my plan to her. It would have to wait until I was finished with Lavender House, anyway.

"I'm going to take a shower," I told her, but she was already asleep.

I left her on the couch and explored the rest of the flat, finding a little kitchen with a view overlooking the water and a bedroom with spare bedding in the closet. I changed out the dusty duvet for the less-dusty option, then found fresh towels and a dressing gown in the bathroom closet. They'd been protected from the dust, and though the dressing gown was more suited to Poa's style than my own, I wanted to wear something clean.

I laid out my loot on the little table in the bathroom, then climbed into the tiny shower once it had heated up. The old toiletries on the edge of the bath did the job, even though they made me smell like an out-of-date rose.

The hot water ran out far quicker than I'd expected it to, and I squealed as the cold blasted onto my head. I leapt out of the shower, grateful that I'd rinsed the last of the shampoo from my hair. The mirror revealed that my eye makeup was still running down my face, and I winced. As I was turning on the tap to wash the black streaks away, I heard something from downstairs.

I stiffened, heart racing.

The thumping noise came again.

Was someone down there? It had been dead silent when I'd arrived.

Adrenaline raced through my veins, and I threw on the dressing gown, which billowed around me as I crept from the bathroom toward the door. A cricket bat painted with countryside scenes hung on the wall near the door, and I pulled it off. It might be art, but I could still whack an intruder with it if I needed to.

You could just use your magic, you know.

I looked over at Poa, then whispered, "Do you hear someone?"

She nodded. *Downstairs.*

Damn it. I gripped the bat more tightly. She was right about the magic, but I'd bring the bat, just in case. I was so out of practice with my power that I was as likely to blow myself up as send an intruder packing.

Carefully, I opened the door to the stairs, trying not to make as sound. It swung silently on its hinges, and I began to creep downstairs, hesitating halfway. Because of the walls on either side of me, I could only see the narrowest strip of the floor below. I'd need to get to the bottom to see who was there.

Heart pounding, I moved as silently and swiftly as I could. Reaching the bottom and turning the corner with the bat raised, I nearly slammed into another person and shrieked as I stumbled backward.

A half-naked man stood in front of me, one hand gripping the towel wrapped around his hips. I stared at him, stunned. The golden light from the fixture overhead gilded his body. He was built like a god, with a face to match. I'd never seen someone so fit in my whole life, and I was suddenly very aware of how much of my own body was distinctly not fit. One might go so far as to say *squishy*.

Not that it mattered in this life-or-death situation.

I dragged my gaze up to his impossibly handsome face—strong jaw, full lips, brilliant green eyes, and perfectly tousled dark hair that was still damp from the shower. I was looking for a threat, and all I saw was stunned shock.

"Who are you?" I demanded, though it came out as more of a squeak.

"Who are *you*?" he replied. "And what are you doing in my house, dressed like a lunatic Victorian ghost?"

I gasped, offended. "Lunatic Victorian ghost?"

"You mean this wasn't intentional?" He gestured from my face to my flowing white gown, and I remembered my streaky mascara.

"There was no more hot water left," I said, focusing on the wrong thing. "And why the hell are you naked in my house?"

"I'm not naked, and it's *my* house."

I glared at him. "I've got the deed."

"So do I."

"That's not possible if I've got it." But he was so confident that he definitely *believed* he did. As much as I wanted to get to the bottom of that, I needed to cover a few important things first. "Convince me you're not going to murder me."

A low laugh burst from him. "What?"

"You're a giant half-naked man in the building I inherited from my grandmother. I have a right to be worried."

He sobered, then stepped back. "You're right. It's still *my* house, but you're right. I can see how you would be worried. You're safe here, though. I've never murdered a single person, and I don't plan to start now."

He sounded genuine, and he'd been so shocked when he'd seen me that I believed his side of events, as inconvenient as they were for me. He didn't intend to do wrong here, even though it was a real pain in the arse to have to argue over who owned this place.

He looked me up and down, a brow raised in a skeptical expression. "Now convince me *you're* not a murder ghost from the nineteenth century."

I laughed, shocked. "A murder ghost?"

He shrugged. "You're dressed like one." He gestured to my streaky face. "And this situation suggests you're a bit unhinged."

"What it suggests is that I ran out of hot water before I could properly wash my face, and then I heard a possible murderer in my new home, so I had to grab the nearest thing to wear. Which isn't mine, by the way. It was my grandmother's." Suddenly, this was all too much. "I'm going to wash my face and get changed, and I'll be back down in a bit. Put on some clothes. Please."

"Gladly." He turned and stalked off, and I couldn't help but stare at the broad muscle planes of his back.

Poa gave a wheezy little whistle. *I could climb that like a tree.*

I rolled my eyes.

"I'm going to change. Don't cause any problems while I'm gone." I walked past her, headed back up the stairs. I wasn't keen on wearing my dirty clothes, but it was better than dressing like a nineteenth-century murder ghost.

When I made it to the bathroom, my makeup was worse than I'd realized. I'd gone all out for my special date with Tommy, and it now ran down my face in a look that could only be described as "deranged comic book villain." I scrubbed the makeup off in the cold water, then put my dress back on. It wasn't the height of fashion, but it was at least clearly from this century. On my way out of the flat, I grabbed the bag of paperwork that the solicitor had given me.

When I reached the main floor, the man was already waiting for me, dressed in a pair of rugged camel-colored work pants and a thin blue T-shirt that did nothing to hide the ridiculous body underneath. He sat in the back corner of the room, in a space that had been turned into a small kitchen, looking relaxed in a chair that was far too small for him. On the table in front of him lay a piece of paper.

I walked toward him, my gaze on the paper.

He crossed his arms over his chest, a maneuver that made his biceps look even more impressive than when I'd first seen them—which was hard to believe—and nodded to the paper. "It's all there."

I set my bag on the table, then picked up the paper. It definitely looked like a deed, though I was no expert. And the name at the bottom was familiar—Albert Whitwell. "My uncle doesn't own this place."

"Albert Whitwell is your uncle?"

I nodded. "How did you meet him?"

"I didn't. I bought the place through a listing agent."

"That can't be possible. My grandmother owned this place, and she willed it to me." I reached into the bag I'd brought and retrieved the documents the solicitor had given me, then handed them over. "It's all right here."

He took them from me and flipped through them, his frown deepening. "These can't be real."

"I assure you, they are."

"Well, so are mine."

"This is going to be a mess, isn't it?"

"Unless you're planning to leave, yes."

I laughed. "I'm not leaving." I had nowhere to go, but I wasn't going to tell him that. Anyway, this was *my* home, and I was going to fight for it.

"Neither am I."

I glared at him, and he glared back. This was getting off to a great start. "I'll send your paperwork to my grandmother's solicitor and we'll see what he says."

"Why should I trust him?"

I groaned. "I don't know. He's a solicitor, and he looks trustworthy. You can get your own, if you want." I was confident that I owned the house, so I didn't care what he did. I just wanted to get this process started so that I could get him out of there.

"What's his name?" he asked.

"Malcolm Ludlow."

He pulled his phone out of his pocket and typed in something that I couldn't see. His gaze scanned over the screen, and then he met my gaze. "He looks legit enough. Let's see what he has to say, and then we'll discuss."

"You mean if you don't like what he says, we'll send it to

your guy."

"Or an entirely new solicitor. But I have copies of the deed, and there's no harm in letting your guy have a look, especially since you'll be paying his bill."

I glared at him but nodded. "Fine. Anything to get this over with."

He pushed the deed across the table toward me, and I took it.

"Where will you go while we sort this out?" he asked.

"Upstairs."

"You want to live here?" He grimaced.

"Yes. I need a place to stay while I fix up Lavender House, and since I own this place, I'll be staying upstairs. You're clearly not using it unless you're a horrific housekeeper with creepy taste in knickknacks."

"I'm not." His gaze flicked to the windows, as if looking toward the ramshackle old house on the hill. An incredulous expression crossed his face. "You're going to fix up that place?"

"Yes." I infused my voice with confidence, though I wasn't loving the skepticism in his.

"Good luck."

"Where will you stay?" I asked, looking around at the workshop. "Surely you don't live here."

"I do." He nodded toward a door. "That's a bedroom."

I looked at it, then glanced around the kitchen, which I only now realized seemed lived-in. Not messy, but there was a teacup on the counter next to the kettle and a box of biscuits near the refrigerator that was partially open.

"Why don't you live in the flat upstairs if you really own

this building?"

"You've seen that place," he said. "Too much stuff. I'm fine down here."

That was strange. Wouldn't he just clean it out? Before I could ask, he said, his voice gruff, "You can stay until we sort this out, but keep to your part of the building."

"Likewise." I shot him a glare, about to turn around, then realized that I had no idea what to call him. "What's your name?"

"Rafe."

"Just Rafe? Like Madonna?"

"Just Rafe." He didn't so much as twitch at my joke.

"All right, then, Just Rafe. I'm Isobel Whitwell. Not nice to meet you."

That made him smile, but it wasn't a particularly friendly one. "Not nice to meet you, too."

I scowled at him, then frowned. "Hang on. You're a supernatural."

"You're only just noticing?"

"I was a bit distracted to start." Now that I'd solidified that I wasn't going to be murdered and I still had a place to live, the adrenaline had faded enough to allow me to notice that he had a magical signature. It smelled like the forest and glowed like the pale light of the moon. "Shifter?"

"Werewolf. And you're a witch."

"I am."

"Well, witch, stay in your part of the boathouse."

"Gladly." I shot him one last glare, then turned and went up to the flat. Maybe if I asked her nicely, Poa would pee on his shoes while he wasn't looking.

CHAPTER
FIVE

RAFE

I STARED at the witch as she stalked away, her hips swaying. I averted my gaze. I shouldn't be staring at her, no matter how beautiful she was. She'd stunned me when she'd walked back downstairs after cleaning the streaks of black makeup off her face, and it took everything I had to shove my wolf back inside.

It recognized something in her, and that was a problem. It didn't matter that she was perfection, with her pale hair and luminous gray eyes. She couldn't be here. I'd worked too hard to find the quiet peace that this place afforded me. I needed it too badly.

I closed my eyes and pinched the bridge of my nose, but all I could see was the outline of her lush curves. I groaned, annoyed with myself. As long as she lived upstairs, I shouldn't be having pervy thoughts about her. I shouldn't be having them about her ever, but it was much worse while she was alone and under my roof.

I didn't know what kind of witch she was, but if she was the kind that could read minds, I didn't want her to see something in my head that would make her uncomfortable. But she was going to drive me crazy, that was clear enough. She was too beautiful, for one. She had skin like cream, with pale pink lips and...

Nope. I couldn't let my mind go there.

Better to focus on her quick wit and the fact that she was willing to go toe to toe with me over this place. She seemed delicate, but she wasn't. She clearly didn't put up with shit from anyone.

Not to mention there was just something...*bright* about her. She'd been scared at first, then angry, but through it all, she had seemed to radiate this light. She was like a ray of sunshine after a year of clouds, and it was annoying as hell.

I *liked* my clouds. At least I was comfortable with them.

And she was a witch, for fate's sake. They were entirely untrustworthy, and I wanted nothing to do with them. I knew it was prejudiced and irrational, but I didn't care. It had been hard enough to find peace after *the incident* with the last witch I'd been involved with, and I was going to protect that peace, no matter what it took.

Which meant staying the hell away from her while the solicitors sorted out this problem with the deed.

I rose from the table and headed toward the simple bedroom that I'd called my own for the last year. As I entered, a tapping sound came from the window that overlooked the sea view to the west. I walked toward it and pushed it open.

A black bird sat there, its onyx eyes staring at me. A tiny scroll was attached to its leg.

"Really?" I asked the raven. "She couldn't have just sent me a text?"

It squawked as if offended.

I raised my hands. "Sorry, sorry. Your mistress would never dream of something so obnoxiously modern. Thank you for coming."

The bird preened, pleased, then stuck out its leg, presenting me with the scroll that had been tied there.

I carefully untied the note, surprised to see my hands so steady—I'd been waiting for this message for months. If the Jade Sorceress could help me, I might be able to find my pack. Every witch to whom I'd gone for help over the last decade had said they couldn't undo the spell of the witch who had cursed me, but a sorceress might be able to, especially one as powerful as the Jade Sorceress.

I'LL SEE YOU. *The seventeenth of this month, noon.*

I STARED AT THE NOTE, my mouth dry. Finally, a lead. I'd been coming up empty-handed for the last two years, but now I had hope.

CHAPTER

SIX

ISOBEL

THE NEXT MORNING dawned clear and bright, the autumn breeze blowing gently through the open window. The fresh sea air was invigorating, and I woke with more energy than I'd had in months. Years, even.

I yawned, stretching every muscle in my body, then sat upright.

Poa, who lounged on a pillow at the end of the bed, stared at me. *You look like you're in a good mood.*

"I really am." There was a lightness in my soul that was entirely unfamiliar. "It feels like a weight has been lifted off my shoulders."

Was the weight named Tommy?

A surprised laugh escaped me. "Yes, probably. I'm really not as sad as I should be about him."

What was sad was how long you stayed with him.

"Ouch." I winced. My cat was ruthless. "But you're right. I guess I just got comfortable."

As if he could tell we were talking about him, a text came through with Tommy's name on it. I didn't even bother reading it—I just deleted.

Was that him? Poa asked.

"It was. I can't believe I stayed with him so long."

Don't beat yourself up. You got together when you were too young to know any better, and you had your own issues.

"Well, I know better now, and I'm going to make some changes."

Like your hair? If a cat could arch an eyebrow, she would have.

"What's wrong with my hair?" I raised a hand to the long, dark mane that had been one of Tommy's favorite things about me.

It could just use a trim, that's all. It's pretty lifeless.

I rolled my eyes. "You don't pull your punches, do you?"

Absolutely not. Would you, if you knew you were right all the time?

I laughed and climbed out of bed. "You know what, you're right. I think I need a makeover."

I could multitask while getting it done. Salons were excellent places to learn about a town, and I could perhaps get leads on local handymen who might be desperate for work. My grandmother had had a hard time finding people to help with the house, but maybe she had only looked in the most obvious places.

Anyway, I'd left my clothes behind in the ashes of my old life, so I needed something to wear that wouldn't make me look like a murder ghost, as Rafe had called me. I glowered at the thought of him, then forced my mind toward more productive tasks.

I had no coffee *or* food, and I wanted to post the deeds to the solicitor, so I needed to go into town, no matter what.

I reached for my phone, grateful that I'd thought to pack a charger in my purse before going to dinner at the Regent. The full battery allowed me to check the account that the solicitor had set up for me. When the login worked and I saw the sum sitting in the account, my breath rushed out.

It was roughly half a million pounds. A giddy little squeal escaped me, and I did a twirl.

Are we rich?

I looked at Poa. "How did you know what I was looking at?"

Please. You think I haven't seen a money dance in my life? Also, I know everything.

"Right, of course. I forgot." I put the phone down and hurried to the tiny bathroom, getting ready as quickly as I could. I wasn't thrilled to put on my old clothes, but I couldn't exactly go into town wearing the clothes in my grandmother's closet.

Poa was gone when I made it into the main room, so I grabbed my bag and headed down the stairs. As I neared the bottom, the smell of coffee greeted me. It was divine, and my mouth watered.

Maybe Grumpy McHottiePants would share.

I reached the main floor and turned the corner to look into the kitchen, but I found him already glaring at me. He must have heard me come down.

"Morning." His voice was gruff and decidedly unwelcoming.

The coffee was going to be a no, then.

"Morning." I turned and headed to the door. "See you later."

He just grunted, and I scowled. What a miserable grump.

I wouldn't dwell on him, though. I'd spent too much of my life thinking about a man, and it was time to think about myself. Poa was waiting in the car when I reached it, already asleep on the seat.

The drive into Charming Cove was short—just five minutes up a winding path away from the sea and back down into town. Using the directions the solicitor had given me, I was able to enter the town from the back, approaching the magical section and skipping the human part entirely.

Like London, Charming Cove had an entire hidden neighborhood just for supernaturals. It was impossible for humans to find Foxglove Lane, which was the main road through this part of town. I had no trouble, thankfully, and was delighted when I finally reached it.

Charming Cove was just about the prettiest place I'd ever seen. Foxglove Lane sat on a small cliff that overlooked the sparkling blue sea. The ocean side of the road had no buildings so that everyone could enjoy the view. Instead, there were narrow, beautifully landscaped gardens sitting right on the edge of the cliff, dotted with wooden benches.

Shops and restaurants occupied the inland side of Foxglove Lane. The buildings themselves were primarily stone with slate roofs, though many of them had been painted white. There were a few in other colors—a cheerful yellow and a calming blue sat side by side, and I promised myself I'd make time to check them out and see what they were.

Farther down the road, I could see the cove and sandy beach that gave Charming Cove its name, but I was pretty sure that was the human part of town. I felt little desire to explore it—the magical part was so beautiful that I was sure I'd never need to leave.

I found a parking spot in front of Margot's Tea & Cake Parlor and pulled in. Poa woke up, her nose twitching. She put her front paws on the dash and stared out at the coffee shop, then looked at me.

"I suppose you want a latte?"

Whole milk, please.

I sighed. "Coming right up, Your Majesty."

If a cat could have grinned, she would have. Instead, she just wiggled her shoulders in a pleased gesture. I climbed out of the car, and the sea breeze whipped my long hair in front of my face. I pulled it back so I could see better and looked across the quiet road toward the ocean.

A strip of grass at the top of the cliff widened in some places to form little gardens. A walking path cut through the grass, running alongside the main road. There were far more blooms than there should have been at that time of year, and I stared for what felt like seconds but must have been longer, because Poa tapped on the window with her claw and nodded toward the shop as if to tell me to get going.

"Fine, fine. Hold your horses." I turned and went toward the coffee shop.

The divine scent of sugar and butter washed over me as

soon as I stepped inside, followed by the scent of freshly brewed coffee. The little shop was cozy and tidy. An older couple occupied a squishy loveseat, each reading a novel while sipping from steaming mugs. I reached the counter, and a woman bustled out from the back. She was probably somewhere in her sixties, with gorgeous silver hair that fell to her shoulders in loose curls.

"Hello, lamb." She wiped her damp hands on her apron and gave me a wide smile. "I'm Margot. What can I get for you?"

"Two small lattes, please. Whole milk."

"Coming right up." Margo turned to get to work on the coffees, and I looked into the pastry case, which was full of the most incredible-looking treats. Croissants, scones, danishes, and sausage rolls lined up in neat, delicious-looking rows. I decided on a chocolate croissant for myself and a sausage roll for Poa. I wouldn't hear the end of it if I ate my croissant without bringing her something snacky.

Margot returned with my drinks a few minutes later and handed them over. "New to town, are you?"

"How can you tell?"

"Well, for one, there aren't that many of us. And for another, I saw you eyeing the gardens like you'd never seen anything like them."

"I haven't." I smiled. "They're gorgeous, even though summer is gone."

"That's the magic in the air. And we love our gardens here in Charming Cove. Different volunteer groups care for each section of the garden, and let me tell you, it's quite the competition. Why, I swear I saw the Bridge Club try to sabotage the Stitch 'N Bitch group's peonies last spring."

"No." I gasped. "That's diabolical."

She laughed. "I know. They're ruthless. Can I get you anything else?"

I pointed out my preferred pastries.

As she packaged them, I asked, "Do you know of any contractors who might be looking for work? I'm trying to fix up Lavender House."

She looked up at me, her eyebrows rising. "Really?"

"Really."

She grimaced. "Sorry, lamb. No one will take that job. Plenty have tried over the years, but the house just kicked them out."

"Not a single person is looking to make a few quid?"

She shrugged. "Maybe. It's been a time since the last attempt. Perhaps there are some young lads who can help you out. Want me to ask around?"

"I'd love that, thank you." I paid for my breakfast, then scrawled my name and number on the back of the receipt and pushed it toward her. "If you find anyone, they can contact me. I'll pay well."

"I'll do my best, lamb, but no promises."

"I appreciate anything you can do."

She winked. "You've got it."

I said my goodbyes, then walked toward the exit. At the door, I turned and asked, "Do you know of a salon in town where I could get my hair cut?"

"Certainly. Minxie's. Go right out the door and head down a few buildings."

"Thank you." I raised my bag of pastries in farewell, then went out to the car. Poa had left the vehicle, though I had no idea how, given her lack of opposable thumbs, and found a spot on a bench across the street.

I joined her, admiring the autumn flowers that rustled in the breeze and the blue sea behind. The wind blew through her whiskers as she turned to look at the bag in my hand.

"Don't worry, I got you a sausage roll."

You're not so bad, you know.

"Why, thank you." I laid the roll out on a napkin and opened her latte so she could lap it out of the cup.

We ate in companionable silence, listening to the waves crashing on the rocks below and the gulls calling to each other as they wheeled overhead. It was one of the loveliest mornings I'd had in a long, long time.

Once I'd finished my truly divine pastry and latte, I headed off to the salon. Poa stayed behind to nap in the sun. On my way, I passed a bookstore and a chippy called Codswollop's. A clothing shop caught my eye, and I decided to stop in after I got my hair done.

I found the salon situated between a small grocery store and an off-license that seemed to specialize in uniquely magical libations. A bell above the door jingled as I entered, and the scent of shampoo and roses greeted me. The space was decorated in ivory and pale pink, and a woman sat in one of the three salon chairs, bent over her mobile as she tapped away at the screen. As soon as the bell chimed, she looked up and smiled at me.

"Hello!" She stood. "Are you in for a cut?"

"I'm afraid I haven't made an appointment, but yes, if you've got the space."

"Well, you're in luck! My last appointment just canceled." She held out her hand. "I'm Minxie, the best stylist in Charming Cove."

I shook it and smiled. "I'm Isobel, and I'm looking for an entirely new look."

Minxie clapped her hands, her face lighting up. "Oh, excellent! A makeover?"

"Yes, exactly." Excitement thrummed through me as she bustled me over to the hair washing station and began chattering about options.

For a moment, I was tempted to give her free rein. She was the professional stylist, after all. But then I remembered that I'd been giving away all of my decisions to Tommy for too many years. I was going to make them myself.

"Short," I said. "Above the shoulders. Something light and fun."

"Got it." She smiled. "You're going to love it, I promise."

I quizzed her about the town as she worked, learning that the weather was almost always good because of all the excess magic in the air and that the clothing shop I'd seen was run by three sisters in their eighties who would rain hell upon anyone who didn't return the clothes to the proper rack when they were finished trying them on.

"Noted." I smiled, liking the sound of Charming Cove already. "What about contractors or handymen? Are there any you know of who are looking for work?"

"Oh, loads. Most of them probably have jobs lined up for

the next couple of months, but I'm sure I can find you some-one. What were you thinking?"

"I just inherited Lavender House from my grandmother. You know, the one on the hill by the sea, just outside of town?"

"Lavender House?" She grimaced. "That changes things, I'm afraid."

"Really?" I shouldn't be surprised, since Margot had said the same thing, but I'd thought perhaps she was exaggerating.

Minxie nodded apologetically. "No one in the area will work there. The house is entirely unwelcoming. In an aggressive way, if you know what I mean."

I didn't, but I just nodded along, disappointed. Maybe I could find some workers from farther afield.

"Are you planning to live there, then?" she asked, picking up the dryer.

"If I can fix it up, yes."

"Well, good luck. Your grandmother tried for years, but no one would do the work."

"I guess I'll have to learn some new skills, then." YouTube could teach me how to repair a house, right?

But in a month?

I shoved away the negative thought as Minxie switched on the dryer. When she turned me around to see my new style in the mirror, I grinned. "Oh my gosh, it looks gold instead of boring. And I didn't realize there was some curl to my hair!"

"Yep. Underneath all that weight was some nice texture. I

did a little spell as I dried it, so it should always look like this when you wake up."

"So, no fiddling with tools or hair products?" I asked, excited about the prospect. "That's incredible."

"Nope. You should wake up like this!"

"Amazing! I can't believe your last client canceled on you. If you can do this, I'd never let you go."

"Well, good." She grinned. "I'll put you on the books for another appointment in a couple months."

I nodded, just hoping I would still be here at that time. If I failed with my grandmother's house...

I shoved the thought away. Since my plan to find help hadn't gone the way I'd wanted, there was no time to waste. I needed to hurry back and learn how to fix up a house, pronto.

The next hour passed in a blur as I stopped at the shop to pick up a few things to wear. The three sisters were as eagle-eyed as promised, but I was careful to replace everything I tried on. In the end, they even gave me some good advice. I decided that when I had more time to shop, I would be back.

On the way to the post office to send the deeds to the solicitor, I spotted a purple sign hanging over a door: *Aurora Coven: Here for all your magical needs.* Hmm, that could be helpful. Contractors might not help me, but a coven could have some resources. I needed to learn more about magic, anyway, if I was going to fully embrace this new life of mine.

After a quick stop at the little grocery store for staples, I looked for Poa on the bench she'd chosen for her nap. There was no sign of her, but that didn't worry me. She could more than take care of herself.

I drove back to the boathouse alone. Thankfully, Rafe wasn't there as I hurried up to my flat and stashed my new goodies. I changed into the trousers and shirt I'd bought, ate a quick sandwich, then headed up to the house to see what I was working with.

CHAPTER
SEVEN

ISOBEL

ANTICIPATION DANCED through me as I climbed the steep, rocky hill toward Lavender House. I could have gone around via the road, which wasn't much farther, but I was so anxious to see what I was up against that I cut straight across the uneven ground toward the ramshackle gray structure.

There was a small cottage about a hundred meters to the east, sitting a bit higher on the hillside. I hadn't noticed it last night, but from the look of the neatly trimmed garden, it was inhabited. I'd have to make a point to meet my neighbor eventually.

As I neared the big house, I realized that the stone it had been built from was actually very pretty. The rest of the house, however...

Rafe had been right—it was in terrible condition. The roof looked like it was on its last legs, and several of the windows had been boarded up, presumably after the glass had been broken. Had my grandmother done that? I couldn't imagine her climbing up there to put the boards in place, but I was grateful to whomever had done it. The chances of water damage inside would be substantially less.

The wind blew my hair in my face as I inspected the suggestion of a front garden. If there had ever been one, it was long gone, supplanted by a path cutting through the rocky hillside that dropped sharply down to the boathouse and sea. The view was gorgeous, but right now, the landscaping looked very neglected. One day, I could put pretty flowers alongside the path, but that was a ways off.

I turned my attention back to the house. I needed to get inside if I was going to figure out how much work really awaited me.

Apprehensive, I pulled the key from my pocket as I approached the door. There was a strangely unwelcoming feeling as I slipped the key into the lock, and a tiny shock raced down my arm.

"Ouch!" I yanked my hand back and shook it, glaring at the door. "You'd better stop that. I'm not going anywhere. And I'm here to help, actually."

The house seemed to groan, and I wasn't sure if it was my imagination or a real noise. I shook my head. So peculiar.

The key was still sticking out of the lock, and I gently tapped it with one finger. It didn't shock me again, so I gripped it and turned. It was a stubborn lock, more due to old age than the house's anger. I wasn't sure how I could tell, but probably because the house didn't shock me again. It took a bit of force to get it to click, but it finally did, and I swung the door open. It made the most awful creaking noise as it did, and I grinned. "You're laying it on a little thick, you know?"

I'd never been one for talking out loud, especially not to inanimate objects. But Lavender House was different. There was a presence here.

The house responded with a godawful stench—rot and mildew and old socks. I covered my mouth with my sleeve and stepped inside, letting my eyes adjust to the gloom. The first thing I noticed was the beautiful staircase that led upstairs. Then I clocked the horrific wallpaper and carpeting, along with the thick layer of dust. Broken glass glittered dully on the ground underneath the window near the door, and a giant spider skittered through a crack in the baseboard.

I blew out a breath, a weight seeming to descend onto my shoulders.

This was *a lot*. There was just *so* much wrong with this place, and I was only in the front room.

"Snap out of it," I muttered to myself.

I wasn't a quitter. I couldn't be—I had to make this work since I didn't have anywhere else to go. Anyway, my trip to the village this morning made me want to live in Charming Cove. I'd felt more at home during my few hours on Foxglove Lane than I ever had in London. And no matter how bad this house looked now, it was my home.

I could feel it.

Problem was, the house didn't agree.

"Are you a ghost?" I asked the empty space around me.

There was no response, but that didn't mean it wasn't a

ghost. Maybe it was playing a more subtle game. Didn't matter—I would beat them at it.

I headed toward the door at the far end of the room, entering an old kitchen that looked like it had been built sometime at the beginning of the last century. It was going to need to be completely redone, no question. Through the back windows, I could see the remains of what had once been a glorious garden. It was in seriously bad shape, of course, choked by weeds bigger than I was.

The bathrooms weren't any better, and I didn't find a single room that wasn't horrible. Some of them might have been fine, but the stench was enough to make my eyes water and colored my opinion of everything.

"You don't feel very well, do you?" I asked the house. "Is there a ghost bothering you? A curse?"

Beneath my feet, the floorboard popped up underneath the rug. I tumbled to my butt, landing hard on the gross old carpet. A cloud of dust poofed up, and I coughed. Behind me, a bathroom door slammed, the noise so loud it made my head hurt.

"All right, all right!" I wasn't afraid, exactly, but I also wasn't stupid. Whatever was in here wanted me gone, and I didn't want to get on its bad side. "I'm leaving. But I want you to know that I'm coming back, and I'm here to help."

The house seemed to groan again, almost in frustration. Like it wanted to be left alone. Well, it was out of luck.

I climbed to my feet and brushed off the seat of my trousers, then headed to the front door. The floor beneath me shifted, ejecting me through the entryway. I stumbled, nearly losing my footing, then whirled around to glare at the house. "I get it, okay? You're grumpy. But I'm going to fix that."

The door slammed in my face.

"Rude." I turned and headed down the hill. I needed to find a way to fix that house's mood, stat. It wouldn't be safe to work there until I got a better handle on what was happening inside.

Poa waited for me at the door to the boathouse, lounging in a patch of sunlight. Her orange, white, and black fur gleamed beautifully, and she squinted up at me through the bright light, her gaze going to my shortened hair. *That's a new look.*

"Do you like it?"

Yes. You look less Little House on the Prairie.

"Um, thanks."

How did it go at our new house?

"Fantastic," I said wryly, looking back up at the place, which seemed to glower at me. "You didn't want to see for yourself?"

She gave a wheezy laugh, which I supposed was the best a cat could do. *No. I knew it would be a nightmare.*

"More like a ghost."

Do you think?

"I don't know. But I've got no skill with the dead. I know where to find someone who might, though."

Who?

"There was a coven in town. I saw the sign on my way to the salon. They should be able to help me." Covens weren't the whimsical groups of forest witches that human fiction depicted them to be. Rather, they were businesses formed by groups of witches to help others solve their problems. There were plenty of supernaturals who couldn't do magic, like werewolves and vampires and witches who had ignored their own skills for too long.

I looked at my phone, realizing that it was almost five o'clock. Time had passed more quickly than I'd realized while I checked out the house. The coven probably shut their door at five, but if I hurried, I'd make it there in time. I looked at Poa. "Want to come?"

She scrunched her face. *There's only a little sun left. I'm not leaving this spot until its gone.*

"Suit yourself." I shrugged. "There might be a handsome tom there, though."

Pass. She rolled over so that her white belly faced the sun.

I grinned and hurried to the car, then drove back into town. I found a parking spot right in front of the coven storefront. As I climbed out, my phone buzzed in my pocket. A text came through from Tommy, then another and another. I deleted all of them, then blocked his number. He hated being ignored, and I loved the idea of how irritated he would be.

The thought put a pep in my step as I walked toward the Aurora Coven, reveling in the wild autumn day by the sea. The wind had whipped up even stronger, and as the sun neared the horizon, it was cooling off. On the sea, the whitecaps tipped the waves, and most of the birds had abandoned the sky.

Inside the Aurora Coven storefront, the room was cozy and welcoming. A fire burned in the hearth, and two witches sat in cozy armchairs in front of it. Bookshelves and plants filled the space, and I immediately felt at home.

Both witches smiled as they stood. One was tall, with long blond hair, and the other wore a pretty scarf tied through her dark curls.

"Hello," said the blonde. "What can we help you with?"

"Hi. I've got a bit of a problem." I blew out a breath, unsure of where to start.

"Let me get you a cup of tea," the blonde said. "I'm Emma, by the way."

"Hi, I'm Isobel."

"Holly." The other woman waved and smiled, then gestured to the third chair in front of the fire. I took a seat while Emma disappeared into a back room.

Holly sat, then leaned forward. "You're a witch."

"I am. But not skilled."

Holly frowned. "I feel your power, though. You're strong."

I winced. It was almost worse to be powerful but unskilled—it was just evidence that I'd neglected my gifts. Holly seemed to notice my discomfort, though, and said quickly, "That's okay, we can help you with that."

It wasn't the reason I'd come, but it was a great idea. I needed to master my magic, and after what I'd seen at the house today, that was the only way I'd be able to fix the place up in time. There was no way I could do all that work with elbow grease alone.

Emma returned with the tea, setting the tray on the little table in front of the fire. It was all so cozy that I was immediately in love. She poured the tea, then handed me a mug and said, "Help yourself to sugar and milk."

"Thank you." I added splash of milk, then took a sip. It was fiercely hot but delicious.

"So, you're new to town," Emma said.

"I am. How did you know?"

"Well, we know everyone." She smiled and shrugged. "But I know you're not just a visitor because I stopped by Margot's for coffee, and she told me about the newcomer at Lavender House."

"That's why I'm here," I said, then I looked at Holly. "Though I could also use help with my power. But the house is my biggest concern right now. I need to fix it up in a month, but it's got a ghost or a curse, or something. I'm not sure what, and I need help finding out."

"I can assist you with that," Emma said. "I'm good with ghosts."

"Fantastic." Relief rushed through me. "Thank you. This is the first help I've managed to find."

Emma nodded, a sympathetic look on her face. "Yeah, that place is infamous. Not a single contractor will touch it."

"I'm hoping they'll change their minds if I can get rid of the ghost."

"I can come by tomorrow morning, if that works for you," Emma said.

"Perfect. Nine?"

She agreed, and I wondered how to broach the subject of my neglected magic. I hated talking about it. I didn't need to, though. Holly leaned forward. "As for your magic..."

"It's that obvious?" I asked.

"Just that you're powerful. I only know about your lack of skill from what you said. But don't worry." Her warm smile was a balm to my embarrassment. "Do you know what your skill is?"

"I don't." Every witch had a specific skill to call her own —I just had no idea what mine was. "I also don't know many spells, but I'm going to need some if I want to fix up this house. Do you maybe have a library of spell books I could use to brush up?"

"Of course." Holly pointed toward the ceiling. "We have a workshop that will be perfect."

"And we can help with pointers, if you need," Emma said.

"Oh, I would love that." How was I so lucky? "I know you're probably closing soon, but would it be all right if I took a peek upstairs before you do?"

"We can do you one better," said Emma. "I've got to make some potions. You can look at the books while I work."

"Thank you. That'd be amazing."

"Good luck, ladies, because I'm out of here," Holly said. "I've been manning the desk all day, and I need a break."

I looked around for a desk but didn't see one.

"Just a turn of phrase," Holly said. "I'm a novice in the coven. There are four of us, and we take turns in this front room greeting possible customers." She gestured to Emma. "Whereas Emma here is our most recent full member." She grinned proudly at her friend. "She was just keeping me company. Senior witches don't have to man the desk."

"No, but we do have to make potions after hours if we didn't finish our work earlier." She grimaced. "Vivienne will not be pleased. It's fish and chips night, and I'm going to be late."

"Vivienne?" I asked.

"My partner Alaric's grandmother. She lives next door to us. I love her to bits, but she gets grumpy if we delay dinner."

I smiled, loving the idea of having family like that.

"Come on," she said, "I'll show you the first floor." She led me up the stairs and into a magnificent workshop. It ran the length of the building, with windows on one side that provided a view of the sea and more windows at the back. Shelves covered the walls, each stuffed full of books and potion ingredients. Herbs hung from the ceiling, and large wooden tables sat beneath. Cauldrons and other tools were scattered across the surfaces.

"This is amazing," I said.

"Isn't it?" Emma smiled. "I moved here a few years ago and have been in love with Charming Cove and the Aurora Coven ever since."

"I can't blame you." She'd clearly built a life for herself here, and suddenly, I wanted nothing more than to do the same.

"You'll find some helpful books over here." She walked to a shelf and pulled out a few, leaving them poking out slightly so I could find them. "They're mostly about housekeeping and construction. A few spells to help you do the work more quickly, to make the materials more cooperative, that kind of thing."

"Perfect." I joined her and took the books off the shelf, then carried them over to the squashy armchairs beneath the back windows. I leaned forward to squint into the darkening evening. There was a walled garden behind the building, and it was beautiful.

I smiled and sat, tucking into the books and devouring

the information as Emma worked on a potion on the other side of the room. It was a companionable silence, and she already felt like a friend.

I'd found another place that felt like home—and come hell or high water, I would find a way to keep it.

CHAPTER
EIGHT

Isobel

By the time Emma finished her potions, it was nearly eight o'clock. I closed the books and put them back on their shelves, biting my lip so I didn't ask if I could borrow them. Emma had been so welcoming that I was sure she'd have offered if it were possible. More than likely, the books were meant to stay in the library. Spell books like these were incredibly valuable, after all.

"Did you find what you were looking for?" she asked as she led me downstairs.

"Some, yes." I had a couple handy new tricks. "But I'd love to come back."

"Absolutely. Anytime." She smiled as she held open the door for me, then locked it. "Well, I need to run. Vivienne will be waiting for her order from Codswollop's."

I grinned and waved as she hurried down the street, then

turned to look at the sea. The wind whipped off the dark waves, bringing a scent of salt and sea that I sucked deep into my lungs.

This place was amazing. Why had I spent so much of my life stuck in dreary London?

Oh, right. Tommy.

I shoved the thought of him away. He was no longer part of my life.

But what was I going to do with that life? Now that I didn't have Tommy to take care of, I had free time. The evening spread out before me—a weird feeling, but a good one. It was too dark to do any work at Lavender House, and I didn't fancy going back to the dusty, frilly flat that I was temporarily calling home.

I looked down the street in either direction, catching sight of a sign that said *The Sea Shanty*. Warm light glowed from the windows, inviting me in. As I neared, I realized it was a pub.

Perfect.

I walked toward it, noticing that across the street, there was a garden with tables overlooking the sea. The tables were repurposed old beer barrels, and the sight made me smile. It was kitschy, but in a charming way. The garden would be perfect for a sunny day, though it was far too windy and cool right now.

Instead, I turned toward the pub and pulled open the wooden door, and was immediately enveloped in warmth and good cheer. The interior was mostly warm wood, with nautical regalia on the walls. It was like stepping back in time, with the little fire burning in the hearth to the right and the small wooden bar with half a dozen leather barstools directly in front of me.

I approached the bar, smiling at the bartender, who was pulling Real Ale out of the polished brass spout.

"Welcome to The Sea Shanty," she said. "What can I get you?"

"Are you doing food right now?"

"We are indeed, and I can recommend the steak and ale pie."

"Perfect. I'll have that when you've got a chance." I pointed to the Real Ale she was pouring. "And one of those, please."

"Not a problem. Find a seat, and I'll bring it over."

"Thanks." I smiled and turned around, looking for a good table. There was a little one right by the fire, and it was just so charming that I couldn't resist.

I took a seat, leaning close to the fire to read the little plaque beneath it: *Burning Since 1602.*

"Wow," I said, unable to help myself. That was cool.

I turned back to the pub and spotted a familiar figure at a table on the other side of the room.

Rafe. And he was looking right at me, a scowl on his face.

How had I not noticed him when I'd come in? He seemed to command the room with his quiet yet massive presence. He definitely didn't seem pleased to see me invading his space.

I grinned cheerily at him and waved.

"Do you know him?" the bartender asked as she approached with my drink.

"Rafe? Yes. A bit. Does he come in here often?"

"Often enough, but he keeps to himself." She shot him a glance. "A shame, really. He could keep to me as much as he likes."

"He's not very social?" Even as I asked the question, I knew the answer. Of course he wasn't social.

"Hardly." She set the beer down. "Rumor has it he's quite well off. They say he made a bunch of money in London, investing or something, then moved out here to build boats as a hobby."

That made sense, given what I'd seen in the workshop.

She smiled. "Your pie will be out soon."

I drank my beer and looked at Rafe, who'd turned away from me. Could I possibly annoy him into leaving the boathouse?

Probably not, if he thought he owned it. Ah, well.

The bartender delivered the pie, and it was as delicious as she'd promised. They really knew how to do food here in Charming Cove, if the coffee shop and this pub were any indication.

When I finished my dinner, I decided to move over to the bar. It was getting too warm by the fire, and I wanted another pint before I headed back for the night. I was tired, but I didn't want Rafe thinking he was driving me away from The Sea Shanty.

The bartender smiled as I approached, and began to pull me another pint. I took one of the barstools and asked, "Has that fire really been burning since 1602?"

"Never put out." She passed me the beer. "And there's the ghost of a female pirate here, Mary MacAlain. They say she cut off the balls of the pirate who stole her ship."

I winced, then grinned. "Well, she certainly didn't take any shit, did she?"

"An icon." Her gaze went to someone over my shoulder, and she smiled. "Not that I'm planning to cut off any balls, Charlie, so don't worry."

A warm laugh sounded from behind me, and I turned. A handsome man with friendly features and warm brown eyes smiled at me, then nodded at my drink. "One of what she's having."

"Coming right up." The bartender got to work on his pint, and he turned to me.

His smile was warm. "Pity you haven't finished your drink. I'd offer to buy you one."

His tone was distinctly flirty, and I smiled. He was about my age and seemed like a nice guy. He definitely gave off good guy vibes, but I'd just spent all of my adult life with Tommy, so what did I know?

"I'm Charlie." He held out his hand, and I took it, immediately noticing the warmth of his handshake. It was a good guy handshake, as far as I could tell.

Something made me look over at Rafe. He was staring directly at us, and there was something in his gaze that I didn't recognize.

I turned back to Charlie. "I'm Isobel. New in town."

"Oh, yeah?" He smiled and took the seat next to me, then immediately stood again. "I should have asked. Is this seat taken?"

"Only if you sit there."

He gave a relieved laugh and sat. "Great."

The bartender handed him his beer, and we got to talking. He was a plumber, which I found to be immensely exciting, considering the fact that I had four broken toilets and exactly no plumbing skills, but I didn't mention the house yet. It was clear what the town thought of that house, and I needed to make this guy like me if I was going to ask him to help. It was sly, but I was desperate.

After about fifteen minutes, two other men entered the pub. They were a similar age to Charlie, and they smiled as they greeted him.

"Isobel, let me introduce you to the guys." He turned and gestured to the shorter man. "This is Lee, who does roofing, and Carlos does electrical work. They work with me."

A plumber, a roofer, and an electrician? Jackpot. They were the damned dream team.

Lee and Carlos ordered their beers, and Charlie invited me to play darts with them. I immediately said yes, liking the vibe of the three guys. Even if they weren't tradesmen, I'd have wanted to hang out with them.

The dart board was in the corner of the room opposite the fire, which meant it was near Rafe's table. He was still there, still looking at me. Not all the time, but often enough that I could feel his gaze.

It gave me shivers, and not the bad kind, which was a surprise.

Nope, I admonished myself. I needed to keep my mind out of that gutter. Rafe was complicated, whereas Charlie and his plumber friends were exactly what I needed. They were friendly and easygoing.

After a couple of games, they all had to leave because of an early job the next morning. As they walked out of the pub,

I looked down at my empty glass. I should go home, but I was having too much fun. Who knew that freedom could be so great? I hadn't realized I was in a cage in London, but I definitely had been.

Decided, I went to the bar and ordered another beer, then another one of what Rafe was having.

The bartender raised her brows at the order but filled it. "You're a brave woman," she said as she handed it over.

"What's the worst he can do? Growl at me?"

She nodded. "Fair enough. I'm just not one for rejection."

"Oh, he can't reject me." I grinned. "We live together."

She leaned on the bar, interest lighting her eyes. "Now that's a story I need to hear. I'm Meg, by the way."

"Isobel. Nice to meet you. And next time I come round, I'll fill you in on the details. For now, I'm on a mission to annoy my roommate."

Rafe

I watched as Isobel approached, a beer in each hand. My wolf hearing had allowed me to eavesdrop on every word she'd said since she'd walked in, and I couldn't help the anticipation that fizzed through my veins. It annoyed the hell out of me, but it was impossible to fight. My body just seemed to come alive around her—my wolf instincts in particular.

Connect, protect.

The instinct surged through me, one I'd never felt before.

68

She stopped by the table, grinning widely as she put the beer down in front of me. Her golden hair gleamed in the light, shorter than it had been last night. The soft curls made my fingertips itch to touch, and I clenched my fist.

"What's that for?" I looked between the beer and her, careful to keep the scowl on my face. It wasn't as easy as it normally was.

"For you." She smiled, a damned ray of sunshine. And like a ray of sunshine, she warmed me. Which was irritating.

"Why?"

"Because you look grumpy, and I want to turn that frown upside down."

I groaned. "Too much."

She grinned. "I know. It was over the top, but I thought it would annoy you, and I couldn't help but try."

"Try to annoy me?"

"Yep." She laughed lightly. "You're just so grumpy. I could try to cheer you up, but...nah. So I'll go with annoying you." She took the seat next to me, her lovely lavender and honeysuckle scent washing over me.

"Well, it's working."

"Good." She sipped her beer. "Why are you sitting over here by yourself, just glowering?"

"I'm not glowering." I took a drink of the beer she'd brought me.

"Oh, you definitely are. You're the grumpiest werewolf I've ever met."

"You've met a lot of werewolves?"

"No, actually. I suppose I can revise that statement to say you're the grumpiest man. It's an even broader category."

"Then you should avoid me."

"Can't, unfortunately, since we live together."

"We live near each other, not together."

"*Very* near." She grinned. "But that would change more quickly if you'd help me fix up my house. I'd be out of your hair much sooner."

"No."

"Oh, come on. Take a break from your boat hobby and help a girl out."

"It's not a hobby." Her words shouldn't have annoyed me, but they did. "It's a business." Albeit one that I didn't need the money from. But my reputation as a reliable craftsman who delivered on time was important to me, and that was more than a hobby.

"Sorry." She seemed genuinely contrite. "The bartender said it was a hobby. I misunderstood."

"It's fine." I sighed. "So, you're not having a lot of luck finding help with the house?"

"No. The locals want nothing to do with it. Aren't you local?"

"No. Moved here a year ago."

"A newcomer like me." She smiled, her luminous gray eyes twinkling. "All the more reason to help me."

"Why didn't you ask the plumbers for help?"

"How do you know I didn't?"

I tapped my ear. "Wolf hearing."

"Damn. Were you listening to everything I said?"

"Can't help it. I try to filter it out." I found that I wanted to annoy her as much as she annoyed me. "Didn't bother, though."

Although I should have. It had been irritating to hear the flirting going on while they'd played darts, and I shouldn't have been irritated by that. She could do whatever she wanted. Hell, it would be better if she got a boyfriend and moved out of my house.

The idea of it made my wolf growl, and I told the beast to settle down. He listened, but barely.

"For your information, I was trying to make them like me before I ask for the help," she said. "No one in town wants to work on the place, so I'm going to need favors instead of just hiring people."

"Good plan. A bit mercenary, though."

"Maybe, but it's a mild form of mercenariness."

"Mercenariness? Is that a word?" Oh hell, was I flirting with her? I never flirted.

She smiled at me. "It is now. I suppose I could say Machiavellian, but I prefer my version."

I couldn't help the smile that tugged at my lips, and it irritated the hell out of me.

Time to go. I drained the last of the beer, then stood. "Thanks for the drink, but it's past my bedtime."

I turned and left the pub, feeling her gaze follow me the entire way out.

CHAPTER
NINE

Isobel

THE NEXT MORNING, I awoke to the same lovely breeze and sound of the waves as the morning before. The bed was so comfortable that I could have snuggled there for hours, but that wasn't on the agenda.

Today, I was going to figure out what was wrong with the house so that I could get to work on it. With any luck, I'd fix it and be able to convince some local contractors to take on the job.

I sat up and climbed out of bed, disturbing Poa, who lay at the foot. She gave me an annoyed meow, then settled back and began snoring again.

"I'm going to meet Emma today at the house. She might have a familiar for you to meet."

Poa perked up, interest on her face.

"We leave in thirty," I said, heading to the bathroom to

brush my teeth. I had a feeling I'd be getting dirty today, so I'd save my shower for tonight.

After dressing in some suitable trousers and a shirt, I brewed myself a cup of coffee and headed downstairs to drink it by the water. My life in London had been so land-bound that being this close to the ocean was amazing. I'd never spent much time by the sea, but that hadn't been from lack of desire. Tommy just hadn't wanted to travel.

The thought of him made me scowl, but it didn't hurt as much as I expected. There was a dull ache there, mostly for the thought of what I'd had and lost. But what I'd thought I'd had was a lie, so I couldn't really mourn it. And if I were honest with myself, we'd been drifting apart for years.

I shook the thought away and headed outside, inhaling the fresh sea air. It woke me up, and I quickened my pace toward the water. As I neared the end of the boathouse closest to the sea, I saw a flash of movement to my left.

Rafe, disappearing around the side of the building.

Was he avoiding me?

Probably. I'd annoyed the hell out of him last night, and as fun as it had been, I'd probably better lay off the guy. We still had to live together, and I didn't want him to dislike me more than he already did.

But there'd been some flirtation there, too—I was sure of it. I'd had fun with him, and for a moment, I'd thought he was having fun as well. He definitely wasn't as bad as I'd imagined, though his avoidance this morning didn't bode well for the future of our relationship.

Not that we had one.

I didn't need another one of those any time soon, and he

was a terrible candidate. I shoved the thoughts away and finished the last of my coffee, then headed back into the boathouse. Rafe wasn't in the main room, so I had to assume he was in his bedroom.

For the best, I reminded myself.

I found Poa in the kitchen, eating shredded cheddar cheese straight out of the bag. She'd made a mess, but I was confident she'd clean up every scrap.

"You have kibble, you know." I pointed to her bowl.

She looked over at it, clearly disdainful, then returned her attention to the cheese.

I rolled my eyes and pulled a granola bar out of the cabinet. "We're late, so finish your cheese, and let's go."

She picked up the pace, and the bits of cheddar were gone in seconds. I ate the granola bar as I headed back down the stairs, Poa on my heels. Rafe was now in the kitchen, and I called out a cheery, "Good morning!"

He grunted, and I smiled.

The walk up to the house on the hill was short, and we arrived just as a small car was pulling into the drive from the other side. I waved at Emma as she climbed out and said, "Hello!"

"Hi!" She waved, then looked at the house.

She'd left the car door open, and a black and white creature leapt out, a pink bow flopping around her neck. The telltale white stripe on her back marked her as a skunk, which was a little odd since they weren't native to the UK. But familiars were often all sorts of odd animals.

Poa stopped in her tracks about five meters from the

skunk and glared. The skunk glared back, then hissed. Poa returned the sound, her back arched.

Emma and I watched silently as the two familiars stared each other down. The last thing we needed was a fight, especially when Poa would end up stinking to high heaven and still expect to sleep in my bed.

The moment passed as quickly as it had come, and the two relaxed. They trotted closer, clearly communicating, even though I couldn't hear what they were saying. After a moment, they headed around the house toward the back garden like two gal pals headed off to have a drink and a chat.

Emma looked at me. "If you have any wine or chocolate back there, you won't have it for long."

"Oh?"

"Penelope is a big fan."

"Can cats and skunks have wine?"

Emma shrugged. "Normal ones? No. But familiars are fine since they're magical. It's never had any ill effect on Penelope, at least."

"Good." I really didn't want to have to monitor what Poa ate or drank since I had a feeling she was the most adorable garbage disposal I'd ever seen.

"Ready to check out your house?" Emma asked.

"Let's do it." I led her toward the front door, which opened with the same horrifying creak that it had made the day before.

We stepped through the doorway, and the house gave an audible groan. It sounded almost like an annoyed human.

"Chill out," I said.

"I'm chill." Emma shot me a sideways glance.

"Sorry, not you. I was talking to the house. Didn't you hear it groan?"

"It's been silent since I walked in."

"Really?"

"You heard something?"

"Yes."

"That's unusual." She gave me an appraising look, clearly storing that information away for later.

I stepped further into the house and shut the door. Almost immediately, an awful stench washed over us. Emma flinched and raised a hand to her mouth, then shot me a glance. "Okay, *that* I noticed."

"We should have probably brought plague masks."

She laughed weakly, raising her arm to cover her mouth with her sleeve. "It's fine. It's probably part of the haunting."

"The house definitely doesn't want me here." I patted the doorframe next to me as if trying to convince it that I meant no harm. "But we're going to change that."

"Definitely." Emma stepped further into the house. Underfoot, the floorboards moved beneath the carpet, creating waves of polyester that were difficult to walk on. She stumbled to a spot by the wall and pressed herself back against it. "I think its extra annoyed that I'm here."

"I hate to say it, but I agree." I'd at least been able to walk last time I'd been there.

"It's not a problem." She drew in a deep breath, pressing her hands to the wall behind her. "I'll see what I can find." Her magic flared on the air, vibrating around me with the scent of honeysuckle and jasmine. "Hello? Is anyone there?"

Silence followed.

She frowned, a glint of concentration entering her eyes. Her magic flared more strongly, a distinct addition to the air that made my skin prickle. She was powerful.

"Any ghosts in the area, I request that you show yourself. Now." The firmness in her voice made me twitch. A strong desire to follower her order filled me, and I wasn't even a ghost.

Except nothing showed itself.

After a while, Emma turned to me, a frown on her face. "If there were a ghost here, they'd have felt compelled to show themselves. They wouldn't have been able to stop themselves from appearing."

"Huh." I leaned against the wall, frowning. "So, no ghost."

She nodded. "Could be a curse."

"I'll need a curse detection spell for that."

"We have the ingredients at headquarters, and I could make one, but it would take a while. The quickest way to get one would be to visit Seaside Spells, the shop at the end of Foxglove Lane. They sell all sorts of potions, and they'll definitely have one."

"Thank you." As much as I wanted to send more business her way, I was in a legitimate hurry. "I really appreciate this. What do I owe you?"

"Nothing. First-timer discount." She grinned.

"No, I have to pay you something."

"How about you come to girls' night?"

"What's that?"

"Some of my friends and I get together on Thursday

night for drinks and a chat."

"That sounds like more of a favor to me than a way to pay you back." All the same, my heart leapt at the idea of having friends. Emma was cool, and I'd love to hang out with her.

She shrugged. "We need fresh blood, and I like you."

"Thanks. I like you, too." Okay, this was getting nerdy. Or sappy. It was getting something, and I needed to chill out. "Where and when?"

"Potions & Pino, the wine bar on Foxglove Lane. Seven o'clock tomorrow."

"I'll be there." I looked around for our familiars, realizing that they'd never joined us. "Good luck finding Penelope. I'm sure Poa has led her around back to engage in some property destruction or some other kind of light crime."

Emma grinned. "Penelope is one step ahead of her. Don't worry about it."

I grinned, then waved her off and turned back to the house. I propped my hands on my hips and frowned. "So, you're not haunted. But there's definitely something going on here. If it's a curse, I'm going to get to the bottom of it and cure you."

The house didn't say thank you, of course. It only acknowledged me by strategically popping a floorboard that sent me onto my butt. I landed with a hard thud, and frustration flared.

No. I wouldn't let this house get the better of me. "Cute, but you can't scare me away. We're going to be best friends, you'll see."

The house groaned again, and I rolled my eyes. "I'll be back."

I left, shutting the door carefully behind me. Poa was nowhere to be seen, but I knew she could take care of herself.

As quickly as I could, I hurried down to the boathouse and got in my car, then drove into town. It was a bit busier at this hour—nearly lunchtime—but I was still able to find a parking space pretty close to Seaside Spells.

I gave the sparkling blue sea a long, lingering look. Now that I lived here, I couldn't get enough of it. The sight, the sound, the scent—it all cleared my mind and gave me perspective.

After I'd had my fill, I turned away and looked at Seaside Spells. The three-story building was made of the same stone as the other buildings in town, but it was by far the quirkiest one of the lot. There were four crooked chimneys and diamond-pane windows on the second floor. The blue sign over the door proclaimed, *Seaside Spells: The Finest Purveyor of Magical Potions & Spells in the United Kingdom.*

"All right, then," I murmured. "You're sure to have what I need."

I crossed the street and pushed open the wooden door, entering the charming space. Dried herbs hung from the ceiling, and the shelves were filled with sparkling glass bottles and objects that vibrated with magic. To my right, a spiral of wands decorated the wall, each marked with a tiny label that displayed its special properties. Cauldrons were stacked against the stairs, and a fire in the hearth burned faintly, a welcome warmth after the autumn chill.

In front of the hearth, a black and white cat snoozed. The creature didn't seem to notice me enter, or it didn't care, because it didn't so much as flick its tail.

An older woman bustled out from the back room, her white hair piled into a neat knot on top of her head. Her floral dress was the epitome of grandmotherly attire, and it made me wish that my grandmother had been more traditional. Or that she'd liked me more, at least. I wouldn't have cared if she'd worn a leather catsuit and driven a Harley-Davidson if she'd shown she loved me.

Whoa.

Where had that come from? I'd known I'd had some demons, but that one had come screaming out at the sight of this woman. I should probably get myself into therapy at some point.

She smiled warmly at me. "Hello, dear. How can I help you?"

I smiled back at her, trying to banish any trace of my thoughts. "Hi. I'm here for a curse-revealing spell, if you have one."

"Oh, certainly." She picked up an enormous bottle of Coke and took a sip.

It was an entirely unexpected gesture, and I blinked.

"Oh, I know it's far too much cola for any one person." She waved her hand dismissively. "My granddaughter tells me that every time she sees me drinking one. But it keeps me young, I say."

"It's your spunky attitude that keeps you young." A child's voice preceded her into the room. "At least, that's what my mum says." She grinned as she stopped just inside the door. She had to be about eight years old, and she sported a pink sweatshirt that went all the way down to her

80

knees. Her high pigtails were decorated with ribbons, and a bruise bloomed under one eye.

The woman laughed. "She's right." Then she frowned at the girl. "Catrina, what happened to your face?"

"Will Bellows." Catrina grinned even wider. "But don't worry, he looks worse."

"You're fist fighting?" The older woman glared. "Why?"

"Because mum said I couldn't give him any more tails." The little girl looked at me. "I gave him a squirrel tail earlier this year. Then a pig's tail. But his mum complained to my mum, and well, here we are." She shrugged and pointed to her eye.

The older woman groaned and pinched the bridge of her nose. "You'll be the death of me, Catrina."

"Didn't you hear me say that he looks worse?"

"I did, darling. Well done. But we're going to need for you to find another way to settle your differences with Will Bellows."

I tried to repress the smile that threatened.

"Sweep the shop, darling." The older woman handed the girl a broom. "Time to earn your keep."

The girl grinned and grabbed the broom, then made it stand on its bristles as she focused her attention on it. Magic swelled in the air, smelling of bubble gum and flowers. As I watched, the broom began to scoot across the floor, doing a reasonably good job of sweeping.

"You're very talented," I said.

"I know." Catrina grinned, but there was nothing particularly cocky about her. She just owned her magic, and I respected that. I needed to be more like this child.

The older woman came out from around the counter. "I'm Cecelia, dear. Owner of Seaside Spells. And this is Catrina, my honorary great-granddaughter."

Catrina bowed, but her broom never stopped sweeping.

"I'm Isobel. I inherited the house on the hill outside of town."

"Ah, so that's why you want the curse-revealing spell." Cecelia went to the shelf along the left wall and began poking through small glass bottles. "That place has something off about it, though I'm not sure it's a curse."

"I'm about to find out," I said.

"Have you looked for a ghost?" Catrina asked.

"Yes, just an hour ago. No luck."

Catrina gave a knowing nod, seeming older than her years. "Smart to go for the curse revealer, then."

"Thanks." I grinned, liking her already. "That's what I thought."

Cecelia walked toward me, handing over a vial of sparkling powder. "You'll need this for the spell. And let me get you the words and instructions." She hustled to the desk and scratched out some words on a paper, then returned to me. "It's a tricky one. If you need help, I can come by after work."

"Thank you." I appreciated the offer, but I didn't have the time to wait. And anyway, Step Two of reinventing myself was to master my magic. I'd already made a good start on Step One, my makeover, but Step Two was arguably more important. "I'm going to try it myself, but if I mess it up, do you have more ingredients?"

"Certainly. Just come back to get them, and I'll help you do the spell."

"Thanks." I couldn't believe how amazingly nice everyone was in Charming Cove. "What do I owe you?"

"Let me see." She went back to the desk and looked through a book, then glanced up sat me. "Forty-five quid with the newcomer discount."

"Thank you." I handed over the money, then waved goodbye to Catrina and Cecelia before turning to leave the shop.

"Can I go with her?" I heard Catrina ask as I made my way to the door. "I want to see the house."

"Once we know if it's cursed, dear. Then you can go and help her get it cleaned up. It's sure to be a big job."

"It's true," I said over my shoulder before I stepped out the door. "I can use all the help I can get."

"Count me in." Catrina saluted.

I smiled back at her. "With your broom skills, you'll be more than welcome."

"I can also provide security."

I looked at her black eye and thought of her story about being banned from giving the local boys tails. "I bet you're even better at that than sweeping."

"I am." Catrina shot her gran a look that said *See? She thinks so, too.*

"I'll see you later," I said. "And thank you again."

CHAPTER
TEN

ISOBEL

LATER THAT AFTERNOON, I walked up to the house, my chest humming with anticipation. This was the first big spell I was going to try in ages. I couldn't believe I'd let myself drift so far away from my craft. Tommy had nudged me in that direction for years, and I hated that I'd let him. I knew I'd allowed it because I'd been so desperate for affection that I'd have put up with just about anything, but that no longer seemed like a worthy reason.

I sucked in a deep breath—I was on the path to *Becoming Not a Doormat*. I would become the door, or whatever. That actually made no sense, but at least I was planning to be in charge of my destiny, and that was all that mattered.

As I neared the house, Poa appeared from beneath the bushes at the side. She wobbled slightly but had a pleased expression on her face.

"Did you have fun with your new friend?"

Penelope is one cool chick.

"I'm glad." My familiar was making friends, and I had a girls' night out tomorrow. We were both on the right track to making Charming Cove our home. "Do you think you could come help me inside?"

She grimaced. *I don't have to clean anything, do I?*

"I would never ask you to." Mostly because I knew she would do a terrible job. "I just need you to lend me some of your power."

That, I can do. She turned and sauntered toward the front door. I was grateful I'd found her here. I hadn't wanted to delay using the spell, and having my familiar's help would increase my power and the odds of success.

As usual, the door creaked loudly as I pushed it open, and the house groaned.

"Do you hear that?" I asked Poa. "The groaning noise?"

I do. It's different than the door creaking, right?

"Yes. Emma couldn't hear it."

Well, she's not as powerful as we are.

"That's patently untrue." But it was interesting that she couldn't hear the house groaning. "We have a connection with it, I think."

Fantastic. Poa's tone was dry.

I smiled at her. "Hang in there, pal. This place will be amazing when we're finished with it."

The house began toek, and I couldn't help but think it was a response to my words. When the floorboards popped up and made the carpet move, I was *certain* it was the house responding. "Don't worry," I told it. "If someone cursed you,

I'm going to figure it out and break the curse. You'll feel better in no time."

The house didn't respond, and I took that to be a good sign. I reached into my pocket and withdrew the vial of powder, which I uncorked and sprinkled sparingly on the floor, making sure to cover as much of the carpet as I could. That accomplished, I went to stand by Poa. She leaned her warm body against my leg, and I smiled.

"Here goes nothing," I said, and began to say the words that Cecelia had taught me. "Powder thee, reveal to me a curse that lingers beneath these eaves." I repeated the words, reaching deep for the magic in my soul, and released it into the room, feeling it sparkle around me as I chanted. Poa's magic added to mine, and the powder began to glow.

It's working! she crowed.

"It's not, though." I frowned at the glow, which was blue. "Cecelia was very clear on the instructions that the powder would glow green if the house was cursed."

Dang. That's not green. You boffed it.

"Did not!" Or maybe I had. "I'll call Cecelia and see what she has to say. There was a phone number on the little paper tag tied to the bottle."

Put it on speaker. I want to hear her confirm that I'm right.

I glared at the cat, then dialed the number on the tag. It rang only twice before Cecelia picked up, her voice still familiar from this morning. "Seaside Spells, how may I help you?"

Poa nudged me with her head and glared up at me. I put the phone on speaker. "Hi, Cecelia. This is Isobel. I stopped by your shop earlier this afternoon—"

"Oh, I know who you are, Isobel. How did the spell work?"

"It glowed blue."

"Blue?" Surprise sounded in Cecelia's voice. "I've never heard of that happening."

"I was afraid you might say that. Did I screw it up?"

"No. If it glowed at all, then you definitely did it correctly. But there's not a curse on that house. It's something else."

"Any idea how I might figure it out?"

"No, I'm sorry. The fact that the powder glowed blue has more to do with you than the spell. You're the only one who can figure out what's going on, since I think it has to do with your power. What's your gift?"

"I, ah, don't know." Embarrassment flushed through me. I was too old a witch to not know what my particular gift was. "I haven't used my magic as much as I maybe should have."

"That's all right, dear. We all have our reasons. But I think that if you learn more about your magic, you'll be able to determine what's wrong with your house."

"Thanks." The advice was more disappointing than anything. Figuring out my magic was a huge task, and one that I didn't really have time for. I also had no idea *how* to figure it out.

"Come back any time you need help," she said. "And good luck."

"Thanks, I'll need it." I rang off and looked down at Poa.

She gave me a grudging nod. *I suppose you didn't boff it.*

"No, but it might have been easier if I had." My head spun with what I'd been told, and I knew I needed a break from thinking about my magic. "I'm going to go clean the back garden. I need to give my mind some time to clear, and I can't keep delaying work on the house."

I'll come with you. I'm sure there's a patch of sun that needs my attention.

Poa accompanied me around to the back. The garden was as wild as I remembered, and I decided to start on the rear wall of the house, where vines grew up over the stone and some of the windows. If I could get those cleared away, the house could breathe better.

I frowned. Why was I thinking of the house breathing? That was odd.

But I couldn't fight the feeling that it was suffocating, maybe because it looked choked by all the greenery on the wall. I had to fix it.

Poa found herself a spot to snooze in the sun, and I found a little shed in the back corner of the garden. Within were some rusty old gardening tools, but they worked well enough once I used a spell to fix them up. I found a pair of leather gloves and pulled them on, then went to the wall and began to tear the dead vines away.

Hours passed as I worked. Using my hands and having something simple to focus on allowed my mind to wander around my problems. It was a less stressful way to look for solutions, and that was the most likely path to success.

By the time it was dark, I was sweaty and filthy. Tiny dead leaves were stuck all through my hair, and dirt covered much of my skin. But the back of the house looked much better, and I was no longer as worried. I had an idea that I could start to work on tomorrow.

For now, I desperately needed a shower and some food. I'd forgot to eat lunch, and I was pretty sure I'd fall over soon if I didn't get something in my stomach.

Poa had abandoned me once her spot was no longer sunny, so I headed down to the boathouse alone. Rafe was nowhere to be seen as I let myself into the main house, but I felt his presence. He was probably in the back room.

Before he could come out and see what a mess I was, I hurried up to my flat. My stomach was roaring as I made myself a quick sandwich and gobbled it down. Once I'd eaten, I hurried to the bathroom, stripping on my way there. I was desperate to get out of my dirty clothes. I might not even wait for the shower to warm up before I got in.

In the bathroom, I reached for the tap and turned on the shower. It groaned as the metal neck of the shower rattled, and I had only a second to feel panic before metal dislodged and a spray of water hit me in the face.

I shrieked, stumbling backward. The water continued to pelt me from where the showerhead had fallen off, and I scrambled to reach the handle. It spun uselessly, and I gave another shriek of frustration. Water continued to spray.

"Isobel?" Rafe's voice sounded from outside the door. "Are you all right? I'm coming in."

I squawked, grabbing for a towel to cover my nakedness. I'd just wrapped it around myself when Rafe pushed open the door and stood there like a rescuing hero. He took in my towel-clad form, and heat replaced the worry in his eyes. It was there and gone so quickly that I thought I might have imagined it.

"I thought you were being attacked," he said.

"I was." I pointed to the showerhead, which was still spraying. "By that."

"Did you try turning it off?"

I gave him a light whack on the shoulder. "Of course I did. But the handle just kept spinning."

As if the shower were offended that I'd tried to stop it, a jet of water hit me in the back of the head. I gave another small shriek of frustration. "I just needed a shower!"

"You do."

"Jerk!" I gave him another little whack, fully aware that I was flirting but unable to help myself.

"You can shower in mine, if you want," he said. "I'll fix this while you do."

"Wow. That's way nicer of you than I'd expected."

He shrugged, then tapped his nose. "It's just that I'm a werewolf, and I have a *fantastic* sense of smell."

I gasped. "Are you saying that I stink?"

"I would never."

"Liar."

A reluctant smile crossed his face, and I was pretty sure that he was flirting back with me.

The smile fell, and the glower returned. "You should go before this room floods."

"Right. Of course." The grump had returned, but at least he was familiar. I left without another word, heading downstairs to his bathroom. I had to go through his bedroom to reach it, and it was far tidier than I'd anticipated. Tommy had been so messy, and I'd assumed it was a guy thing. More likely it was the fact that I cleaned up after him.

I scanned the room as I walked toward the bathroom

door, unable to help myself from trying to learn a little more about him. But it was so *empty*. Maybe that was one reason it was so tidy: Rafe just didn't have a lot of stuff. Like, it was barren. Prison-cell barren.

The lack of evidence of hobbies and enjoyments was weird, like he was someone who worked one hundred percent of the time.

Or he was a total weirdo serial killer.

Nah.

I would get serial killer vibes off him if that were the case, right? Totally. And as much as he was a miserable grump, he wasn't a murderer.

I definitely wanted to know why he was so grumpy, though, and why there was so little in his flat. I shook the thought away. I was *not* going to get involved with a guy—even if only to figure out what his damage was. I was still recovering from Tommy and regaining my sense of self. No way in hell would I let a man interrupt that.

His bathroom was just as tidy as the bedroom, but it smelled divine. Whatever products he used filled the air with the scent of the forest and sandalwood. Fortunately, his shower had no problems at all—perfect temperature and water pressure. A quick inspection showed that his showerhead looked shiny and new, so maybe that was why.

Once I'd cleaned off and wrapped myself in the towel again, I headed out into the main part of the boathouse. Rafe was already back downstairs, and he averted his gaze from me.

"Is it off?" I asked.

"Yes. I fixed it for now, but we'll need to get you a new showerhead."

"Why didn't this happen the first time I showered?"

"Probably because I was showering at the same time, and it cut the water pressure in half. Once you were the only one showering, it couldn't handle any more. It was just too old."

"You really know your house stuff, don't you?"

He grunted.

"You know, that makes you the perfect candidate to help me fix up Lavender House." I grinned at him. "I'd be out of your hair sooner if you did."

"Don't press your luck. I'll get you a new showerhead and install it, but that's it."

"We'll see." I smiled at him, then turned to leave. Over my shoulder, I said, "Thanks again, Rafe."

He didn't reply, of course. But I was sure I could feel him smiling.

CHAPTER

ELEVEN

ISOBEL

I WAS at the Aurora Coven headquarters bright and early the next morning, armed with a plan to figure out what was wrong with my house. The idea had started forming while I'd been cleaning the garden the day before, but it had solidified when I'd woken at three a.m. with my mind racing.

Fortunately, Holly was at the desk again.

"You work a lot," I said as I let myself in.

She grinned. "It's an apprentice's duty." She gestured for me to sit in the chair across from her.

"Thanks, but I've got work to do. May I use the library again?"

"Absolutely. Have you figured out what's wrong with the house?"

"Not yet. It's not a ghost, and it's not a curse. But I have a connection with the house—I'm sure of it. I just need to amplify that, and then maybe I'll be closer to an answer."

"Oooh, I like how you're thinking." She tapped her chin. "So you think your power is giving you a connection to the house?"

"Yep. I just need a spell to give my magic a boost, and then perhaps I'll be able to understand more about what's going on."

"I have just the spell for you. Come on." She rose and hurried. She selected a book that looked far older than the rest and carried it over to the table. "There's something in here that will enhance your powers."

She flipped through the pages, finally landing on a short spell. "You'll also need some conduits. We've got some crystals that will help." She pointed to a basket on the shelf near the door. "Choose about half a dozen of those."

"Thanks." I went over to the basket and sorted through colorful rocks. They were all shapes and sizes and textures, but I was primarily drawn to the amber-colored ones. They buzzed with power when I touched them, and I chose some that glittered with an internal yellow fire.

As I searched for the last one, Holly asked, "Have you ever thought of joining a coven?"

"Hmm?" I turned, torn away from my focus on the rocks. "A coven?"

"Yes. For work."

"I don't know." The idea was enticing, though. Exciting, even. I would need to find something to do with my time when I finished fixing up the house, and the money my grandmother had left me wouldn't last forever. "Maybe."

"Emma left her position as apprentice to become a full-time member, so theoretically, there might be space if we have enough work to go around. That's the one thing I can't guarantee."

The hope in my chest banked a bit. This wasn't a huge town. How much work could a coven bring in?

"Don't worry about it," I said. I was just grateful these witches wanted to be my friends. I didn't want to add the pressure of them trying to find me a job. "I've got a lot on my plate with the house right now, and who knows what the future will bring?"

"Well, think on it. I bet you'd make a great addition to the team."

Her words warmed me, and I smiled. "Thanks."

"I'm going to head back downstairs to keep an eye on the desk. Once you've got your crystals and you've memorized the spell, will you put the book back?"

"Will do."

She headed downstairs, and I finished choosing my crystals and memorizing the spell. I carefully put the book back, then headed downstairs and said goodbye to Holly.

"See you at Potions & Pinot tonight," she said. "Glad you're coming."

"Thanks." I grinned at her, excitement fluttering within me.

On my way out of town, I stopped by Margot's Tea & Cake Parlor, picking up a traditional Cornish pasty for myself and a sausage roll for Poa. I was going to need her help at the house, and I wanted to have a bribe on hand.

Fortunately, Poa accepted the offer of a sausage roll in

exchange for her assistance, and after she'd eaten, we headed up to Lavender House.

As usual, it made its displeasure known as soon I entered, but I ignored it. Poa hissed, and I couldn't blame her. Cats' noses were probably more sensitive than humans', and this place stank.

Be quick, Poa said. *I can't take much more of this. And if you expect me to live here, you have your work cut out for you.*

"Can't argue with that." I resisted a grimace as I entered the main room and set the crystals on the ground at equal intervals along the walls. They hummed with power in my hands, and I was glad Holly had such excellent conduits to loan me. Once they were in place, I went to the middle of the rough circle they created. I sat cross-legged on the ground, and Poa climbed into my lap. Her warm body was a comforting weight on my legs, and I looked down at her, pleased.

She glared. *What? I might as well be comfortable.*

"I wasn't complaining. I like having you there!"

Well, don't get all marshmallowy with feelings, all right? I'm not that kind of cat.

"I wouldn't dream of it."

Let's get this show on the road. I'm to meet Penelope for lunch.

"On it." I drew in a deep breath and pressed my hands to the ground in front of us. I wanted to make a connection with the house, if that's what my power was actually connecting me to.

Poa began to purr as I let my power fill me. Slowly, I recited the words I'd memorized. They were in Latin, and I wasn't great with Latin, but I could feel that they were working. Magic thrummed through me, growing in strength.

As it did, I could feel the house like it was a limb. Instinct made me lie down on the dirty floor to increase my physical connection to it. Poa gave an annoyed hiss but resettled herself on my chest, a heavy, purring weight whose magic enhanced my own.

As I continued to chant the words, I felt the connection with the house strengthen...and then a distinct sense of discomfort swirled through me. There was also the grumpiness that I'd been noticing since I'd entered, but now I had an idea of why.

The house didn't like the condition it was in.

The fact that the house had any opinion at all was strange. It should be an inanimate object, with the strange goings-on attributed to a curse or a ghost, but the house was alive in its own way. There was an enchantment woven through its walls that was far older than I was. I could barely sense it, but I was sure it wasn't evil, like a curse would be. The enchantment wasn't meant to cause problems, I was sure of that. It was more like it had given the house personality. If I tried harder, I could probably get a good grip on what it was and how to remove it.

The house seemed to shudder at the thought.

"I won't!" I called out. "I won't remove the enchantment, I promise." It would be like killing the house. If the house had a personality, that meant it was alive. Kind of. It didn't matter that it hadn't been born—I couldn't just tear the enchantment away and kill it.

I was going to have to find a way to live with it.

"Can you tell me how this happened to you?" I asked. "I want to make you feel better."

The house was silent, and I realized it was too much to ask it to speak. But that didn't mean I couldn't speak to it and try to get its cooperation. "I can tell that you're alive," I said. "Sort of. And that you're uncomfortable. You probably don't like being in such a state of disrepair, is that it?"

No response.

"Anyway, I'm going to fix you up. Then you'll feel better."

As if it wanted to disagree, the house popped a floorboard beneath my butt.

"Ouch!" I cried as it smacked me.

Poa was dislodged, and she tumbled off, then stalked toward the door, hissing at the house as she went. The house seemed to hiss back, popping a floorboard under the carpet she walked on. It jostled her to the right.

"You're both going to have to learn to get along."

The house groaned, and Poa hissed again.

"Whatever." I threw my hands over my head and closed my eyes. "I can do this."

I climbed to my feet, determined to get started on cleaning up the house. I'd got answers today, though not as many as I wanted. I still didn't know how the house had come to be alive, and I hadn't actually convinced it to chill out on me. Until its attitude improved, I wouldn't be able to get contractors up here.

Which meant I was on my own.

"I'm going to work on this carpet, okay?" I told the house. "If we get this up, your floorboards will be able to breathe.

Then we can discuss some refinishing options. You might like a nice coat of varnish."

The house didn't respond, and I felt crazy for talking to it. But it couldn't hurt, right? All living things wanted to be in control of their destiny, but a house would have a hard time doing that. Whoever had enchanted the place hadn't thought of that, perhaps, and it was the main reason the place was in such a bad mood: no control over its destiny, and then it had fallen into a state of disrepair.

Well, I was going to fix that.

I spent a sweaty afternoon pulling up the carpet using some more tools I found in the shed. Fortunately, I'd read a spell the other day that helped me increase my strength and speed, so it went more quickly than it would have otherwise.

I still had a long way to go, but at least I managed to get all the gross carpet out of the house and into the back garden. Disposing of it would be another matter, but I'd cross that bridge later. I covered the carpet with a couple of old tarps I found to keep it from becoming waterlogged in any potential rain, then returned to the house to inspect the floors. They were beautiful, wide beams that needed some refinishing, but they would be gorgeous when I was done.

"That's better, isn't it?" I asked the house.

It didn't give me any indication that it was happy with the change, but the floorboards had stopped popping up. The place still stank, and a door slammed in my face even though there was no breeze, but I decided to call it a win.

By the time late afternoon rolled around, I was exhausted and still needed to coordinate someone to pick up the discarded carpet. I also needed a break from the house and its slamming doors.

I left through the front door. For the first time since I'd been there, I spotted a woman outside of the little cottage on the hillside to the east. She was too far away for me to see details of her features, but her white hair and posture suggested that she was older. Perhaps she would know how the house had come to be enchanted. If she'd lived here a long time, it was possible.

Instead of heading down to the boathouse, I cut across the hillside toward her. Poa joined me, coming out from a hiding spot beneath a log. It took me a while to get to the cottage due to the uneven terrain, but I made it before the woman had retreated indoors.

Up close, she looked to be in her late seventies. She tended to a garden of autumn flowers that bloomed in a gorgeous profusion of yellows, oranges, and reds. The cottage behind her was a tiny postcard-perfect stone building with smoke wafting from the chimney.

"Hello!" I called out, hoping I didn't startle her.

She looked up, then smiled. "Hello, there. Are you the new girl?"

"The new girl?" I smiled. "I guess I am."

"I thought so. Margot mentioned someone had moved in with that moody werewolf."

I nodded. "He's definitely moody. I'm Isobel. This is Poa." I pointed back to Lavender House. "We're trying to fix that place up, and I was wondering if I could ask you a few questions."

"Certainly, dear. I'm Judith. Would you like some tea?"

"That sounds amazing."

"Excellent. Come in."

I hesitated in the doorway. "I'm pretty dirty."

She waved a hand dismissively. "Let me take care of that."

I watched as she squinted her eyes and muttered an incantation, her magic swelling on the air. It was faint, but a moment later, I was clean enough to come into her house. I'd still need a shower, but I was much better.

She gave me a pleased smile. "I'm not particularly skilled with my magic—never been much of a witch, as hard as I've tried—but I've really worked on that cleaning spell."

"Well, it worked great." I grinned at her. "Thanks."

"Now come in." She gathered up the blooms she'd collected, and I followed her into the little cottage, immediately swept away by how beautiful the place was. It was cozy and welcoming, with pastel landscapes on the walls and comfortable-looking furniture. She gestured to the kitchen table, which sat in front of a large window overlooking the sea. "Have a seat. I'll put the kettle on."

I did as she said, watching as she put the flowers in a vase and then filled the kettle. There was something so comforting about being near her. I'd say familiar, but I was sure I didn't recognize her. She had a faint magical signature, and I wondered if she was a witch like me. If she was, she didn't have much power. Or she hid it well.

"Have you lived here long?" I asked.

"On and off my whole life." She smiled as she picked up a tin. "Chocolate biscuits?"

"Yes, please."

Judith laid out a tray of biscuits and tea, then carried it to the table. After she'd set my cup in front of me, she poured a saucer for Poa and added a generous splash of milk before putting it on the floor in front of her.

Poa looked up at me. *See? She knows how to treat a cat.*

"She says thank you," I told Judith.

Poa got to work on her milky tea, and I waited for Judith to finish pouring her own cup. It felt rude to rush her, no matter how excited I was to possibly get answers.

Judith passed the plate of biscuits to me and said, "Now, tell me how I can help you."

"The house is enchanted to have a personality," I said. "Almost like it's alive. I was wondering if you knew anything about the previous inhabitants."

Interest flashed in her eyes. "Enchanted, you say? I'd always thought it was a ghost or a curse to make it uninhabitable, but that's very interesting."

"Have you been inside?"

"A few times, long ago." She smiled. "But no, I don't know the last people to live there. It's been a very long time since it was inhabited. Seventy years or more."

Darn. I'd been hoping for more information.

"There's a chance my mother knew, though. Perhaps I could look in her old papers and see if she had anything that could help you. She collected bits of local lore."

"Oh, that would be amazing. Thank you."

She waved a hand. "Don't think anything of it, dear. I'm happy to help."

My chest warmed. I liked having her call me dear. I wasn't sure why I felt such a connection with this woman.

Maybe my soul was just so starved for familial affection that I was seeing something that wasn't there. My own grandmother and parents had been so distant that I was looking for it anywhere I could find it.

I hadn't felt the same with Cecelia, however, even though I'd liked her very much. With a flash of embarrassment, I realized I'd been silent a little too long. I took a bite of a biscuit to give me a chance to compose myself.

"Great biscuits," I said. "Thank you."

"Any time, truly. I'll look for those papers and deliver them to you if I find anything, all right?"

"Oh, I hate for you to go to the trouble." I thought of how uneven the hillside was between our houses. "I'll stop by tomorrow to see if you've found anything, if that works for you."

"Perfect. I look forward to it." She smiled again. "Perhaps tomorrow, I'll be delivering good news."

I hoped so, because I had no other leads at all.

CHAPTER
TWELVE

ISOBEL

I WAS PRETTY high on life as I headed into town for girls' night. My tea and biscuits with Judith had been a balm to my soul for reasons I didn't want to explore too deeply. Going down that path meant facing the demons of my past, and I wasn't interested in that right now. Maybe never.

Instead of driving, I decided to call a cab. For me, girls' night meant a few glasses of wine. I had a feeling it meant the same for the other women since we were meeting at a place called Potions & Pinot, and I certainly shouldn't be behind the wheel in that situation.

At the sisters' clothing shop, I'd bought a dress in a silky fabric that was shot through with tiny sparkles. It was shorter and cut lower than the things that Tommy had liked me to wear, but that could be said of most dresses. Which meant I loved it, of course. I'd even picked out a pair of strappy, heeled sandals, which I'd been unable to resist. I wouldn't be walking far in those shoes, but that wasn't the point of them.

Poa was nowhere to be found as I left the boathouse, but I did see Rafe. He was walking out of the sea, shirtless and dripping water like some kind of ocean god. I halted dead in my tracks, unable to stop myself from staring. His body was insane, even more beautiful than I remembered from the first night I'd met him. Maybe because I wasn't afraid for my life now, I could get a proper look at him.

And wow.

He had the kind of body built by years of hard work, tall and broad, with clearly defined muscle that made my palms tingle at the idea of touching him. He was just...perfect.

And now I was totally objectifying him.

Embarrassment shot through me, and I winced, feeling heat bloom in my cheeks. That was inappropriate. He was a person, not a pin-up model in some magazine from the eighties. I shouldn't be ogling him.

He'd also stopped when he spotted me, and as I met his gaze, I saw something in his eyes that made me blush even hotter. There was no denying what I saw in his stare— attraction. Like, a lot of it.

We stood ten meters apart, but I could feel the connection between us like we were joined by a live wire.

"Um, I'm going out." I hiked a thumb toward the driveway, where I could hear the cab approaching.

"All right." He swallowed hard, and I could see his Adam's apple bob.

It took more effort than it should have to tear myself

away and walk toward the cab. But if I put a little extra sway in my hips, who could blame me? His gaze burned into me, and I was vain enough to want to present a good front—or back, as the case was. I didn't need to be in pursuit of a relationship to do that.

The driver was a woman in her mid-fifties with brilliant red hair and dainty features. I thought she might be some kind of pixie, but I didn't ask since it was sometimes considered rude.

"Aren't you all dolled up," she said, looking back at me in the mirror. "Looking lovely. Got a hot date?"

I grinned. "Girls' night."

"Even better. Does that mean I'm taking you to Potions & Pinot?"

"Indeed it does. Is it popular for girls' nights?"

"They keep the place in business, though I prefer the cocktails myself. They make a mean Manhattan."

"I'll have to try one."

"Tell them Anita sent you. They'll make you a proper one."

"I will." I settled back into the seat as she pulled onto the main road into town. "Have you driven a cab around here a long time?"

"Twenty-five years. Wouldn't leave Charming Cove for all the money in the world."

"It's a gorgeous place," I said, looking out the window at the darkness. The full moon lit up the night, shining on the sea that I could see far in the distance. "I don't suppose you know any handymen or contractors in need of work?"

"For Lavender House?" She scoffed. "Not a chance, darling. That place is haunted."

"Not haunted, exactly. It's been enchanted to have a personality, and it's grumpy about the poor state of affairs it's been left in." At least, I was pretty sure that was the case.

"Well, as soon as it stops smacking the workers on the arse with floorboards, they'll start working there. Can you guarantee that?"

"No, definitely not." I sighed, totally able to see why people wouldn't want to work there. I had a lot at stake, and a family connection. A paycheck couldn't compete with that.

We reached Charming Cove, and Anita turned onto Foxglove Lane and headed toward the wine bar. She pulled over right outside. "Call when you want a ride home," she said as I handed her the fare.

"Will do. And thank you."

She nodded. "Anytime."

I straightened and turned to Potions & Pinot, excitement thrumming within me. I was actually more excited than I'd been for my first date with Tommy. Even better, this excitement had less of a sickly feeling of nerves. Back then, I'd been a kid with my first boyfriend. Now I was a grown woman about to drink a bunch of wine with some new girlfriends. That was a different kind of excitement, and an easier one.

The bar itself was dimly lit by a quirky collection of vintage chandeliers, and the muted teal and burgundy walls gave it a cozy ambiance. Plants decorated the walls, sitting on shelves of varying heights.

I spotted Emma and Holly almost immediately. They sat

with two other women at a high-top table, and there was one seat remaining for me. I walked over, already smiling.

"Isobel!" Emma stood and pulled out the barstool for me. "So glad you could make it. Love the dress."

"Thank you for inviting me." I grinned at everyone.

Emma made the introductions, explaining that the red-haired woman was Aria, granddaughter of Cecelia from Seaside Spells. She owned the Enchanted Garden outside of town and supplied most of the potion ingredients for the town's businesses. The dark-haired woman was Tabitha, aunt and primary caregiver to Catrina, the feisty eight-year-old.

"She's a real pistol," I said before sipping the glass of white wine that Emma had poured me. "I like her."

"Me, too." Tabitha took a gulp of her wine. "Now, if I could just get her to stop picking fights with the local boys, we'd be in great shape."

"They're bullies," Aria said. "And she always wins."

Tabitha smiled and shrugged. "Good point. She's a peacekeeper."

I didn't ask how Tabitha had come to be the primary caregiver of her niece, but since they didn't mention Catrina's mother, I assumed it had to be a sad story.

"So, we hear you're fixing up Lavender House." Aria leaned forward. "That's a big job."

I blew out a breath. "No kidding. But I think I know what's got a bee in its bonnet." I told them what I'd learned today, but no one had any idea about who had enchanted the house. It had happened long before our time.

"It's pretty impressive you were able to figure that out," Emma said. "I didn't get a hint of an enchantment."

"And you were able see something with the curse revealer spell that even my grandmother hasn't seen before," Aria said before turning to the other women. "Gran told me that she saw a blue glow. It should have been green or nothing."

"See?" Holly nudged Emma, a gesture that was blatantly obvious.

"I'm getting to it, Holly," Emma said to her. She turned to me. "My very impatient friend over here mentioned talking to you about joining our coven. I think it's a great idea, especially considering your unusual talents. You've got power, Isobel. If you're interested, I'll talk to the other members."

"I would have talked to them if I could have," Holly said. "But I'm just an apprentice, and it would have more weight coming from Emma."

"Thank you," I said, loving how included I felt. "But I'm not sure about my powers. I don't know what my talent is."

"You'll figure it out," Emma said. "It definitely sounds unusual, and the coven could benefit from a talent like yours."

"Once I figure out what it is."

"Just consider it. If we think there's room for someone new, I'll let you know."

"Thanks." I grinned.

We spent the rest of the night gossiping about work and relationships. Aria was married, and Emma would be getting hitched in the summer. Tabitha and Holly were single, but both had options on the horizon, as they put it.

"What about that werewolf you live with?" Holly bobbed her eyebrows up and down. "He's quite fit."

I remembered the sight of him walking out of the sea. "He is indeed."

"Total lone wolf," Tabitha said. "Every woman in town thinks he's a catch, if you ignore his grumpy personality, but he hasn't given any of us the time of day."

"That's not what Meg said about him and Isobel." Emma grinned widely and pointed at me. "He was totally into you at The Sea Shanty, she said. Kept staring at you all night, looking tortured."

"Yeah, tortured by the fact that he has to live with me," I replied.

"Not that kind of tortured. *Sexy* tortured."

I rolled my eyes and laughed, but I couldn't help but think of the look in his eyes when he'd seen me tonight. Something they'd said about him had caught my attention, though. "What do you mean, lone wolf? Isn't there a pack in town?"

"Not one that he's a member of."

"Don't werewolves need to be part of a pack?" I asked.

Aria nodded. "They're like family. But as far as anyone can tell, he doesn't have one."

Sadness shot through me. I knew what that felt like, and I wouldn't wish it on anyone. Perhaps that was why he was grumpy.

"Maybe they kicked him out," Holly said. "Could be he did something shitty."

It was possible, but not probable, unless there were werewolf politics involved. He was a fundamentally good guy, I could feel that about him. If he really didn't have a pack, I didn't think it was through any fault of his own. I moved the subject away from him, though. I didn't need to think about him any more than I already did.

My phone began to buzz with incoming text messages, and I pulled it out of my handbag, frowning down at the screen. An unknown number was texting me.

I opened the screen, immediately spotting the messages, one after the other.

I'M SO SORRY. *Please take me back. I was wrong.*

I GLARED AT THE PHONE, annoyance and disgust streaking through me.

"What's wrong?" Emma asked.

"My ex. I blocked his number, but he must have got a new one." I turned the phone around so they could see the numbers.

"Ugh," Aria said. "It's like he sensed you were talking about another man and felt the need to blow up your phone."

"It's a bit stalkerish," Holly said.

"Kind of, if he weren't so lazy." I blocked the number and put the phone back in my bag. "But if Tommy is anything, it's fundamentally lazy. That's why he wants to keep me around so badly. I did everything for him."

"What a loser," Tabitha said. "And I can guarantee that's

LINSEY HALL

not the only reason he wants you around." She looked me up and down. "You're hot."

I grinned, flushed with pleasure. "Thanks."

"You sure you're not worried about him?" Emma asked.

"Annoyed, yes. Worried, no. He's not violent, never was. He's just annoyed that I left and probably had a few pints too many." But I was getting sick of his messages. I wanted him out of my life entirely. "I might need to get a new number, though."

"I think that's a great idea," Aria said. "Kick him to the curb once and for all."

I liked that idea and shoved Tommy from my mind. He'd lost me, but that wasn't my problem.

The rest of the night passed in a blur of laughter and wine. We didn't finish until the bar closed down at one. Outside on the street, I called the cab company for Anita, but it went straight to voicemail.

"Oh, no," Holly said. "Did you take a cab in?"

I nodded. "I figured I'd have some drinks and wouldn't be able to drive back."

"Well, that was smart, but the cab company closes at midnight."

"Crap." How the heck was I going to get home?

"I've got some sober-up potions in my flat, right above here. Let me get one, and then I'll drive you home."

Sober-up potions—I should have thought of that. I'd had enough to drink that the idea of going upstairs in my heels sounded like a bad idea, so I told Holly I'd wait for her on the street. The wind was chilly as I huddled in the recessed alcove of the wine bar's door, but it didn't take her long to return.

"Here, I brought you one, too." She handed me the tiny vial before throwing hers back.

I drank mine, grimacing at the bitter taste. Almost immediately, my head felt clearer. "Thanks. This will really help me out tomorrow when I have work to do."

"They're the perfect remedy after a girls' night." She waved for me to follow her. "Come on, let's get my car."

Rafe

I TURNED ONTO FOXGLOVE LANE, wondering if I was being an idiot. I'd spent the last several hours in wolf form, running underneath the full moon. It was a pleasure that I allowed myself rarely, since I usually felt worse afterward—as if being in that form reminded me of my lost pack.

But with the full moon and the sight of Isobel still in my mind, I'd needed the run. Anything to release the tension that bound me up tightly whenever I saw her. She threatened my hard-won peace, and I really couldn't afford to lose what little serenity I had.

Of course, I had my meeting with the Jade Sorceress soon, so hope was on the horizon. With any luck, I'd have answers about my pack. That kept me going. Kept me sane.

When I'd returned home from my run about half past midnight and she hadn't been home, I'd realized she'd probably stayed out beyond the time that the cab ran. So I'd hopped in my car and driven into town like a lovesick fool.

Or maybe I was just being a decent roommate. I didn't want to live with her, but I also didn't want her stuck in town on a chilly autumn night. As I pulled up to the wine bar, I saw two figures walking toward the side street. Both wore dresses, and one was unmistakably Isobel. Even if she weren't the most captivating person I'd ever seen, my wolf would have recognized her.

She must have heard my car approaching because she looked over her shoulder. I pulled up beside them and rolled down the window.

"Rafe?" She frowned at me. "What are you doing here?"

"Um." This was the part where I felt like an idiot. "It got late, and I realized you weren't home."

"Oh, and you remembered the cab wouldn't be running!" the woman next to her said. "How thoughtful!"

"Very thoughtful." Isobel sounded a bit suspicious, and I couldn't blame her.

"So, do you want that ride?" I asked.

"Yes. Thank you." She turned to Holly. "Thanks anyway."

"Sure thing." Holly smiled. "And don't forget that offer about joining the coven."

The idea of her joining the local coven was a new one. It would make her life here more permanent. Not that it already wasn't. She had a house, for fate's sake, and even though it was in bad shape, she was determined to change that. I wanted her out of the boathouse, but if she moved up the hill, she wouldn't be going that far. I didn't think I could survive having her so close.

Isobel walked to the passenger door and climbed in. Immediately, her honeysuckle scent enveloped me. I inhaled deeply, unable to help myself, and hoped she didn't notice.

"Thanks again," she said as I turned the car around and headed toward home.

"Sure." I shot her a sideways glance. "But don't get used to it. I'm not doing it again."

"All right, Grumpy Pants."

I rolled my eyes and repressed the smile that tugged at my lips. We rode in silence to the boathouse, but that was somehow worse. I could hear the faint sound of her breathing, and it was enough to drive me to distraction.

We arrived, and I climbed out, grateful to have the space and fresh air. It didn't last long, however. When I went to push open the door to the boathouse, I found it locked. Isobel, who must have expected me to open it and walk right through, bumped into me. She made a startled noise and stumbled backward.

I spun, gripping her shoulders gently to keep her from falling.

"Sorry." She looked up at me, so beautiful in the moonlight that it made my heart clench. "I thought it would be unlocked."

"Me, too." My voice came out huskier than it should have, but who could blame me? Her scent was wrapping around me again, and the warmth of her bare skin beneath my hands made me burn. There was just something about her that stole every rational thought from my mind. She was intoxicating, and the tension that bound us together was delicious.

"Rafe?" she whispered, putting a hand to my chest. It burned into me. Her gaze was even worse—luminous and all-seeing, piercing my soul in a way that left me laid bare.

"Yeah?" I looked down at her lips, full and soft, and something tightened within me. I desperately wanted to kiss her. From the way she tilted her mouth up toward mine and licked her bottom lip, I was fairly sure she wanted me to. Comingled regret and relief tugged at me as I said, "You've had some drinks. We shouldn't."

She smiled. "You're worried about my consent?"

"You don't exactly like me."

"Oh, I like you just fine. It's you who doesn't like me."

Right now, that was patently untrue.

"I took a sober-up potion," she said, stepping closer. "But considering how much you dislike me, I should be worried about *your* consent."

Dislike her? I could never.

I liked her far too much. Wanted her far too much. She looked delicious in the moonlight, all creamy skin and luscious pink lips. The sight, the scent, the closeness of her made me want to taste every inch of her.

It was more than I could bear.

Unable to stop myself, I leaned down and pressed my lips to hers. She was impossibly soft, tasting of wine and strawberries. She wrapped her arms around my neck, and I pulled her closer, pressing the full length of her body against mine.

The feel of her was enough to make my head spin, and she kissed me with a passion that stunned me. One second, she was sweeping her tongue over my lips, and the next, she was pulling away and gasping.

"I don't even like you," she said.

"I don't like you, either." *Lie.* But I shouldn't like her. And kissing her like this was a terrible idea. "Sorry. I shouldn't have." I stepped away from her and turned to open this door.

This time, after a bit of a push, it opened. It hadn't been locked at all—which would have made no sense, since I hadn't locked it—but rather had just been stuck.

Before she could say anything, I disappeared into my room like the coward I was.

CHAPTER
THIRTEEN

Isobel

I DREAMED OF THE KISS. How could I not? It was the single most incredible physical experience of my life. Nothing with Tommy could have ever compared. Rafe was just so overwhelmingly physical, with his strength and height and beauty.

And he was an incredible kisser. I'd felt like the center of his world, and the pleasure that had rushed through me had been like nothing I'd ever experienced before. He'd swept me away, making me lose all rational thought as I'd disappeared into the kiss. I'd forgot where I was—hell, I'd almost forgot *who* I was. Every part of me had been focused on him and the feeling of his mouth on mine, of his strong hands around my waist. As soon as I'd realized how far I'd lost myself, I'd panicked.

I don't even like you.

My words echoed in my head. They had been a lie. It didn't matter how grumpy and moody he was—I still liked him. But I didn't want to. I couldn't afford to fall for another guy, not when I was finally finding myself.

Ugh. Enough of that.

I forced myself out of bed. There was no time to lie here daydreaming, and no point. He'd made it perfectly clear that he regretted the kiss just as much as I did. Anyway, I would be living with Rafe until I heard from the solicitor, who reported that he was having a hard time getting solid answers, so I needed to keep things nice and casual between us.

I started the day with a quick trip to the hardware store to pick up supplies for the work ahead of me. Of course, I had to swing by Margot's for a pastry and coffee, and I spent a lovely few minutes chatting with her while she made the latte. It was amazing how quickly I was starting to feel at home in Charming Cove.

By the time I made it back to Lavender House, it was nearly nine. I had a long day ahead of me and would only manage it with the help of a bit of magic.

Poa was nowhere to be seen as I collected my supplies from the boot and headed into the house. Immediately, that familiar stink rose in the air, and one of the remaining blinds went up and down as if discontented.

"Oh, chill out," I said. "I'm here to help."

Air seemed to rush out of the door, as if the house were giving an irritated sigh. I smiled. My life was full of grumps lately—the house, the wolf I lived with, and even Poa if she didn't get her snackies right when she wanted them—but I knew they were lovely on the inside. They just needed a little care.

Not that I cared about the wolf. That would be beyond foolish. I did my best to shove him from my mind and turned my attention to the job at hand.

First things first. I drew in a deep breath and recited the spell that would give me enhanced strength and speed. Every time I used my magic, I felt a little more confident in it. There was no doubt that ignoring my power for so long had been bad for it. The magic inside me had been left to go rusty, but I was changing that.

Once I finished reciting the spell, I felt the faint buzz of power through my whole body. Energized, I got to work.

I spent the next two days cleaning out the house, removing all the horrible kitchen cabinets and bathroom fixtures. It was a lot of hard labor, but my magic made it easier. Every night, I returned to the boathouse exhausted and dirty. Rafe was never anywhere to be seen, as if he knew I was coming and wanted to avoid me.

He probably did. He'd even managed to fix my shower without me seeing him. I thought I heard him downstairs occasionally, but he was always gone when I left to go to Lavender House.

I hardly saw Poa, either, and the days were a blur of work and sleep. The house didn't make it any easier, of course. Every time I entered, it complained. And every now and again, it made its dislike for me known. Blinds fell on my head while I was removing them, and water shot me in the face while I tried to fix a toilet using instructions from the internet.

Things were moving forward, but not as quickly as I wanted. I really needed help. Unfortunately, my second visit to Judith hadn't revealed any new information about how the house had come to be enchanted, but she'd promised to look in one other place. I was less hopeful she'd find anything, but there was always a chance.

It was my seventh day in Charming Cove when I started to remove the wallpaper. By midafternoon, I'd stripped all of it and bundled it into the garden, where I'd been putting all the rubbish. As I looked at the pile amid the weeds, the autumn breeze blew my hair off my face.

"You might need to hire a skip for that." A woman's voice carried from the far side of the garden fence, and I turned to see who it was.

Judith stood there, a smile on her faintly lined face and a picnic basket propped on top of the fence railing.

I grinned. "I think you're right. There's no way I can haul all this away on my own. Better to have a company bring out a big bin and deal with it."

"Clever girl." She nodded down at the basket. "Brought you some cookies and lemonade—the American kind."

At the sound of her words, my stomach growled. It'd been too long since breakfast, and a snack sounded divine.

"Thank you." I approached, stopping on the other side of the fence. "You didn't have to come all the way over here. I would've stopped by your house if you'd called me."

"Oh, I know. But it's nice to get out." She looked at the house, interest on her face. "And if I'm being honest, I wanted a glimpse inside—see how you're getting along."

"Come in, I'll show you." I gestured for her to follow me

to the garden gate, and I led her into the house, pointing out the newly removed carpet and wallpaper.

"Well, I'll say, it really does look better in here!" She shoved her

basket at me. "Here, you look famished."

I took the basket and carried it to the front porch. The weather was still nice, and the porch was probably cleaner than the dusty kitchen. We sat on the two rickety chairs and I opened the basket to reveal a glass bottle of what looked to be homemade lemonade. I raised it and showed her. "Did you make this yourself?"

"I did indeed. I've got some lemon trees in my sun room. In fact, your cat has been in there all morning, sunning herself right next to them. I think that girl likes lemons."

"Really?"

"She was licking one pretty enthusiastically."

I laughed at the image of Poa licking a lemon. "She's a weird one."

I poured some of the fizzy lemonade into one of the glasses that Judith had included in the basket, then handed it over. Once we had our drinks and biscuits, Judith said, "I'm sorry to say that I didn't find anything in the attic like I thought I might. Except squirrels." She grimaced. "However, I have one more place I can check tomorrow."

"Oh, thank you." I was disappointed, but not surprised. It would have been too lucky.

We spent the next thirty minutes chatting, and I found that I liked Judith even more than I'd realized. She was everything I could have wanted in a grandmother, and I hoped I'd get to see more of her.

Once she'd departed, there was still enough light left to start on another task in the house. I really ought to get the electricity sorted so I could start working after dark.

I returned to the house and looked around for my next job. As expected, the house grumbled at my arrival, but at least it didn't hit me in the butt with a loose board.

The hearth in the main living room caught my eye, and I went over to check it out. As expected, it was filthy, clogged with debris that had fallen down the chimney.

"I bet if I clean this out, you'll feel a lot better."

There was no response from the house, and I supposed I should have been grateful.

I got to work clearing the hearth and trying to pull the debris from the chimney. I hadn't got very far before a massive plume of dust and soot exploded from the fireplace, coating me.

"Ugh!" I cried, stumbling away. "What did you do that for?"

The house seemed to cough, the chimney expelling more gross, powdery stuff over me.

"Uncool." I took a few more steps back, using the inside of the my shirt to rub off my face.

In front of me was a pile of new debris that had fallen out of the chimney, primarily leaves and other bits that looked like the makings of a squirrel's nest. Or maybe a rat's nest. I was no rodent expert. I started to clean it up, grumbling as I piled it into a massive bin bag. As I was hauling the bag toward the door, a floorboard popped up and smacked me in the butt. I dropped the bag, seething.

"You know what, I'm leaving." I turned on my heel and

stomped toward the main door, hoping to make a point to the house. I knew in my gut that it wanted me to clean it up. But it was behaving like a toddler, and I was getting sick of it. Maybe I could scare some sense into it. "You'd better be nicer when I come back, or I'll stop fixing you up. I'll even install some really hideous lighting and wall fixtures before I leave."

The house seemed to shudder as I walked out. Was that bad for the structural stability? Crap, I shouldn't annoy the house too badly.

I walked down the hill. The weather was unseasonably warm for early autumn, with the early evening sun shining down upon me.

When I neared the boathouse, I spotted Rafe to the side of the building. He was washing his car with the hose, spraying water on the big Land Rover–looking thing. I knew nothing about cars, but it was big and rugged enough to suit him. A worn T-shirt stretched across his broad shoulders as he hosed the suds off the vehicle. His jeans hugged his thick thighs in a way that made my heart race a little faster than I liked.

He looked over at my approach, and surprise flashed on his face when he saw the state I was in. A laugh burst out of him. The smile lines that creased his eyes made him look somehow more handsome, and I scowled.

"It's not funny," I said.

"You look like a chimney sweep. So it is a bit funny." His smile hadn't faded, and his good humor made me forget the last few days he'd spent avoiding me.

"I'll show you funny." I grinned and reached into the

bucket at my feet, fishing out the damp sponge and throwing it at him. It splattered against his chest, soaking his shirt.

"Hey!" He grinned and turned the hose on me, spraying my right arm. He was careful to keep from soaking me entirely, because it wasn't *that* warm outside, and I laughed.

How long had it been since I'd felt this joyful with someone else? I hadn't felt this way with Tommy in a *long* time, if ever. Rafe and I still didn't get on, of course. Despite that kiss, I knew he wanted me out of his place as soon as possible. Hell, maybe because of the kiss. He'd clearly been bothered by it, even though he'd instigated it.

Our moment was there and gone before I realized it, which was for the best. I stepped back. "I've got to get cleaned up. Thanks again for fixing my shower." It was the first time I'd seen him to be able to thank him. I turned to go, then hesitated and looked back. "You know, if you could fix my shower that quickly, you really would be perfect for helping me fix up Lavender House."

He smiled. "It's not going to be so easy to get free labor out of me."

"I'm not giving up." I winked, a little shocked at my own flirtatiousness, then went upstairs to my flat.

It took forever to get the grime off, but the water pressure and heat were so perfect that I didn't mind a bit. As I was drying myself, I heard Rafe call up the stairs: "There's food down here if you want it."

I felt my brows rise. That was unexpected.

"I'll be down in a minute!" I dried my hair as quickly as possible, then threw on an overlarge T-shirt and some leggings. Thick socks completed the look—although no one with any style would call it a *look*—and I headed down to the main level.

I felt the faintest shiver of anticipation as I turned the corner at the base of the stairs. Would I really find him cooking?

As soon as I spotted him in the kitchen, I blinked in surprise. He was standing in front of the hob, ladling pasta into two big bowls.

Yeah, I hadn't seen this coming.

And of course, he'd changed into another thin T-shirt that hugged his perfect shoulders and tapered at the waist. Where did he buy these things? The Grumpy McHottiePants store?

"What's all this?" I asked. "You're being *nice*. It's weird."

"I wouldn't call this nice." He walked to the table and set the bowls down. "I'd just call it *having extra food and not wanting to waste*."

"Uh-huh." It was clear from my tone that I didn't believe him.

"Don't get used to it." The gruff boatbuilder was back, but I could see beneath the surface now.

I took the seat that he indicated, then accepted a glass of red wine. The spaghetti Bolognese in front of me looked divine, and smelled even better.

He got right into eating, not bothering with conversation, so I did the same. The first bite exploded with savory, tangy tomato sauce, and a small moan of pleasure escaped me. Embarrassed, I looked up to see if he'd noticed. His gaze flashed to mine, and I swore I saw the faintest bit of heat there.

I swallowed and said, "It's really good."

He grunted.

All right. Conversation was going great. I briefly considered eating in silence but decided that was a bit too weird for me.

"So, what brought you to Charming Cove?" I asked.

He shrugged. "Best weather in the UK, and I saw this place come up for sale. It was perfect."

I frowned. There was no way this place had gone up for sale through normal channels, not since my grandmother had owned it. "Where did you see it for sale?"

"On Magical Realtors Monthly. I'd been keeping an eye on it, looking for a place to move on to."

"Huh." I sipped my wine. That was a legit site. It shouldn't surprise me, since he struck me as an honest guy. But what the heck was going on? I really needed the solicitor to get back to me.

But it was the other thing he'd said—that he was looking for a place to move on to. Like he didn't want to stay in one place too long. I wanted to know more about that.

Before I could ask, he spoke. "What about you? Didn't you have a life back in London or wherever before you came here?"

"I did."

"It's nice to inherit such a big house, but you left a whole life behind." Even though the words were prodding, the tone was not.

"Not really." I thought of Tommy, and for the strangest reason, I wanted to tell him all about the whole mess.

Nope. That was a terrible idea. Also, it was way too

embarrassing to share. Instead, I went with, "I was ready for a fresh start, and the house became available at exactly the right time." I winced. "That sounds terrible. I'm not glad my grandmother died, of course not. I'm actually sad I didn't get a second chance with her now that I'm an adult. It's just that I didn't know her. Only met her once when I was a kid. It didn't go well."

I could still remember my disappointment. I'd been so excited for that visit when I'd been seven. But her disinterest had been clear, even to someone as young as I'd been. I'd found out later my mother had needed the babysitting for the weekend, which meant my gran hadn't even wanted me there. After that, I'd avoided trips to Gran's—not that there had been many.

I could see the concern in his eyes, but he clearly didn't know what to say.

"Anyway," I said, "the house isn't mine outright. The will stipulates that I need to fix it up within a month of starting. I have no idea why she wrote it that way, but it's definitely going to make things hard."

"That *is* odd," he said. "What happens to it if you don't succeed?"

"It goes to my miserable uncle."

He frowned. "There's got to be a reason she did it that way."

"I know, I just have no idea what it is. I can't fail, though. I *want* to stay—I love it here." To my surprise, I heard myself add, "I also have nowhere else to go."

Suddenly, I was feeling way too vulnerable. "What about you? Shouldn't you have a pack somewhere?"

His jaw tightened, and the air turned tense. I could feel the shift and suddenly regretted the question. I should have gone lighter with my subject change—asked him about his boats or something. Packs were a big deal to wolves, and I'd approached it way too blithely.

When the silence lengthened, I decided to cut my losses and change the subject. "Um, thanks for dinner. It was delicious." I stood. "I'll do the dishes."

"I've got it, don't worry."

"I insist." I grabbed his plate and hurried away. I washed up as quickly as possible, then headed for the stairs. "Early morning for me. Um, thanks again for dinner."

And I scurried away like the awkward little mouse I was.

CHAPTER
FOURTEEN

RAFE

THE NEXT MORNING, Isobel was gone when I woke. Even before I opened my eyes, I could sense that she wasn't nearby. Werewolves had better senses than other supernaturals, and mine seemed to be extra sensitive where she was concerned. We were also some of the few supernaturals who had fated mates, and the fact that my soul came alive whenever she was nearby made me pretty damned certain she was mine.

Which was all kinds of bad news.

Despite what it sounded like, a fated mate wasn't a sure thing. Rather, they were the person most perfect for you in the entire world. That didn't mean things would work out or that they wouldn't blow up your life. In fact, the pressure created by that kind of expectation often had negative conse-quences on a relationship—especially when the mate wasn't a wolf.

ROMANCE RULES FOR WEREWOLVES

Still, I'd spent the night tossing and turning with dreams of her, just like I'd spent every other night since she'd arrived. The kiss had been a mistake, but I couldn't get it out of my mind. I was doing a piss-poor job of avoiding her, if last night was any indication.

I'd made her dinner, for fate's sake. That had been a terrible idea. Cooking for her was the exact opposite of maintaining my distance, something I desperately needed to do. The last relationship I'd had with a witch had ended horrifically, and I couldn't afford for that to happen again.

Logically, I knew it was prejudiced and possibly irrational, but I'd lost so much to a witch. And that relationship had just been proof of my terrible judgment. I couldn't trust myself when it came to women, that was clear enough.

I needed to get her out of my house as quickly as possible. Her solicitor still didn't have an answer, and I'd contacted mine as well. He was coming up blank, too. It made no damned sense.

Which left me with only one option.

I rose, and after getting ready for the day, I headed up the hill toward Lavender House. It was still early, and the pale morning light did nothing to enhance my confidence that we would actually fix the house up in time. It was a wreck, with a roof that looked more like a suggestion than an actual structural feature, not to mention the windows and front garden. The inside was probably even worse.

I was nearly to the porch when Isobel walked outside, her curls wrapped in a bandanna and a flush across her cheeks. She was so beautiful that she took my breath away, and I stopped dead in my tracks.

Surprise flashed on her face. "Rafe? What are you doing here?"

"I thought about what you said, and if it will get you out of my place sooner, then I'm here to help."

Hurt flashed in her eyes, and guilt tugged at me. I hadn't wanted to hurt her, but I didn't know how to fix it.

She smiled before I could figure it out and said in a cheerful voice, "Excellent. I could use all the help I can get. Come inside."

She turned and headed through the door. I followed her, careful to keep my eyes off the jeans that clung to her curves. Staring at her arse was absolutely against the rules.

As soon as I entered the foyer, the scent of rotten eggs washed over me.

"Sorry about that," she said. "The house is ornery. It's got a personality, and it doesn't like being in such a terrible state. I'm hoping that fixing it up will calm it down."

She was right about the state of the place. The foyer was bare, unfinished wood and walls that needed some serious attention. And that was before I even looked at the broken windows.

"I've already ordered replacement windows," she said, "though I've no idea how to install them. Yet."

The confidence in her voice made me smile.

"Do you think you could work on the kitchen?" she asked. "And the bathrooms? They need cabinets, and a boat builder sounds like just the person for the job."

"I can do that."

"Excellent. I'll be around. Shout if you need me." She turned and headed into another part of the house.

I found the kitchen, which was an empty shell except for the old appliances that had probably been too big for her to lift. I'd have to get those out of there.

It was a nice space, with a view overlooking the green hills behind the house and a large fireplace on one wall. I spent the morning measuring and making plans for the cabinets in the kitchen and all bathrooms, then went in search of Isobel to confirm they were what she wanted.

I found her in the living room, standing on a footstool as she tried to pry a piece of rotten trim off the top of the wall. She jerked it hard, and it came away faster than she expected, because she stumbled.

I reacted on instinct, rushing forward and catching her before she landed on the ground.

"Ooof," she said.

She felt warm and perfect in my arms as I lowered her to the floor. She turned, gazing up at me, her luminous gray eyes impossible to look away from. "Thank you."

Her voice was soft, and she was standing so close that her scent washed over me. It took everything I had not to inhale deeply, not to pull her toward me.

"Sure." I stepped back, putting some much-needed distance between us. "I've got some plans for the kitchens and bathrooms I wanted you to approve."

Delight flashed on her face. "Really?"

"Really."

"Oh, my gosh, thank you. I can't tell you how much I appreciate it." She gestured to the house. "I can do the easy stuff like tearing out old carpet and even refinishing the floors. Although that's probably not as easy as I think. But

133

building—or even installing—kitchen cabinets is probably beyond me. At least, if I only have a month to learn."

"Less than a month now."

"Exactly. Show me the plans."

We went out onto the porch, and I showed her what I had in mind for her kitchen. Her enthusiasm was contagious, and it was hard not to feel a little of it myself.

It was odd, but nice.

Don't get used to it, I thought.

After we looked at the plans, I got back to work. The house occasionally made its displeasure known, popping a floorboard under my feet or slamming a door at my arse, but it was easy enough to ignore. The stench was harder, but even that disappeared eventually, as if the house tired of fighting. Or maybe we really were making if feel better, like Isobel hoped.

She brought me a sandwich at some point, but I was lost in the soothing motion of working with wood. Fortunately, I had everything I needed down at the boathouse for my current project, as well as all the tools required to craft the cabinets. I'd started out in cabinetry years ago, once I'd realized that I needed to work with my hands to find peace, and had only recently made my way to boats.

We toiled until it grew dark. I found lanterns and brought them up to the kitchen so that I could keep going, but we'd need to get the electrical up and working as soon as possible.

"Knock, knock." Isobel's voice pulled me out of my trance, and I turned. She'd showered and changed into a clean pair of jeans and a jumper that hung loosely off of one shoulder, and she was so beautiful that I had to glance away. "It's getting late."

"Really?" I frowned, looking down at my watch. It was nearly nine-thirty. Surprise flashed through me.

"You've been in the zone." She held up a basket that I hadn't noticed because I'd been so distracted by her beauty. "I brought you dinner. And a beer."

"Thanks."

"Well, don't get used to it." She walked toward the middle of the room and pulled a blanket out of her basket, then laid it on the ground.

"Don't get used to you bringing me dinner?"

"Or a beer." She pulled one out of the basket and opened it, then handed it to me. "I always did this for my boyfriend. Every night, dinner and a beer as soon as he got home from work. Then I did the washing up." She sounded disgusted with herself, and I wanted to know more.

"Every night?" I sat on the blanket when she did.

"Yep." She pulled two paper-wrapped Cornish pasties out of the basket and handed one to me. It was warm from the oven, and I recognized the distinctive crimped crust of Margot's Tea & Cake Parlor. She must have picked them up earlier in the day and heated them in her oven.

"If you did all that, then what did the miserable sod do?" I asked.

"Mostly just watched footie and took me for granted, I'm realizing now." She sipped her beer. "But I'm done with him, and I've got a new life. I'm not a doormat anymore."

"A doormat?" A surprised laugh escaped me. "I have a hard time believing you were ever a doormat."

"Well, I was. Trust me. But I'm getting better. It's like I just had to wake up and get out of that old life, you know? He was an expert manipulator, Tommy was. I had no idea how well he'd played me until I'd wasted way too much time on him." There was a hint of sadness to her voice, and it made something violent seethe inside me.

She looked over at me. "Did you just growl?"

"Um." Had I? "Maybe."

"Is that a werewolf thing?"

"Yes." Although I hadn't noticed that I'd made a noise. I'd been too busy fantasizing about punching this Tommy bastard. "I don't like the idea of your boyfriend hurting you."

As soon as I said the words, I knew they were too much. I should have kept them to myself.

"That's unexpectedly sweet."

"Don't get used to it. I'm a miserable grump, remember?"

"Oh, right." She smiled. "I almost forgot. But maybe I'm willing to revise that. You've been very helpful today."

"Just trying to get rid of you, remember?" I made my voice gruff, wanting to return to the safety of being a bastard.

"Ah, yes. There's the miserable grump I remember." But still, she smiled.

"Good. Don't forget it." I finished the pasty and stood. "I'm going to get back to work."

"It's late. You should quit."

"Soon enough." I spoke without looking at her, hoping she would go. As long as she was near me, it was difficult to stay in my protective bubble. "I'll see you later."

"All right." If she sounded a bit hurt, there was nothing I

could do about it. And when she finally left, I breathed a sigh of relief and got back to the kitchen.

I finished the project I'd started in the pantry, then went outside. The cool moonlight bathed my skin, and I breathed a sigh of relief. A run would sort me out. At the very least, it would help me fight this endless desire to kiss Isobel.

As the night air came alive around me, I called upon my wolf and shifted into my animal form. My clothes disappeared, and my senses grew twice as strong. Soon, I stood on all fours, feeling immensely better. Then I began to run.

CHAPTER
FIFTEEN

Isobel

RAFE SPENT the next three days helping me at the house. The second morning we were working, he arrived just as I was finishing the spell that would give me enhanced speed. At his request, I enchanted him as well.

It made all the difference. He was so incredibly skilled that the kitchen came together in no time once he was able to work more quickly than his usual pace—which, as far as I could tell, was already quite fast.

I was really starting to feel hopeful about this place. The house was still grumpy, but less so. It would need to get a lot better before I could convince an electrician or plumber to come in. And the roof would need professional help, but I really couldn't let innocent people up there if I was worried the house would find a way to fling them off.

On the third day, during a lunch of cheese and pickle

sandwiches that I'd packed for us, I asked Rafe why he'd chosen to work with wood. We sat on the porch, with the autumn breeze blowing our hair back and the sea sparkling in the distance.

He hesitated before answering, and for a second, I was pretty sure he wasn't going to talk at all.

"I used to be an investor. I liked numbers because they were simple." He didn't say it, but I was pretty sure he'd liked the fact that numbers weren't people. "And that worked out well for me, for a while."

I remembered what the bartender had said about him making a lot of money, but he didn't mention that. "But?" I asked. "There's clearly a *but* coming."

He nodded. "I was unfulfilled. There was just something so cold about it all. So I decided to refinish my kitchen. I wanted a project to do with my hands, and it needed some work."

"And you weren't keen on having people in your house, mucking about with installing a new one."

He smiled. "True. There was that added benefit."

"Where was this?"

"London, about six years ago."

"Wow, you would have been young."

"Twenty-six. Once I started refinishing on the kitchen, I realized how much I preferred working with my hands. It was...calming. I can disappear into the work. So I left my job and started to learn woodworking. First cabinetry, then boats."

"So you started a whole new life?"

"Essentially."

"Did you get a job with a cabinetmaker?"

"No, I did it on my own. Self-taught."

"So you could avoid people."

He just shrugged. But in this whole story, he'd made no mention of getting a job, which meant he'd must have been very good at investing, even though he'd been super-young.

"You're a talented guy, aren't you?"

"Just at one thing." He smiled. "But that's good enough for me."

It wasn't just one thing, but I didn't say it.

"All right. I'm back to work." He packed away the rubbish from lunch, then headed to the kitchen. As I watched him walk away, I realized that in all of the story he'd just told about his life, there had been no mention of his pack.

There was damage there, I was sure. Something about his life was just so...solitary. That couldn't be good for a wolf.

And yet, he was totally unwilling to talk about it. Not that I should be interested. I was starting to like him a little too much, and I still didn't want to fall for someone so soon after Tommy.

We avoided each other for the next few days, though I did always make a point to bring him lunch. It was different than it was with Tommy, though. Rafe was helping me out in a big way, and the least I could do was make him a sandwich. But we didn't talk as much, even though I could feel his eyes on me every time I walked by.

On my twelfth morning in Charming Cove, he didn't show up at Lavender House. In fact, he was gone before I even woke. I knew because I'd peeked into his open bedroom

ROMANCE RULES FOR WEREWOLVES

door and found it empty. He hadn't been up at Lavender House, either, and he didn't show up all day.

Where did Grumpy McHottiePants go? Poa asked in the afternoon. *I thought he'd be here.*

"Me, too."

You sound disappointed.

"I shouldn't be. He doesn't owe me anything, and he's already helped me so much."

You miss him.

"I don't. I just need the help with the house."

Liar.

My familiar could see right through me, but I didn't confirm it. "I'm getting back to work."

Rafe

I SHOULD HAVE TOLD Isobel that I wouldn't be at Lavender House today, but I'd been an absolute coward instead. I rarely felt any kind of nerves, but I was meeting the Jade Sorceress. It felt like she was my last chance to remove this damned curse, and I needed to focus only on that.

I'd left while it was still dark. The drive to London was a long one, and I couldn't be late. My mind spun the entire way there, hours of thinking about what was at stake.

The Jade Sorceress lived and worked in Shoreditch, an eclectic neighborhood entirely dedicated to supernaturals. Humans didn't know it existed and couldn't enter—if they tried to turn onto one of the streets, they had a sudden and overwhelming desire to go the other way.

I found parking about a quarter-mile away from her address and left the car, walking past potion shops and cafés specializing in enchanted coffees and cocktails.

The Jade Sorceress lived in a brick Victorian building with an ornate external staircase at the side. The iron spiral rose to the top floor, where the door to her flat was surrounded by lush potted greenery.

At five to two, I knocked.

She opened the door almost immediately, and her power washed over me. Relief made the tightness in my shoulders loosen a bit. A sorceress as powerful as she was would be able to remove this curse, surely. She was definitely the strongest one I'd encountered over the years, and I'd been to plenty of them.

"Rafe." She smiled, gesturing me inside. Her long skirts shifted around her as she stepped out of the way. She was in her mid-seventies, with a wild mane of silver hair and bright blue eyes that felt like they could gaze into the soul.

"Thank you for seeing me."

She nodded. "You're welcome. Come with me."

I followed her down the hallway, which was lined with bookshelves that were packed full of volumes with names like *A Witch's Guide to Hexes* and *Understanding Devious Spells*. She led me to a room at the back of the flat that was empty except for a round table draped in purple velvet and an antique armoire with a mirrored front.

"Please sit." She gestured to one of the two chairs that faced each other around the table, then took the other.

I did as she commanded, my heart pounding. A crystal ball waited in the middle of the table, the interior of the glass swirling with dense gray smoke.

"Put both hands on the table." She held her hands out for mine, one on each side of the crystal ball. My pulse accelerated as I did as she bid, and she rested her palms on top of the backs of my hands. "Now tell me about your curse."

Her blue eyes pierced me as I began to speak, and I could feel the faint buzz of her magic against the back of my hands. My tone was wooden, and the words came out in exactly the same order they alwayss did. By now, I'd told so many witches and sorceresses what had happened to me that it was a routine.

Her brow creased as she listened, and then she looked down into the crystal ball. She was deathly silent, not even breathing, and the smoke inside the glass turned brilliant gold.

That had to be good, right?

She frowned.

Damn.

"I'll be back in a bit. Stay here." She released my hands and stood, then walked toward the armoire behind her. Instead of opening the door, she stepped right through the mirror, which rippled like water as she disappeared.

"Well, shite." I sat back in the chair, looking around. Did this mean she could help me?

I waited, the minutes turning into an hour. When she returned, she looked paler than she had when she'd gone in. "It took a bit of time and effort to make your potion," she said, "but it's done." She handed it to me, a small cup with a dark liquid inside. "Drink."

"All right." I took the cup and drank the liquid in one quick gulp. It tasted sickeningly sweet, and I winced.

"Now stand." She gestured for me to join her next to the table.

I did as she commanded, letting her put her hands on my shoulders. She stared into my eyes as she began to chant in a language I'd never heard before. Her magic filled the air with power, making it spark around us. I could feel it seeping into my skin, past my muscles and into my bones.

I grimaced. It hurt like hell.

The Jade Sorceress didn't look much better. The rest of the color had drained from her face, and there were dark shadows forming beneath her eyes. But the brilliant blue of her gaze brightened, burning into me, and I gritted my teeth.

This had to be working. No other witch or sorceress had made me feel so damned miserable, and they'd never looked as shattered as she did.

I was nearly blind with the pain when she stumbled back and collapsed, her head slamming into the floor. I snapped out of my agony-induced trance and knelt, worry surging through me.

"Sorceress?" I laid a hand against her neck, feeling for a pulse as fear spiked.

Had I killed her? She was so pale, so still.

A faint pulse beat against my fingertips. Thank fates. I looked around the room for a pillow to put beneath her head, but saw nothing. Should I leave her to find one?

She gasped and sat up, her eyes wide and blind. She blinked, shuddering slightly, then looked at me.

"Are you all right?" I asked, putting my hand behind her back in case she lost her strength and fell backward.

She ignored the question. "There's nothing I can do for you."

My shoulders sagged. Damn it. But there was no arguing. She'd clearly tried her best, and it had knocked her unconscious. I shoved away the desperate disappointment and asked, "Can I get you anything? Call anyone? You had a bad fall."

"I'll be fine. Just help me up."

I did as she asked, sincerely doubting her words. "You're very shaky."

"I know. It'll go away in a while." She looked at me. "I'm sorry. I had hoped I could help, but the curse is just too strong. The witch who did this was powerful, and there's an element to the curse that I couldn't quite see. Without that information, I can't devise a proper cure."

I nodded, having heard this before. "Do you know of anyone else who might be able to help?"

She gave a soft laugh, but it wasn't a joyful sound. "Someone more powerful than me? Because that's what they would have to be. And no, I don't know of anyone."

I wasn't surprised to hear it. I'd been looking for years and hadn't found anyone, either. "Thank you, anyway."

She nodded. "Now help me to the living room."

I did as she asked, getting her set up on the couch and paying her fee. She insisted that she didn't need any more help, so I left, feeling like I was a hundred feet underwater.

CHAPTER
SIXTEEN

Isobel

RAFE NEVER APPEARED at Lavender House, and I spent the rest of the day working on the upstairs bedrooms. I painted them beautiful shades of pale blue, sage, and rose, but I was unable to stop thinking of him.

When I was done for the day, I joined Emma, Holly, Aria, and Tabitha for drinks at Potions & Pinot. It was another girls' night, and I'd been looking forward to it. Once again, I had a fantastic time. But *unlike* the last time, I was smart enough to call Anita the cab driver before midnight. She dropped me off at the boathouse right before her shift ended, and I let myself in, eager to get out of the chilly autumn air. My dress was too thin for the weather, but it was so beautiful that I'd been unable able to resist wearing it again.

A light from the kitchen caught my eye, and I spotted

Rafe sitting at the table, a bottle of whiskey and a glass in front of him.

That was unusual.

I didn't know him well, but he wasn't a big drinker, as far as I'd seen. I approached, noticing the sag to his shoulders.

Worry shot through me. He definitely wasn't himself.

He didn't seem to notice me approach until I was right in front of him, and he looked up, surprise on his face.

"You look beautiful." His words weren't slurred—he would never lose control like that—but he was definitely drunk.

"Thanks." I smiled through my concern and took a seat.

Something was up with him, and I wanted to find out what. But I couldn't just ask him. He might be drunk, but he'd never answered my questions before.

I nodded toward his bottle of whiskey. "Mind if I have some?"

"Help yourself."

I poured more into his glass, then took a sip. It burned, and I tried not to wince. I really wasn't a whiskey person, but I wanted him to feel like I was joining him, not interrogating him.

"I went out with the girls tonight," I said, searching for the best way to bring up the subject of why he was drinking like a fish. It came to me in an instant. As much as I hated the idea, it was the only way: I would have to share first. "Want to hear something depressing?"

"Why?"

"Because I know you're feeling awful, and I'm hoping

that if I tell you something crappy that happened to me, you'll tell me what's happened to you."

"That's an interesting approach." He took the whiskey and sipped it.

"Is it working?"

"Depends on how terrible your story is."

"Pretty terrible." The corner of my mouth tugged up in a smile. "You can judge for yourself."

He gestured for me to continue.

"All right, so I went out with the girls tonight. And it was nice," I said. "I didn't really have any friends back in London." Sharing the worst part of my life sucked, as it turned out. I'd already told him a little about my relationship with Tommy, but this was the really bad part.

He was looking at me, concern and interest in his eyes, but he said nothing, which was smart. This was hard enough without hearing his voice. If I stared into the distance, I could pretend he wasn't even there while I shared.

"Anyway, it was just Tommy and me. Or at least, I thought it was. I gave him my whole life, like an idiot."

"You're not an idiot."

"I was."

He shook his head. "There's nothing you can say that will make me believe that."

I smiled. "Thanks, but wait until you hear my story."

"All right, keep going."

"So, just before I came to Charming Cove, we had a date at a fancy hotel. *Way* nicer than any place he'd ever taken me, so I thought he was going to propose. I'd given him my whole life, so of course I thought that." A bitter laugh escaped me, but it was more at myself than anything. "I got to the hotel and went up to the roof like I thought I was supposed to. I'd found a letter from him that was meant for her, I think. Or maybe it was a reminder to himself. Anyway, all the staff seemed surprised to see me. I thought it was because I wasn't dressed right, but apparently, it was because I was the *second* woman to arrive that night."

A low growl escaped him, and I glanced over. His brow was furrowed, and anger lit his eyes. "He was cheating on you."

"Yep." I took another sip of the whiskey. "There he was, with another woman. She was beautiful, too. Crazy beautiful."

"You're beautiful." His tone was low. "The most beautiful woman I've ever seen."

My gaze flashed to him, and I had to stifle a gasp. He was drunk, but not that drunk—he meant it.

"The worst part was, I'd have said yes if he'd proposed. And it would have been the worst thing in the world. I can see that now. But I was just so blind back then. I'd needed to *see* his betrayal to leave." I sipped the whiskey, wishing I'd been stronger sooner. That I hadn't wasted so many years on him. "Anyway, that's my shitty story. What's yours?"

He heaved a sigh, and I looked up at him. His gaze searched mine, heavy with pain.

Suddenly, I was scared about what he might say. Because my story had been bad, but I was pretty sure his would be worse.

~

Rafe

I COULDN'T BELIEVE I was about to share this, but her story had been so honest, and the pain in her eyes had been so real. The whiskey made it easier to talk, though. Much easier. "When I was nineteen, I fell in love with a witch. At least, for a while. But I was nineteen, so I was an idiot. And like an idiot, I broke up with her on Valentine's Day."

She winced. "That's bad."

"I know." I nodded, taking a sip of the whiskey. "It was an impulse that day. I kept seeing all these couples together —sharing coffee, taking walks, even riding a tandem bike, for fate's sake."

"A tandem bike?" I smiled. "That's almost comedically romantic."

"They wore matching jumpers." I couldn't remember the most important part of my life, but I could remember that ridiculous detail. "In that moment, I realized I couldn't give her what I was seeing all around me. I felt like I was leading her on."

"Oh, no. So you didn't wait?"

"No. Obviously, I should have. But I felt like a liar." How stupid I'd been.

"So you broke up with her."

"I tried to explain, but she was angry." I could still see her face and the storm in her eyes, though she'd banished her name from my memory. "She was powerful. Immensely so, in a way that I hadn't realized. She cursed me to forget my pack, and for my pack to forget me." The words tasted bitter on my tongue.

She gasped. "What?"

I nodded, my gaping hole still ragged at the edges. "I didn't even know that was possible. But one moment, I was staring at her, feeling guilty as hell and realizing I'd made a mistake, and the next I felt something being torn from my soul."

"You can't remember them at all?" Her voice was soft, worried.

"Not at all. And they can't remember me. At least, that's what she told me. I've been looking for them for over a decade now, so I believe her. Unless they never wanted me to begin with." It was a fear that had developed over the years. What if they *did* remember me, but they were glad I was gone?

"They wanted you." She reached out and gripped my hand hard. "They did."

"How can you be sure? I have no way of knowing the truth. I know only what she told me."

"I know." She sounded so confident that I wanted to believe her, but it was impossible. "She was unhinged."

"I realize that now. I'd been too young to see it then. Too self-absorbed."

"It was a jerk move, breaking up with her on Valentine's. But you meant well, and the punishment definitely didn't fit the crime."

I gave a bitter laugh but had run out of words.

"And you've been trying to get the curse lifted all these years?" she asked.

I nodded. "She disappeared after that, and I can remember her face, but she must have taken her name from my memory. I haven't been able to find her to get her to remove the curse. Instead, I've been to countless witches and sorceresses, but none have managed it."

"And today was the same?"

"Today was worse. I went to the Jade Sorceress, and she couldn't do it."

She winced, then tried to smooth her features. "She's powerful."

I nodded. "The most powerful one there is, as far as I could tell. It took me two years to get an appointment."

"And she didn't succeed." Her voice was low with sadness. "Did she?"

"She didn't. And she also said she didn't know anyone else who could help."

"So you're out of options, especially if you can't find the witch who did this."

"Pretty much." I'd known this day would come eventually. Maybe it was for the best that I give up hope.

That was just too dark, and my head was swimming from the whiskey. How much had I had? I enjoyed a dram every now and again, but never like this.

"I think you'd better get to bed." Isobel's voice sounded from above me, and I realized I'd put my head on the table.

"Yeah." I rose, slightly unsteady on my feet.

"Come on." She wrapped an arm around my waist and led me toward my bedroom.

"I never drink this much." And I could feel it swimming though my veins, making my head spin.

"I can tell." She stopped by the side of my bed, and I untangled myself from her and fell onto the plush surface.

This was not my finest moment.

"I'll leave a glass of water on the nightstand."

"Thanks." I draped an arm over my face, and darkness took me.

CHAPTER
SEVENTEEN

ISOBEL

I DREAMED of Rafe that night, and the sadness that had been haunting him for over a decade. No wonder he was such a grump. No one was meant to forget their entire family, but for a werewolf, pack was everything. Losing them would be like losing a limb. It was just so damned tragic.

And what a miserable cow that witch had been. If I could get my hands on her, I'd give her a pig's tail like Catrina did to her enemies. In fact, I wouldn't stop there. Perhaps the eight-year-old could help me give her a pig's snout as well. She deserved it.

Actually, she deserved to be in jail. Meddling with some-one's mind like that was pure evil, and illegal. Determination buzzed within me as I climbed out of bed. The sun was rising, and I had a lot of work to do. Not to mention, I had to check on Rafe.

What lit a fire under your butt? Poa asked from the end of the bed.

"How can you tell I've got a fire under my butt?" I asked her as I pulled on fresh clothes.

Your face. It's all serious, and your eyes are pretty freaky.

"Good." I wanted to find that witch right now and make her reverse her curse. I also wanted to punch her. Before or after I gave her a pig's snout, I wasn't sure. The snout *would* be a bigger target.

Well, if you need any help kicking ass, I'm here for you.

"Thanks." I smiled at her, convinced she could read my mind even though she said she couldn't. "I'll let you know."

I left her to nap on the bed and headed downstairs, finding Rafe still in his bed. The warm sunlight gleamed on him as he slept, one strong arm thrown over his head and his face peaceful in slumber.

"Five more minutes," I murmured, then went to the kitchen to make him breakfast. After the day he'd had yesterday, it was the least I could do.

Once I had the bacon and egg sandwich on a plate, I knocked on the doorframe of his room and called out in a singsong voice, "Breakfast is ready."

He sat bolt upright, rubbing his face. "You scared the hell out of me."

I grinned. "Sorry. I don't want it to get cold, and there's loads of work to do today, so you need to get up and get started."

He groaned, but he didn't sound as tortured as he'd been last night. I was pretty sure he'd want me to act normal, so I did. He might not even remember he'd told me.

"Breakfast is on the counter," I said. "I'll meet you at Lavender House later."

"You're not coming?" He sounded distinctly grumpy, and I smiled.

"Eventually. I just have an errand to run."

He grunted. "Well, don't take too long. That house doesn't like me."

"That house doesn't like anyone."

"It tolerates you."

"Barely." I headed toward the door. "See you later."

It didn't take long to get into town, but I didn't head to the hardware store, which was where Rafe probably thought I was going. Instead, I went to the Aurora Coven. Rafe had tried every witch he could think of to help him with his problem, but he hadn't tried *me*.

I might be unpracticed, but I was sure I had a gift for sensing curses and enchantments. I'd figured out what was going on with the house, after all. And I'd seen a blue light when I'd used the curse detector spell, which was something Cecelia said never happened. I had the skill—I was sure of it —but I needed to hone it.

For the first time ever, I didn't drop in at Margot's. Normally, her coffee and pastries were my first stop in town. Life was too short to live without Margot's. But today, I had a mission that left no time for scones.

I parked right in front of the coven and walked to the door. The brass handle buzzed with magic as I turned it, which I was pretty sure hadn't happened before. Oddly, there was no one in the front room, even though it was after opening hours. Maybe whoever was meant to watch the desk was in the kitchen or workshop. "Hello?"

No one responded.

Voices sounded from the back of the building, so I headed toward the door on the far side of the room. It was shut, so I stopped and knocked, calling out, "Hello? It's Isobel."

A moment later, the door swung open. Emma stared at me, the most massive grin on her face. "Isobel! You opened the front door!"

"Um, yes?" I looked back at the door, then at her. "Was I not supposed to?"

She grinned even wider, though it shouldn't have been possible, given how big her smile already was. "It was locked!"

"No, it wasn't."

She ignored that and grabbed my arm, pulling me inside the room. "Come in."

I followed her, realizing that the room was *full* of witches. There were ten total, and all but Emma sat in chairs that faced each other around a circular table. They were clearly having a coven meeting, and I'd just barged in. I wanted to disappeared through the floor.

"I am *so* sorry," I said. "I didn't realize you were having a meeting. I thought the shop was open."

"It wasn't." A woman in her forties with a sleek bob stood, her gaze on me. Interest glinted in her eyes as she walked closer. Magic radiated from her, and it was obvious that she was a very powerful witch. Probably the coven leader. "Emma, are you sure you locked the door?"

"I did." Emma's grin was still there, and when I spotted Holly, she, too, was smiling.

"What's going on?" I asked. "You're all very interested in the fact that the door was locked, but I'm sure it wasn't."

"This is a big deal," Emma said. "Only a witch who belongs here can open the door if it's locked."

"She's not even a member yet," muttered a beautiful witch who still sat at the table.

"Lily." Hazel's tone was chiding, and the witch shut her mouth.

"Lily's a piece of work," Emma whispered to me. "But she's our piece of work."

"What's going on?" I whispered back. "This is all a bit strange."

Before she could answer, Hazel spoke. "Emma is right, this is a big deal. But first, I'm interested in hearing why Isobel has come today."

I looked at all the expectant faces staring at me and suddenly felt overwhelmed. "Um, it's okay. You're clearly in the middle of a meeting."

"You're the subject of the meeting now," Hazel said. "In a good way, I mean. You opened the door."

"Are you sure you didn't just forget to lock it?" I insisted.

"Very sure," Emma said. "Now spill."

I blew out a breath, suddenly feeling like I was under a microscope. But I needed the help, and Rafe was counting on me, even if he didn't know it. "I think I have the gift of reading curses and enchantments, but I haven't got a good handle on how to use it. I've been practicing," I hurried to say, "but I really need to learn to use this power ASAP."

Should I tell them about Rafe and why I needed control of the power?

"For Lavender House?" Emma asked.

"Yes," I said, latching on to that explanation. And I really should have thought of that. This power could help me figure out the specific details of how Lavender House had been enchanted, and that could help me fix it.

Also, I shouldn't be throwing away my own goals for a man. True, he was in a horrible state and needed help, but I had a bad history of putting men before myself, and I needed to work on that.

"I think we can help you with that." Hazel gestured and said, "Come here."

I went to her and stopped right in front of her. As I did so, Emma said, "Hazel is particularly good at reading other people's magic and diagnosing problems."

"I'm just going to lay my hand on your chest, all right?"

I nodded, and she pressed her palm to the middle of my breastbone. I drew in a deep breath, feeling the warmth of her palm and the buzz of her magic. It flowed inside me, a fizzing sensation that made me giggle.

I snapped my mouth shut. "Sorry."

Hazel smiled. "Don't worry about it. My magic has that effect." She frowned. "Although I'm sensing that your power is quite tangled up inside you."

"What do you mean?"

"Have you been ignoring it?"

I winced. "Maybe a bit. For the last ten years."

She blew out a breath. "That's not good. Magic can't be left alone with nowhere to go. It requires a witch to keep it in order. It's a partnership, and you weren't doing your part."

"I know." Heat flushed my cheeks, and I wanted to sink into the floor. "I had some...life things going on. But I want to get back on track and embrace my power."

"Good. Because you've got a lot of it." She removed her hand, and the fizzing sensation faded. "We can help you untangle it. You'll still need to practice to become proficient, but it will be much easier to get caught up."

"Oh, fates, thank you so much." I looked around the room and found nothing but friendly, understanding faces.

I felt tears prick my eyes. I hadn't expected to feel such emotion, but having all of these supportive, smiling women staring at me was the most wonderful feeling. Even Lily, who had been a bit snobby a moment ago, was looking at me with an understanding expression.

"I say we get started now," Hazel said. "We were nearly done with the meeting, anyway, and since everyone is here, it's a good time. And if Isobel is meant to join the coven, there's no time to waste."

Meant to join the coven.

I'd never been meant to do anything in my life. I'd kind of just floated along, but now I had goals.

It felt wonderful.

Hazel gestured for everyone to stand. "Let's move this to the garden. Lily, will you please collect the athames? Holly, the crystals?"

"On it!" Holly hopped up and ran from the room, excitement glittering in her eyes. Lily followed, albeit a bit more slowly. But she gave me a smile as she passed, and I smiled back.

"Do you have a familiar, Isobel?" Hazel asked.

"I do. Shall I call her?" I sure as heck hoped it worked.

"Yes, she'll need to be here for this." Hazel turned back to the women who were leaving the room. "The rest of you need to call your familiars as well, if you have them." She shot me a look. "In an ideal world, the familiars would attend the meetings, but none of them listen to orders unless they think it's important."

"Hopefully, this will qualify," I said, smiling. I wanted to see everyone's familiars, and magic always worked better when they were present.

"Oh, it will. A new coven member is a big deal." She held up a hand in a *slow down* gesture. "Not that it's official yet. Let's get your magic untangled, and then we'll talk. I realize we haven't even asked you if you want to be a member."

I do! I wanted to shout. But I just smiled and nodded, trying to play it cool. "I would, I think."

"Good. I like the feel of you. You've got good energy."

"Thanks." A grin spread across my face.

"Now, come one. We'll go out back. It's the perfect day for this."

I followed her to the back garden, which was a beautiful rectangular space that stretched out from the house. It was surrounded on all sides by high stone walls covered in vines. Autumn flowers bloomed in profusion, and their scent filled the air. The sound of running water came from the back of the garden.

Familiars were appearing out of thin air to join their

witches—a skunk, two cats, a large gray rat, and tiny teacup poodle—and I realized I'd better try to call Poa to me.

Poa? I need you. I called to her with my mind. I'd done this in the past and it had worked, so hopefully, she'd listen to me.

A moment later, she appeared, staring up at me with annoyance. *This had better be good.*

"It is, I promise." I gestured to the other witches and their familiars, and she turned to look at them.

Now this is what I'm talking about. Approval sounded in her voice. *Finally, you're hanging out with some real power.*

"I've got real power," I said, offended.

But it's a mess.

"Not for long. That's why you're here."

Oh, good. Let's get this show on the road.

EIGHTEEN

ISOBEL

HAZEL WAS DEFINITELY RUNNING this show. In her white dress and colorful jeweled belt, she looked like a bohemian princess as she swept her arm out in front of her and removed the grass from the ground with a shower of sparks. A perfect circle of fresh earth remained, and all ten witches took up positions around it. Half the witches had familiars, and the animals stuck close by their sides.

"You'll be in the middle," Hazel said. "But give me a moment to prepare the space." She went to the center of the circle and knelt, drawing a delicate gold athame from a hidden pocket in her skirt. The ceremonial blade was inset with gems that glittered in the bright autumn sunlight, and she used the tip to draw a circle in the dirt about a meter across. She then pressed her hand to the soil and hummed a note that was so pure and beautiful, it didn't sound human.

Lavender sprouted at the edges of the circle, and fresh green grass grew in the middle.

Hazel smiled and looked up at me. "Lavender. Unusual, but how appropriate, given that you own Lavender House now."

"It's normally another type of flower?"

"It depends on the person, but I haven't seen lavender before. It's ancient and powerful." She rose and gestured for me to step inside the circle.

I did so, with Poa jumping over the lavender bushes to follow me. Once I was in the middle, Hazel went to the last open space in the ring of women surrounding me. She raised her hands, her athame pointed toward the blue sky. When she spoke, it was in a voice that vibrated with power. "Witches, begin."

In a synchronized motion, each witch knelt and pointed an athame at the dirt in front of her. Their movements were so perfectly choreographed that they'd clearly done this before. The ceremonial blades were all different colors and styles—silver, gold, bronze, and even obsidian. Each witch drew a different symbol in the dirt, though I couldn't make out the details from where I stood. I craned my neck to get a look at everyone, and they were all intensely focused on their work.

When the designs were done, the witches sank their blades into the soft, dark dirt and began to chant in low voices. They were so quiet that I couldn't make out the individual words, but I was pretty sure they were each saying something different.

Magic swelled, sparkling brightly despite the sunlight. It

swirled golden through the air, rushing around me in a spiral. Flowers budded from the symbols etched into the dirt, beginning to fill the circle with colorful blooms. More and more sprouted, drawing closer to me with every flower, until the entire earthy space was filled with fresh new growth.

The scent was incredible, and I drew it into my lungs. As I did so, the magic in my chest began to loosen. It was the strangest feeling—I hadn't even realized it had been tight. I'd lived this way so long that I'd become used to it. But I could actually *feel* the power untangling, just like Hazel had said.

Poa leaned against my leg, her purrs vibrating through me. I could sense her joy, as if the magic inside her was feeling better as well.

Poor Poa. I'd had no idea that my familiar was also uncomfortable, but she was definitely happier.

The entire process felt like it was over in seconds, but I wanted it to last longer. It had been incredible.

As the golden sparks faded, the witches stood. "Well?" Hazel asked.

"I feel better." I drew in a deep breath. "I hadn't even realized I'd felt bad. But everything just seems...aligned? I don't know how to describe it."

I do. Poa looked up at me. *Amazing.*

I gave her an apologetic smile, guilt tugging at me. "I'm so sorry. I had no idea you were all tangled up, too."

Well, it's better now, so let's forget it.

"Wow. That's unexpectedly forgiving."

She glared at me. *Don't get used to it. You owe me tuna.*

I grinned. "There's the Poa I know and love."

She purred and rubbed against me, and warmth filled my chest. She was definitely feeling better.

Hazel walked toward me. She held out a hand toward my chest, stopping before she made contact. "May I?"

I nodded.

She pressed her hand to the same spot as before, and her magic flowed into me. She grinned broadly as she removed her hand and stepped back. "You're a Reader. The most powerful one I've ever felt, in fact. With practice, one day, you'll be able to read any spell, curse, or enchantment that has been placed on a person or object. Eventually, you'll be able to undo the magic if you desire."

Wow. I'd heard of Readers, but I couldn't believe I was one. I looked from Hazel to the other witches, turning in a circle to make sure I could see all of them as I said, "Thank you so much. I can't tell you how much I appreciate this."

"Tell us by practicing," Hazel said. "Emma will take you up to the workshop to help you get started. We want you at full power if you're planning to become an apprentice."

I wanted to salute but resisted. "I'll get there. Thank you again."

Emma led me upstairs, and Poa stuck close to my heels. Penelope joined her, and as they communicated in their silent familiar language, I had a bad feeling that they were planning something.

"This is fantastic," Emma said as she walked into the workshop. "The coven hasn't had a Reader in years. And I mean *years*. It's been at least a couple decades. This is going to be so helpful with our work."

Her words thrilled me, filling me with an intense desire

to start practicing. I wanted to be the best damned Reader this coven had ever seen.

"We're going to start with enchanted objects," Emma said when we stopped beside one of the tables. "You touch them and see what you can feel."

"All right. Let's do it."

We spent the rest of the day practicing my power. I felt guilty about spending the time away from Lavender House, but if I could use this gift to more accurately identify the spell that had been placed on it, I could perhaps improve its mood even faster. With any luck, I could make it cheerful enough to let workmen inside.

In the long run, the time spent practicing would be worth it.

Emma and I finished as it was getting dark, and I felt much steadier in my magic. It would still take a lot of practice to fully come into my power, but I had faith I could do it. I'd learned so much from her in such a short time, and she'd even told me about Avalona, a tiny island just off the coast of Cornwall where my magic would be enhanced, if I wanted to try it there.

I definitely did.

On the way back to the house, I stopped at Codswollop's and ordered two fish and chip dinners with an extra piece of fish for Poa. Then I headed toward the boathouse. Lavender House was lit with lanterns, no doubt because Rafe was still up there working. I parked the car, planning to bring the fish up to him, when I spotted the vase of red roses on the ground in front of the door.

I frowned. "What the heck?"

I climbed out of the car and knelt by the flowers, pulling the card out. My heart pounded as I flipped it open, finding a message that made me grimace.

I WAS the worst sort of sod. Please call me. I still have my old phone. I want to explain. Love, Tommy.

"UGH." I crumpled the note up. Why was he trying so hard? He'd spent most of our relationship ignoring me or telling me the laundry needed to be run. Why did he suddenly have to have my attention?

Was it because I was withholding it?

Probably.

And I was going to keep withholding it. I'd do one better, actually. *Two* better.

First, I dumped the roses in the trash, then called Mr. Ludlow, the solicitor. He had no news about the deed to the boathouse, but he did agree to send a letter to Tommy threatening him with legal action if he didn't leave me alone. I didn't know what kind of legal action I would take, and Mr. Ludlow didn't seem particularly bothered by the details.

"I dislike the idea of this bounder harassing you," he said, his tone stiff. "I will take care of it."

I smiled down at the phone as I rang off. That Mr. Ludlow was a good sort.

My last call was to Emma, requesting that she and the coven put a spell on the boathouse to hide it from Tommy. I didn't know how he'd found me, but Emma said that she'd see to it he forgot.

My smile was even bigger as I put the phone away, and I was more grateful than ever for finding my way to Charming Cove.

I left the boathouse and headed toward Lavender House, the takeaway bag gripped in my hand. I'd only made it a few steps when the door opened and Rafe stepped out. He was clearly leaving for the night, so I turned around and went back into the boathouse to set out dinner. I found plates and silverware in his small kitchen and laid the food on the table just as he was walking in.

He was soaking wet from the top of his head almost down to his knees, with his shirt plastered to the broad planes of muscles on his chest.

I laughed. "What happened to you?"

"Your house had some opinions about how I did the plumbing on the new kitchen sink." He sounded grumpy, but I could see in his eyes that he wasn't. Not very, at least.

"You were there all day without me? And you even did some plumbing?"

"Not well, it seems." He gestured to himself.

"Thank you, though. I really appreciate it." I gestured to the food. "And I brought dinner. But don't—"

"Get used to it, I know." He shot me a smile, then headed toward his bedroom. "I'm going to get cleaned up, and I'll be out soon."

"All right." He hadn't mentioned the roses, so I had to assume he hadn't seen them. Thank fates for small favors.

Since it felt weird to sit and eat without him, I walked to

the side of the building that contained his tools and the two unfinished boats. I lifted up the tarp that covered one of the two boats, then gasped. It was *gorgeous*. I'd never seen such beautiful and precise woodworking. And even though I wasn't an expert, I could tell that this was something special.

No wonder my kitchen was coming along so quickly. It was child's play for him.

"Finding anything you like?" His voice drew my attention toward the kitchen, and I looked up.

"Sorry, I was snooping." I let the tarp drop back down. "But you're crazy talented, Rafe."

"I do all right."

"Sorry I called it a hobby. I can see it's not."

He shrugged, but there was half a smile on his face. "Dinner smells great, thanks."

"It's the least I could do." I used my power to call on Poa, knowing that she'd want her fish to be at least a little warm. If I let it cool too much, I'd surely face her wrath. When she didn't come right away, I added the mental note that there was fish for her.

She appeared in the kitchen immediately, sitting on a chair.

"Seriously?" I asked her.

What? You expect me to eat on the floor?

"I would never. But don't put your feet on the table."

She harrumphed but did as I requested, keeping her feet on her plate as she dug into the fish. Rafe smiled down at her, and there was a genuine fondness in his eyes that I hadn't noticed before.

"You like her, don't you?" I asked as I approached.

Everyone likes me. She spoke without once slowing her eating.

"I do," he said. "Always liked cats, but she's special."

Poa did a little shimmy.

Rafe and I ate, the table characterized by the initial silence of a good meal. Codswollop's really was excellent, I realized. What did Charming Cove not have?

"Where were you today?" he asked after he finished his fish. "I thought it was just an errand."

"It was, but it took longer than I thought." I drew in a deep breath, both excited and nervous to tell him what I'd learned. "I think I can help you."

"Help me?" He looked up, and then understanding dawned. "Last night wasn't a dream."

"Um, no. You told me everything. At least, I think it was everything."

"It was." He sighed heavily. "I really didn't want to lay all that on you. It's a lot."

"It's a hell of a lot, and it's horrible. I can't believe you've been living through that."

"I'm fine."

"You're *not* fine, and pretending otherwise doesn't help." I'd been pretending the same thing with my life, and it sure as hell hadn't worked for me.

"Wait," he said, his brow creasing as he thought. "If I told you the truth, does that mean your story was also true? I didn't just dream that?"

"Unfortunately, you didn't." I winced.

"That bastard." His words were a growl, and I smiled. I quite liked having a werewolf on my side.

"Ignore him," I said. "He's old news, and we're focusing on you."

"I'd rather focus on you."

His tone made me blush. There was something more to it that made me think of long kisses and longer nights. His expression turned slightly chagrined, as if he realized how the words could be interpreted.

"Anyway," I said, "let's talk about what I did today."

"All right. It was about me somehow?"

"It was. And about me. For the last ten years, I've been a bit of a loser witch."

He glared. "Don't call yourself that."

I shrugged. "Why?"

"I don't like the idea of anyone speaking negatively about you. Not even you."

"Wow." I sat back in my chair, surprised. "You're not nearly as jerky as I thought."

"Much to my shame." He looked like he wished he'd never said anything. "But please continue. Let's stop talking about me."

"Okay, okay. Back to me. I'm a witch who has ignored her powers for too long."

He nodded.

"But I'm done with that. I want to embrace my magic. And while I've been here, I've realized that I've got a gift for reading spells and enchantments. Even curses. So I went to the Aurora Coven to get help with that." I smiled at the memory. "And it went well. Really well. They helped me untangle my magic, and I think that with some practice, I can maybe help you with your curse."

ROMANCE RULES FOR WEREWOLVES

Hope flared in his eyes, but it was gone so quickly that I could have imagined it. "I've been to so many witches and sorceresses, Isobel. It's not that I don't believe you're powerful, but I'm a lost cause."

"I really don't think you are. It's obvious that the witch who cursed you was extremely powerful, and that's one of the reasons it's been hard for the other witches to remove her curse. But it's also possible they weren't able to properly read every element of the curse itself. Do you know if that's the case?"

"It was. The Jade Sorceress said she couldn't see all of it and made me drink a potion. Then she tried to draw the curse out of me."

"Bingo." I gave a triumphant little fist pump. "The potion is used as a cure-all. When combined with a powerful witch's or sorceress's magic, it can be used to remove most curses. *Most* curses."

"So that means you might be able to help?"

"If they hadn't used a potion to help them, I would know that they'd been able to read every element of the curse because they'd have removed it in another way entirely. Basically, it means there's hope."

He went still, and my heart fluttered. I wanted to be able to help him so badly.

"That would be...incredible." His voice was soft.

"I'm committed," I said. "I won't give up until I remove the curse. I promise."

He frowned. "No. Don't make that promise."

"Why not?"

"The last sorceress who tried collapsed. She was in bad

shape. I don't want that to happen to you."

"I'll be fine. We'll take it slowly. Want to try now?"

"That's not really taking it slowly."

"I know, but I just want to get a feel for it. I've got to start somewhere, and I'd like to get an idea of what I'm working with."

He hesitated.

"Come on. Let me try."

"If you're sure. But if you feel faint at all, stop immediately."

"Will do. And I have Poa here to help me."

She had laid down on her chair and was having a nice post-dinner bath. Fortunately, she had the good grace to not stick her leg up in the air to lick her bum—a move I called the *turkey leg*—but that was probably because we were with Rafe. If it was just me, she had no shame.

"Poa?" I said. "Can you help?"

Him? Yes. I like him.

"Great." I looked at Rafe. "She likes you. Now stand up."

He did as I commanded, standing in front of me with a stalwart expression on his face. It was almost as if he were trying *not* to have hope, and it hurt my heart for him.

"I'm going to press my hand to your chest," I said, planning to mimic what Hazel had done with me. I'd only practiced on inanimate objects with Emma, so this was going to be an entirely different process.

He nodded, and I pressed the flat of my palm to his shirt. Immediately, I could feel the curse inside of him. It was dark, like a heavy fog that filled his soul. But I felt more distant from it than I should—like it was just out of reach.

An idea came to me, but it was probably ridiculous. There was no way I could ask him to—

"What's wrong?" he asked.

"Huh?" My gaze flashed up to his.

"You look doubtful."

"Um, yeah. I had an idea, but..."

"What is it?"

I drew in a deep breath. "Take off your shirt."

His brows rose. "What?"

"I can feel the curse, but I think this would work better if I touched your bare skin." I could feel the heat rush to my cheeks as I said it.

"Okay." His voice had turned a bit rough, but surely I was imagining it.

When I glanced up to meet his eyes, however, the heat in their emerald depths made it clear that I hadn't been imagining anything. Memories of the kiss flashed in my mind, and I tried to drive the thought away.

I stepped back as he pulled off his shirt, careful to keep my gaze directed over his right shoulder. I certainly couldn't look at his eyes, and staring at his chest just felt like too much.

"Okay, I'm going to touch you again," I said, trying not to sound as breathless as I felt.

CHAPTER
NINETEEN

Rafe

I'M GOING to touch you.

Isobel's words echoed in my head, and my heart hammered against my ribs. It took everything I had not to close my eyes and clench my fists. I didn't want her to know how she affected me, but it was going to be impossible if this went on for too long.

To make matters more difficult, she was standing so close that I could see the silver in her eyes, and her scent was a drug. I inhaled, trying for subtlety. In the ideal world, I'd stop breathing entirely. Since that wasn't an option, I should at least try to look unfazed.

Her palm was warm against my chest, electric. Heat roared through me, and I trained my gaze at a spot on the wall over her head. When her magic flowed through me, I had to bite back a moan.

This was not part of the deal.

The process seemed to last forever yet end too quickly. But when she drew her hand back, I could finally breathe. I chanced a glance at her face and saw the faintest flush to her cheeks. Her bottom lip was damp where she must have licked it, and it took everything I had not to pull her into my arms and kiss her.

Why the hell was this so difficult?

And how were we going to keep avoiding what was clearly between us?

She cleared her throat. "All right, so I've got a bit of an idea of what's going on. But we're going to need to go to Avalona Island."

I frowned, her words temporarily distracting me from the thoughts running through my head. "Where?"

"According to Emma, there's an island about three miles off the coast of Charming Cove that has a whole lot of magic. It's a special place to the coven, and it'll help enhance my power so that I can get a full read on your curse."

I cleared my throat. "So we're going to an island to do more magic?"

"Yes. Tomorrow. I just need to find a boat." She frowned. "I hadn't thought of that."

"I have a boat. But we need to work on your house."

"Right. I know. But we can just pop over really quick in the morning."

"House first," I insisted. "You have a deadline. I've been like this for a decade."

"But you're miserable."

"I'm fine." She gave me a hard look, and I sighed. "I'm used to it, okay? I want to get your house finished."

"To get me out of here, right?" She arched a brow.

"Exactly. It won't do me any good to find my pack if you're still in my house, driving me crazy." That didn't make much sense, but she'd just been touching my bare chest. I was far past sense.

"Won't you go live with them if you find them?"

She had a point. All I'd wanted for the last decade was to find my way back to my family. "I would, actually. But I won't leave until your house is finished."

She smiled. "So you really do like me?"

"I tolerate you."

"Sure, Mister Built-Me-A-Custom-Kitchen."

"It's literally the only thing I know how to do."

"Not the only thing. But you're darned good at it."

"Then just let me do it. We'll focus on your house, then we'll go to this island and deal with my issues."

"We'll do it tomorrow. Because I want to do this," she insisted. "And I don't like being told no."

I groaned. "Fine. But house first."

"Good. House in the morning, island in the evening. Deal?"

She looked so damned stubborn as she stared at me, jaw set and face determined. "Deal. As long as we make good progress on the house tomorrow."

She grinned. "I have a plan for that, actually."

"You do?"

"Oh, I do." She moved toward the stairs. "And now, I'm off to bed. Your turn to do the dishes."

I looked back at the paper takeaway containers. "Sure, I can do that."

"Good. See you in the morning!"

Isobel

OF COURSE, I tossed and turned with dreams of Rafe. The feel of his firm chest beneath my palm was burned into my memory, and I couldn't shake the sight of his face.

He'd looked *tortured*.

Like, jaw clenched and eyes burning. *For me.*

No, that was crazy. He'd probably just been miserable. Neither of us was in a place in our life where a relationship was a good idea. And he was leaving. There was no question that I would break this curse on him—for the first time in my life, I was truly confident of something. And when I did, he would go join his pack. But there was no way in hell I was leaving Charming Cove. It was home. I'd been here almost two weeks, and I knew it like I knew my own face.

When I woke, still hot from dreams of Rafe, I found him in the kitchen, having made the coffee. "Ready for a big day of home reno?" he asked.

"Beyond ready." How had this become my life? Handsome man handing me coffee while being enthusiastic about building me a custom kitchen?

Frankly, I had no idea. But I was going to lean into it. Hard.

I took the coffee he gave me, then sipped. He looked perfect leaning on the counter, his jeans slung low on his hips and his worn T-shirt hugging his shoulders. He hadn't yet put on shoes, and even his feet were attractive. That wasn't fair. Frankly, I was pretty sure it wasn't even natural.

I spun on my heel and marched toward the door.

"Don't you want breakfast?" he called after me.

I turned back. "You made breakfast?"

"Well, yes. I'm a werewolf. We eat a lot."

I nodded. "Right." I just hadn't expected him to make breakfast for *me*. "What is it?"

"Ham and egg sandwiches."

One of my favorites, of course. But I didn't want to play it too easy. I couldn't get used to cozy breakfasts around the kitchen table with him. *That way be heartbreak*, I told myself in my most ridiculous internal pirate voice in order to make it less serious, but it didn't work.

"Can I take it to go?"

"One step ahead of you." He held up paper towels, which presumably he planned to wrap the sandwiches in.

Damn. He was perfect.

"Great." I nodded, going for my best *cool girl, I don't care* expression. He looked at me like I'd just passed gas, so I probably didn't nail it. But he brought me the sandwich all the same, and I thanked him before scurrying away like the awkward mouse I was.

I didn't wait for him because I needed a bit of space after the dreams I'd had. And though running away wouldn't make him forget what a weirdo I'd been, a girl could hope.

As I climbed the hill, I ate my sandwich. It was delicious,

and I should have expected that after the Bolognese he'd made. I needed to stop expecting him to be anything but perfect. Even his grumpy exterior was appealing to me.

I polished off my breakfast as I stepped through the front door. As usual, the house groaned its annoyance. I tilted my head and said, "That doesn't sound as annoyed as the first time I walked in."

In response, the floorboards shifted under my feet.

Right. Still too irritable to get contractors in, but I clung to the idea that things were improving.

I closed my eyes and drew in a deep breath, calling upon Poa. I'd need her help with this, and she hadn't been around at the boathouse. She appeared a few moments later, grumbling indistinctly.

"If you'd woken earlier, Rafe would have made you a sandwich," I said.

You need to lock that one down, ASAP.

"Oh, shut up. We need to get to work."

What are we doing?

"Testing out my new power on the house. I bet I can learn more about what's bothering it."

Lead the way. She sounded resigned, but I'd take it. Any time she cooperated, I was grateful.

I led her to the center of the house, then sat on the bare wood floor and gestured for her to climb into my lap. She grumbled as she did so but began purring as soon as her weight settled onto my legs.

I closed my eyes and pressed my hands to the floorboards, calling upon my magic. It was so much easier to access now—I didn't even need help from crystals or other conduits for power. The Aurora Coven untangling my magic had made all the difference in the world.

Carefully, I began to study the enchantment that had been placed on the house. It was easier than it had been with Rafe, possibly because it was an inanimate object. Or maybe because the witch who had placed the spell hadn't been as strong.

Whatever it was, visions began to bombard me. The process was similar to what had happened with Rafe, but I could see more detail, like a woman who—very strangely—reminded me of Judith. They looked nothing alike, but there was something similar in their mannerisms.

The images shifted to show the woman placing a glowing crystal into the walls of the house. She put it right on top of a crossbeam in the wall, then watched as a workman boarded it up and painted it over. When he was done, I swore I could still see the glow of the crystal. If I focused, I thought I could feel it as well.

Was that the heart of the spell? The heart of the *house*?

It had to be.

I needed to find it.

The vision faded, having shown me all it was meant to.

Well, that was interesting. Poa leapt off my lap, and I rose.

"You could see it, too?"

Yes. There was something familiar about that woman.

"She looked like Judith."

Ah, lemon tree lady. If Poa could have grinned, she would have. *She has a lovely sunroom and an excellent selection of treats.*

"That's where you've been while I've worked on the house?"

Of course. But do you think she knows more about this house than she's saying?

"I think she's more connected than I'd realized." Whether *Judith* also realized that was the question. I'd need to make some time to talk to her.

But first, I wanted to locate that crystal. I walked throughout the house, trying to spot the wall where the crystal had been hidden. I found it to the right of the hearth that had coughed up dust on me, located in the distinct square depression in the wall that I'd seen in the image.

I laid my hand on the wall, and the outer edges of the depression glowed purple. I fed some of my magic into it, imagining the wood disappearing so that I could see inside.

It didn't exactly disappear, but I did find the pressure release latch. When I pushed just right, a small square section of the wall popped open like a door. Heart pounding, I opened it fully.

Inside, the crystal glowed. It was surrounded by all sorts of debris, probably brought in by some long-ago rodent. I could feel its magic like a second heartbeat, and the house seemed to make a noise of protest.

"Don't worry," I said, "I'm not going to hurt anything. I'm just going to clean away the debris in here." I didn't know what it was—an old mouse nest, maybe?—so I got a pair of gloves and a bin liner and carefully cleaned out the cubbyhole, leaving the crystal sitting in a nice, open space.

The house seemed to sigh in relief.

"That must feel better, huh?" I asked.

It didn't respond, but it also didn't smack me in the butt with a loose floorboard, so I was going to count it as a win. For the first time since I'd started here, I had the strongest feeling that I was actually getting somewhere with the house.

"What's that?" Rafe asked from behind me.

I turned to see him wearing his work boots and tool belt, and if I were being honest with myself, it was the sexiest sight I'd ever seen. Even Poa made a noise of approval.

"It's the heart of the enchantment. The heart of the house, really." I turned back and shut the wall. "I think the house will be happier now. Let me know if it's easier to work here. If it is, we can try to convince some contractors to come. Maybe I can even get a clean bill of health from the coven, something to show workers so they'll believe there's no magic in the house that will mess with them."

He nodded. "I'll let you know how it goes today. You can find me in the kitchen if you need me."

"Thanks." I watched him go, grateful to have his help. I had less than two weeks to finish fixing up Lavender House, and there was so much left to do.

We worked until midafternoon. Over a lunch of sandwiches and crisps, Rafe planned out how long it would take his boat to get to the island. We decided to leave with enough time be back in the harbor by nightfall.

When two o'clock rolled around, I went to collect him. The kitchen was looking fabulous, with all of the beautiful cabinets installed and the doors going on. I sighed happily as I stared at it, imagining baking cookies in there on a cold winter day, the fire in the kitchen hearth blazing.

Okay, that was enough fantasizing. I called out, "Time to go!"

"I just need a few more minutes to finish these cabinet doors," he said.

"Nope. We need to get moving so I have enough time on the island."

He straightened from his spot on the floor, where he was attaching a cabinet door. "I really think we should wait until the house is done."

"No. It's just a few hours. You're helping me, so I'm going to help you. And I need to master my magic, anyway, so this is practice that I desperately need."

That seemed to mollify him, so he stood and put the screwdriver on the counter. "Fine. Let's go."

I clapped. "Excellent!"

"How are you always in such a good mood?" he asked as we left the house.

I shrugged. "I don't know. This is a nice life."

He looked around at the scenery—all the green hills and sparkling blue sea and white gulls circling on the breeze—and said, "I suppose it is."

"Will you miss it when you go back to your pack?

"Assuming we find them, yes. Definitely."

So he was going back for sure. I'd asked the question just to confirm what I'd heard last night, but I didn't want to focus on that. Instead, I gave him a playful poke on the shoulder. "Are you doubting my skills?"

"I would never." He put his hand to his heart.

"Good." I grinned. "Because I can do this. I know I can."

We'd reached his car, so he stopped and stared at me, giving me a long look. "I believe in you. Truly."

The seriousness in his tone took my breath away. It was as if he saw through to my insecurities and wanted to banish them.

It made me feel all kinds of warm inside, and that was no good. "Thanks." Flustered, I turned to the car and climbed in.

TWENTY

Isobel

Rafe drove us down to the Charming Cove harbor, which I'd yet to visit because it was in the human part of town. The harbor was a beautiful little place, with a stone breakwater protecting the cluster of boats inside. Shops and restaurants surrounded it, and happy people ate ice cream from the Mr. Whippy truck in the harbor parking lot.

The humans in Charming Cove were known to be the happiest in England, and though it was attributed to the weather, the meteorologists couldn't figure out *why* this particular spot in Britain was so much nicer than all the rest.

The supernaturals knew, though--it was the magic in the air.

Rafe parked at the far end of the lot, and I climbed out.

"Did you bring anything warm to wear?" he asked. I held up my little jacket, and he frowned. "I'm not sure that'll be enough. I should have thought of this sooner." He went to the back of the car and popped open the boot. A few moments later, he pulled out a big jumper and handed it to me. "This will do."

I took the soft fabric, which smelled gloriously of sandalwood and leather, just like him, then frowned at him. "What will you wear?"

"I'll be fine."

"In that T-shirt?" He certainly *was* fine in the thin fabric, but not in the way he meant.

"Really, don't worry about me." He gave me a glare, which was so reminiscent of the first time I'd met him that I stepped back.

"All right, all right. I won't bother you about it."

"Good." The grump softened. "Now come on."

He led me toward the docks, heading down to the end of one of the little piers. Tied up in the very last spot was the most beautiful wooden boat I'd ever seen. It was fairly large —almost thirty feet, if I had to guess—and had a cabin underneath the mainsail.

"You really built this?" I asked.

He nodded.

"I can see why you kept it instead of selling it." I admired the sleek lines of the craft and the way the varnished wood gleamed in the sunlight.

"It wasn't good enough to sell," he said.

I laughed. "That's not it. You're sentimental about it, so you kept it." When he didn't argue, I asked, "Was this the first one you built?"

He nodded shortly, climbing onto the deck and turning

around to offer me a hand. I followed him, clutching his jumper tightly to my chest so that I didn't drop it in the water.

He reached into his pocket and pulled out the paper I'd given him earlier that day with the coordinates for the island. I found a seat in the cockpit on one of the wooden benches, and he set about preparing the boat to leave. From inside the cabin, he fetched two long cushions for the cockpit benches and handed one to me. I put it beneath my bum and resettled myself, then watched as he climbed back onto the deck.

"Can I help with the ropes or anything?" I asked.

"They're called lines, and no. I've got it."

He certainly did. He worked with such confident grace that it was clear he was just as comfortable running boats as he was building them.

"When did you learn to sail?"

He stilled briefly, his big hands holding one of the lines gently. "I don't know."

"Oh." The word escaped me on a soft breath. "You mean, you just knew? From your past life, you think?"

He nodded. "As soon as I stepped on a boat, I knew what to do."

"Wow. That must be...weird." I'd wanted to say *horrible*, but he already knew it was horrible.

"Weird is one word for it."

He turned to the outboard engine and started it. Within minutes, we were pulling away from the dock. He stood at the helm, so confident and handsome that I wanted to snap a photo. He just looked so natural behind the gleaming wooden steering wheel. But playing paparazzi would be too odd, so I resisted the urge.

Instead, I settled back onto the comfy cushion and watched the marina go by as he navigated expertly through the crowd of boats. Gulls circled in the sky above, calling out to each other as the breeze blew my hair back from my face.

Soon, we were at sea, with small waves splashing against the sides of the boat. It was cooler out here, and I pulled on the big jumper, luxuriating in the scent and softness. I caught him looking at me, but he glanced away as soon as I noticed him.

As the mainland shrank, I faced forward in hopes that I could see the island. There was nothing but open sea, however, and after nearly an hour, I turned back to him. "Are we close?"

"We are." He frowned, his gaze scanning the horizon. "Did she mention if it was hidden? We should be seeing it by now."

"No, but it makes sense that it would be. Otherwise, humans could know it was out here, right? You would already know, since you sail around here."

"Most likely, yes. I know the coast around here pretty well."

"Right, then I'm going to see what I can—" The sight ahead cut off my words. The air shimmered, a vision so wondrous that I almost gasped. "Do you see that? It's like a beautiful pearly haze."

"No." His frown deepened. "But I do feel an intense desire to turn back."

"That means we're close."

"Are you sure? Because it could just mean there are rocks up ahead."

"I'm sure."

He leaned to the side and lifted up the top of the bench I wasn't sitting on. It was a hatch, and inside, I spotted life jackets. He pulled one out and tossed it to me. "Put this on."

"Why?" The sea was quite calm.

"In case you're wrong and I'm right."

"You think we're going to sink?"

"No. But in case I'm wrong, I don't want anything to happen to you."

I smiled, unable to stop the little surge of warmth. "That's really sweet."

"I'm not sweet." He glared at me, sounding grumpier than I'd ever seen him.

"Mm-hmm. Sure." I put the life jacket on, cinching it tightly to satisfy him. He nodded his approval. "Aren't you going to put one on?"

"Hadn't planned on it, no."

"That's all kinds of ridiculous. Do you really want to put me through the trauma of trying to keep your unconscious body afloat?"

He shot me a wry look. "I thought you didn't believe there were rocks ahead."

"Well, I don't want to be wrong, now do I?" I pointed to the seat where the life jackets were stored. "Put one on."

"Fine." He rolled his eyes, but he smiled and did as I asked.

I returned my attention to the pearly haze that filled the air ahead of us. The island was definitely there. I could feel it. My magic could feel it, like I was being drawn forward.

But that didn't mean there were no dangers between us and the land. Instinct told me to dip my hand in the water, and it was so strong that I did as it commanded. Immediately, I could feel the presence of underground rocks, just as Rafe had feared. It was odd that Emma hadn't warned me about them, but maybe she'd known I wouldn't need the warning and that I'd follow my gut. I'd never had such a strong instinctual tug before. It was impossible to ignore.

"What are you doing?" Rafe asked.

I'd had to lean pretty far over to reach the water, and my bum was unceremoniously in the air. "I wanted to check for dangers in the water."

"That's something you can do?"

"Not normally, but this place is special." I sank my hand a bit deeper into the cold sea. "You're going to want to veer to the right a bit. I think there are some rocks up ahead."

He turned the wheel, and the boat drifted a bit to the right. "Good?"

"Yes, that should be fine." I guided him through the water for the next ten minutes until the haze parted to reveal a small, rocky island covered in trees that sat atop a high hill. I grinned. "We made it."

He gestured to the small wooden dock that protruded off the island. "Is it a clear path to that dock?"

"It is. You can head directly toward it." I pulled my hand out of the water and straightened, trying to loosen the crick in my back.

He navigated the rest of the way, slowing the boat as we

neared the dock. When he was close enough, he turned off the engine and jumped ashore, stopping the boat before it could drift into the dock. Then he tied off the lines to the little metal bits that stuck off the dock— I had no idea what to call them—and it was all done so quickly and seamlessly that I couldn't help but give a little clap.

He arched a brow. "Seriously?"

I shrugged. "What? You did a good job."

"You're just too much sometimes," he said, but he was smiling as he said it.

"I'll take that as a compliment." I stood and took off the life jacket, then put it in the boat's cabin.

He held out his hand to help me onto the dock, and I took it, unable to help the shiver that raced up my arm when my skin met his. I'd never felt such an electric connection with anyone before. His eyes flashed as they met mine, and I thought he might be feeling the same thing.

He let go as soon as he could, though, and took off his life jacket to throw it in the boat. "Lead the way."

I nodded and started up the dock, following the pull of the magic. As soon as I stepped onto the rocky land, I felt the magic whoosh up through my feet. I gasped, stopping dead still as it flowed through me.

"This place is amazing," I breathed. "Do you feel it?"

"I don't."

Probably because he was a wolf and not a witch. I closed my eyes and absorbed the power, then opened them and continued toward the interior of the island. It was a rocky ascent up a steep hill, but scrubby flowers grew in the gaps between the stones, and rugged little trees gave me the occasional handhold to keep from slipping. As we neared the top, I spotted some abandoned cottages and made a note to ask Emma why no witches lived in them anymore. They were falling down, so it had clearly been a while since they'd been inhabited.

Maybe the power was just too much to deal with on an everyday basis. It was already starting to make me jittery.

"Do you know where we're going?" Rafe asked from behind me as I reached the top of the hill.

The land was flatter up here, and there were far more of the twisted, ancient trees that grew no taller than the top of Rafe's head. They formed a small forest in the middle of the island, and I pointed to it. "There. I can feel the power emanating from the grove."

I headed toward it, breathing deeply of the magical air. The pearly fog that had concealed the island was thicker in the grove, and up close, I could see that it sparkled with silvery magic. I reached out a hand to touch it, and the sparkles danced around my fingertips. I laughed, filled with the purest joy I'd ever felt.

As we walked through the trees, large, luminescent moths fluttered around us. They were beautiful, fluttering in the air around the gnarled tree branches. The trees themselves seemed to breathe, emanating a wisdom I'd only ever seen in sentient beings.

"This place is special," Rafe said. "Even I can feel it."

I smiled. "It really is."

We reached the middle of the grove, which was marked by a circle of thick green moss. I had to guess that the space had been cultivated long ago by the witches who'd lived here because it was so round and devoid of trees.

"It's perfect," I murmured as I walked into the middle of the clearing.

Rafe followed, and I turned to him.

All around, wind rustled through the leaves. They seemed to sing a wordless song that filtered through my soul, making me feel connected to the island and the power within it. I'd thought I might call Poa to me once I arrived— she'd refused to ride in the boat—but there was so much power in the air that it was unnecessary. In fact, I didn't think I could handle any *more* power.

Rafe stopped in front of me, and I looked up at him. There was an intensity to his eyes that had nothing to do with the magic. When his gaze lingered on my lips, I couldn't help but think of the kiss we'd shared that night after the bar. Everything in me ached to stand on tiptoe and press my lips to his. From the heat in his eyes, he was thinking something very similar.

As if to remind me of my purpose, a sparkling shimmer of silver magic darted between our faces. I gasped, laughing slightly.

"You're the most joyful person I've ever met," he said, and there was the faintest tone of wonder to his voice. It was entirely unexpected.

"It's easy to be so when I'm here." I smiled up at him.

"Not just here." He shook his head, as if reprimanding himself for what he'd said. "What do I need to do for this spell to work?"

"Right." I cleared away any thoughts of romance and raised my hand to press it to his chest. "May I?"

He nodded.

I laid the flat of my palm against him, then frowned. "I think..."

I trailed off, but he finished the sentence for me. "I need to take off my shirt, don't I?"

I nodded, blushing slightly. I really shouldn't be blushing —it was downright ridiculous. But I just couldn't help it. Being close to him made me think all kinds of thoughts I didn't want to share. Unfortunately, my face had other ideas, because it just *loved* broadcasting my embarrassment to the world. I could feel the heat flushing my cheeks.

He reached for the hem of his shirt and pulled it over his head, revealing the smooth planes of muscle that my fingertips itched to touch. I'd never objectified anyone so much in my whole life as I did with Rafe, but I'd also never been around someone so insanely beautiful. He was a work of living art.

"What are you thinking?" he asked.

"That I need to do my laundry."

"Mm-hmm." His murmur of agreement was clearly disbelieving, and when I looked up to meet his gaze, the heat in his eyes had only flamed hotter.

This was *so* not the place. Dark was falling, and I could smell rain on the air. I needed to do my thing before the weather turned and we were forced to leave.

"Here goes nothing," I said, raising my hand to press my palm to his skin.

Just like last night, my hand tingled, and heat raced up

my arm. His breathing stilled as if he were holding it. I realized that I was holding my breath, too, and forced myself to inhale. Sweet, rain-damp air entered my lungs, and I called upon my magic.

It filled me with such a rush of power that I gasped and had to press my hand harder to Rafe's chest to keep from being blown away from him. A vision flashed in my mind, bright and clear. Rafe and a woman stood within a circle of massive standing stones, each rock tall and straight, their sides decorated with sacred carvings.

I know this place.

Then darkness took me.

CHAPTER
TWENTY-ONE

Rafe

Thunder cracked as Isobel collapsed to the mossy ground. My fear spiked, and I dropped to my knees. "Isobel!"

I cradled her head, searching her pale face for any sign of consciousness. Her skin had turned white right after surprise had flashed in her eyes, and she'd passed out. Now, dark shadows colored the hollows beneath her eyes.

"Isobel, wake up." I lifted her to me, cradling her against my chest. Fear like I'd never known surged through my veins as lightning struck far in the distance.

I was a curse.

I'd hurt her just like I'd hurt the Jade Sorceress, and I hadn't even realized it would happen.

In my arms, Isobel jerked and gasped, pulling back slightly to look up at me. Her voice shook as she said, "I saw where she performed the spell."

"I don't care about that. Are you okay?"

"Yeah." She gave a shaky little laugh. "More than okay. I feel great, actually."

"Great? You just collapsed."

"It was the magic. I couldn't handle it." She patted the moss next to her. "Anyway, the ground is soft."

"If you say so." I looked her up and down, searching for any sign of injury. "You're sure you're not hurt?"

"I'm sure." She pushed herself to her feet, and I joined her.

Lightning struck again, and I counted the seconds until I heard the thunder. It still wasn't raining, but the storm was coming. The houses I'd seen on our hike up here weren't nearly sound enough for us to weather a storm at this time of year. "I didn't see this storm on the forecast, but we should leave before it arrives. It could be a big one."

"Agreed. I don't think I can handle more magic tonight, anyway, and I've got a good lead for us to follow."

As long as there was a storm threatening, I couldn't think about my curse. I was more concerned with getting her to safety. I grabbed her hand and pulled her along. "Let's go."

We hurried from the clearing, and she released my hand to more easily navigate down the narrow path that led to the dock. The wind whipped up as we ran, and I kept my eye on the storm, which rolled closer with every minute. We were nearly to the dock when Isobel tripped on a loose rock. She stumbled and fell, crying out.

"Isobel!" Fear lanced me once again, and I knelt by her side. "What hurts?"

"My ankle." She pointed to her right ankle, her face scrunched in pain.

"I'm going to pick you up." Before she could protest, I swept her into my arms and raced for the boat. The scent of rain grew heavier in the air, and I knew the storm was only a few miles away.

"Will we make it back in time?" she asked as I stepped onto the deck and lowered her to the bench on the starboard side of the cockpit.

I looked at the lightning that cracked in the distance, counting the seconds before I heard the thunder. "We should, just barely."

"Good. Those houses didn't look sound," she said, glancing up the steep hill to where they sat.

I untied the lines and tossed them aboard, then turned on the engine and piloted us away from the dock. I'd memorized the route around the rocks and was able to go much faster as we left the island.

"Put on the life jacket," I said, nodding to where it sat next to her.

"You put yours on, too." She donned hers, and I did the same, liking that she'd insisted. I didn't have a memory of a time when someone had cared about me, and it was strange. But nice.

The waves were picking up as I sped back to shore, pushing the engine to its limit. There was just enough wind that I could assist the motor with the foresail, and we made excellent time. All the same, rain began to fall as we neared the harbor, and the heavy droplets soaked us in seconds.

"You can go in the cabin!" I shouted over the roar of the deluge.

"I'm fine!" She huddled away from the rain.

She wasn't fine, obviously. But it was more likely that she didn't want to attempt climbing down into the cabin with her bad ankle. I wished I could help her, but the storm was really on our tail now, with the wind whipping hard enough that I had to lower the foresail immediately. It would take all my focus to get us back to the harbor safely.

Isobel hung onto the side of the boat as the waves buffeted the hull. As soon as we reached the protected waters behind the jetty, relief rushed through me.

We were safe.

Assuming we didn't get struck by lighting. The storm was still a couple miles off, however, and we made it back to my slip in one piece.

"Stay there," I said as I pulled alongside the dock and hopped off to take care of the lines. "I'll get you when we're tied off."

"I'm fine. I can walk." She rose, then winced.

"You can't, so sit down." My voice cracked with command, and she did as I said.

I had the boat tied off in seconds, then returned to the cockpit to lift her. She wrapped her arms around my neck, and I cradled her against my chest as I stepped onto the dock.

"Don't you want to put the cushions back in the cabin?" she asked, massive raindrops splattering on her face.

I laughed at the idea of worrying about cushions right now. "No. We're going."

201

She smiled up at me, and even in the deluge that drenched her, she was still somehow the most beautiful woman I'd ever seen.

I ran toward the car, then set her down on the seat as gently as I could before shutting the door and hurrying to my side. Once I'd closed us into the car, the lack of rain and wind was profound.

Isobel heaved out a breath, then began to shiver. Shit, was she going into shock? "Are you okay?"

"Yeah, just cold."

I turned on the heater, letting it blast over us. "How's your ankle?"

"Hurts, but I'll live."

"We're only ten minutes from the boathouse, and I can call a healer to meet us there."

"It's just a bit sprained. No need for a healer. All I really want is a hot bath."

"Humor me." I sent a quick text to the Katia, the healer I'd met when I'd first moved to town, then started the drive toward home.

The weather worsened, and rain lashed the windscreen as I slowed to a crawl through town, afraid that someone might dart in front of the car on their way to shelter. By the time I pulled up to the boathouse, Isobel's teeth were chattering. I parked as close to the door as I could, then helped her out, sweeping her into my arms before rushing her into the warm boathouse.

She laughed as I slammed the door behind us. "This is all a bit dramatic, isn't it?"

"Hardly. You're white as a sheet."

"Goes with my Victorian murder ghost persona."

"It was lunatic Victorian ghost, actually." I'd never forget the ridiculous thing I'd called her when I'd first seen her. "And yes, it does suit that. But I'm going to take you upstairs now."

"Good. I could use a cup of tea and a bath."

"Coming right up." I took the stairs two at a time, then deposited her gently on the floral couch in the living room. For all the work we'd done up at Lavender House, she hadn't touched a single thing in the flat. Every surface was still covered in knickknacks, so many that it made my skin crawl.

Isobel must have caught me looking at them because she said, "Poa won't let me remove them. She loves the attention of all those little eyes. They're creepy, though." She gave a little shudder.

I looked at the figurines on every table and had to agree with Isobel—it was very eerie the way they stared. "I'll check on the healer's progress while I brew the tea. Don't move."

"I'm fine. I don't need a healer." She sounded exasperated, but she didn't move.

I pulled my phone from my pocket as I walked to the kitchen and put the kettle on. Katia had responded that she'd be by in twenty, and we were nearly to that mark. I typed out a quick response telling her to let herself in and come up to the flat, then turned my attention to making tea. By the time I carried the cups to the living room, Katia was knocking on the door at the top of the stairs.

"Come in," Isobel called.

Katia, who was somewhere in her mid-forties and ran the health clinic in town, was wrapped up in a hooded floor-length raincoat. She pushed the hood back from her hair and smiled, but there were shadows under her eyes that made her look tired. "What's the emergency?"

"*Not* an emergency," Isobel said. "I twisted my ankle, and Rafe freaked out."

"Well, let me check it." Katia walked closer, then knelt on the floor by Isobel's ankle, which she had propped on the couch next to her. She'd taken off her boot, and her socks had kittens printed all over them. It was almost ridiculously cute. Katia held her hand over Isobel's ankle. "May I?"

"Sure, thanks."

Katia touched her ankle, and a moment later, Isobel cried, "You can't heal me. You're exhausted. I can feel it in your magic."

Katia gave her a weary smile. "We had quite a day at the clinic. Lots of healing to do."

"You should have told Rafe. This is nothing. You'll pass out if you try to use any more magic."

"He made it sound like an emergency." Katia looked at me. "It's not, by the way. A very mild sprain that should be better in a few days."

Relief rushed through me, but I didn't regret my actions. I did feel bad about Katia coming all the way out here, though, especially when she was tired. "Can I give you a ride back?"

"I'm fine, I brought my car." She rose and turned her attention to Isobel. "I've heard about Lavender House. It's all over town that you're trying to fix it up on a deadline. If you can't put weight on your ankle, come into the clinic tomorrow. A good night's rest will have me ready to heal you in a jiffy."

"Thank you." Isobel smiled up at her.

I walked Katia to the door and down to the main floor, paying her exorbitant house-call fee.

"I can tell you like that one." Katia winked, then turned and left.

Like that one? Katia didn't even know me. How could she tell anything?

I shut the door behind her and returned upstairs. Isobel was attempting to rise from the sofa, and I hurried toward her. "Hang on, I'll help you."

"I'm fine." She tried putting weight on her bad ankle and winced. "Okay, maybe a little help."

"Where do you want to go?"

"To the bath. I'm desperate for a long, hot soak."

I nodded, then hoisted her into my arms and carried her to the bathroom. She sat on the edge of the tub and turned on the water. Within seconds, steam began to rise. "Perfection."

"I'll go fetch your tea."

"Thank you." She gave me a long look. "You really don't have to take care of me, you know."

I gestured around me, indicating the knickknacks that had somehow managed to invade even the bathroom. "Of course I do. If you fall *anywhere* in this place, you'll take out half a dozen of Poa's creepy admirers."

She looked at a little porcelain puppy that sat on the back of the cistern and winced. "Good point. She would kill me for that."

"Glad you're seeing reason. You can't get on that cat's

205

bad side." I couldn't believe I was joking with her, but that had definitely sounded like a joke.

"You're just too good, you know that?"

I gave her an incredulous look. "That is patently untrue."

"It's really not. I've been watching you, you know." She gave a little laugh that morphed into a grimace, and it was cute as hell.

Cute as hell?

I was losing my mind.

"I mean, not watching you in a stalkerish way," she continued. "But around. Day to day. And you're good. Like, a really good person."

"All right, I'm leaving." I turned and headed toward the living room to get her tea. I didn't want to admit it to myself, but I *liked* taking care of her. I shook my head. Better not get used to it.

By the time I returned to the bathroom, she had my jumper off and was working on the buttons of her jeans. She looked up, her gaze catching mine. Heat flushed her cheeks, and she nodded toward the little ledge on the bathroom sink. "You can put it there."

I nodded and did as she asked. "I'll be just outside the door in case you fall."

"I'll be okay on my own. Seriously. You go do your thing." She turned to face the tub and made a squeak of pain as she put weight on her ankle.

"Like I said."

"Fine." I could actually *hear* her roll her eyes. "And thank you."

I felt a smile tug the corner of my lip but said nothing as I left. After shutting the door behind me, I went to the kitchen to get a chair to sit in, then put it by the bathroom so I could hear if she needed help.

Eventually, she called through the door, "Are you out there?"

"I am."

"What are you doing?"

"Sitting."

"On what?"

"A kitchen chair." I smiled. "What's with the twenty questions?"

"Don't know." There was an audible shrug in her voice. "Just want to know you, I guess."

"By knowing what I'm sitting on?"

"You can know a lot about a person by what they choose to sit on. For example, you could have gone for the floor. Or a cushy chair. Or a stepstool."

"And what would that have told you about me?"

"I'm still working on that bit."

I smiled again, unable to help myself.

"How about you tell me something real, then?" she asked. "Like why your room is so barren. There's nothing in there."

I sighed, not particularly fond of this question.

When I didn't answer, she continued. "Like, are you a secret serial killer?"

I laughed. "What about a tidy room leads you to think 'serial killer'?"

"It's more than just tidy, it's empty."

She had a point. "Fine. Since the alternative is you

thinking that I'm a serial killer, I'll tell you." I shook my head and smiled as I leaned back against the wall. "I've moved around so much that I got sick of throwing things away. And since I don't remember my friends and family, I don't have any important mementos."

"Oh, wow, that sucks." I could hear contrition in her voice. "Sorry, I didn't think about that. I shouldn't have poked so hard."

"Don't worry about it. When I think about it from your perspective, it *is* a bit weird. Most people decorate their places. Pictures on the walls, that kind of thing." I shrugged, looking toward the window that I could see the other end of the hall. "The outdoors is so beautiful here that I don't feel any need to hang pictures. And I don't look at the walls, anyway. I look at my work."

"Fair enough." There was a pause. "So, you have nothing from your previous life. Is that because you forgot everything after she cursed you?"

"Yeah. I woke up outside, with no memory of where I lived or what I did. I remembered my first name and her face. From there, I had to figure things out."

"Wow. That's...intense."

"Yeah, it wasn't the best part of my life."

"But you built something amazing."

"I built *something*, at least." And that was the most I could say about it. After all, I would hardly call it amazing, since I felt the need to move around every couple years. Nothing ever felt like home, no matter how hard I tried. "The water has to be getting cold. Are you ready to get out?"

"Done talking so soon, huh?"

She knew me too well after too short a time. "It'll be an early day tomorrow. We've got a lot of work to do."

"All right." I heard water sloshing as she rose and waited, wondering what I should do. Did she need help?

When she cried out in pain, I launched myself upright and through the door.

"Hey!" She had a towel wrapped around her and was standing on one leg. "Knock first!"

"I heard you cry out."

"Well, yeah. I put weight on my ankle like an idiot. But I'm okay."

"Do you need a ride to your bed?"

"Um...yeah, actually. Can you give me a minute in here, though? I can balance while I brush my teeth."

"Sure." I left, shutting the door behind me, then leaned against it and squeezed my eyes shut.

She'd looked so damned beautiful, it had turned my mind to pudding. With her cheeks flushed from the heat and her hair piled loosely on her head, she'd been gorgeous. Everything in me pulled toward her, and the wolf's soul that was part of my own howled with its longing.

I rubbed my chest. "Settle down."

It didn't work that way, of course. It wasn't a separate being who would listen to commands. It was part of me, and as such, it was stubborn as hell, just like I was.

"Okay," she called out. "I'm ready."

"Coming in." I returned to the room.

She still wore the towel, and I was careful to keep my gaze on her face. Not that that was much better for my equilibrium. "Ready?" I asked.

She nodded, and I lifted her into my arms. Her flat was so tiny that I reached her room seconds later and deposited her on the bed.

"Can I get you anything?" I asked. "Water? Pajamas?"

She shook her head and pointed to a water bottle at the side of her bed. "I'm good."

There were no pajamas near her, though. So if I wasn't getting her any, that meant she didn't wear any. And that was *definitely* something I couldn't dwell on.

"All right. Call if you need anything." I headed toward the door. "Actually, I'll sleep on your sofa."

"You don't need to do that."

"I'm fine." I left before she could argue anymore. I didn't want her falling on her way to the bathroom.

Of course, the sofa was tiny, and when I sat on it, a cloud of dust poofed upward. I leaned my head back and closed my eyes. This was going to be a long night.

CHAPTER
TWENTY-TWO

ISOBEL

WHEN I WOKE, I could hear someone puttering around in the kitchen. "Rafe?"

"I'll be there in a moment!" he called.

I laid back on the pillow and stared up at the ceiling.

You've got a good one.

I popped my head off the pillow and looked down at the foot of the bed. "Poa? Where have you been?"

Doing important things, but I came in late last night and found him on the couch, asleep. Then I found you in here, like the princess and the pea.

"The princess and the pea? Hardly."

Well, there might not be a hundred feather mattresses under you, but you're on the bed, and he wasn't.

"Because it's my bed!"

You could have invited him in. It's what I would have done.

211

I groaned and flopped back on the pillow. "I can't with you right now."

Well, maybe you can *get me a sausage roll and latte from Margot's.*

"When hell freezes over." I squeezed my eyes shut. "We've got a ton of work to do today. There will be no time for sausage rolls. You'll be lucky not to be commandeered into service."

As if I would ever.

I laughed.

"Knock, knock." Rafe said the words rather than knocking, and I looked up to see him carrying a cup of coffee. He wasn't alone, though. Katia the healer was beside him, holding her own mug.

"Katia?" I asked. "Why did you come back?" I was certain she'd told me to come into her office today if I needed her to fix my ankle. Which, from the faint throbbing, I did.

"This one here." She hiked a thumb at Rafe. "Called me early and promised to pay double my house-call fee if I would be here before eight."

"Rafe." I scowled at him. "You didn't have to do that. It's so early."

"Oh, I don't mind." Katia grinned. "It really is quite a bit of money." She walked toward me. "How are you feeling?"

"The ankle still feels a bit crap, honestly." I looked at Rafe, unable to help the smile on my face. "Thank you, really."

He just nodded. "I'll be in the kitchen."

Before I could say anything else, he turned and left the room, coffee in hand. Katia watched him go, then said, "I'm pretty sure he intended that coffee for you. But then you spoke and scrambled his mind."

I laughed. "That's ridiculous."

"It's really not. I've never seen him like this."

"Have you seen him much?"

"Well, no. And that's the point. He's always been alone. But with you, he's distinctly *not* alone. He seems more whole, somehow."

"Are you a therapist as well as a doctor?" I joked.

"No, but I've got an eye for this. People's wellbeing is kind of my thing. That's what it is to be a doctor, especially a small-town doctor."

"Fair point." I liked her a lot. She had a good energy about her.

Katia set her coffee on the bedside table and reached for the end of the duvet, holding her hands over it and looking up at me. "May I?"

"Of course."

She pulled the blanket back, then winced. I leaned over to look. "Yikes."

No kidding. It looks like a purple melon. Poa hopped off the bed. *I can't watch this. And I smell bacon.*

"I can fix you up in no time," Katia said. "But it's a good thing Rafe called me. You wouldn't be able to walk on this today."

"Thank you for coming back," I said.

"Thank you for waiting so nicely. Not all my patients understand when I need to rest to regenerate my powers. But then you're a witch, so it works similarly."

I nodded, understanding entirely. If a witch wore herself

out, it took time to recover her magic. Werewolves and vampires were different, as were pixies and gremlins, so they didn't always understand.

Carefully, she pressed her hand to my ankle and hummed. Her magic swelled on the air, and a gentle warmth flowed through my ankle. The pain slowly faded, and the bruising and swelling disappeared before my eyes.

"That's amazing," I said.

"Thank you." She smiled and stood. "I'm quite good at my craft."

I loved her confidence.

We said our goodbyes, and she left. Once she was gone, I leapt out of the bed and sneaked into the bathroom. I was still naked, and the last thing Rafe needed so early in the morning was to see my moon-white arse.

After brushing my teeth and washing my face, I found a set of work clothes and put them on, then tied my boots and headed into the kitchen. Rafe was just putting the bread on top of two bacon and egg sandwiches. At his feet, Poa demolished her own.

"Thank you," I said. "Let me know what I owe you for her visit."

"Don't worry about it."

"You can't keep taking care of me."

He just grunted and handed me a plate with my sandwich. "Eat."

"All right, all right." I smiled and took the plate, then ate, totally ravenous. When I was finished, we headed up to the house together.

We spent the day painting the walls and working on the

cabinets. I was obviously in charge of paint, given that I lacked Rafe's incredible skill with wood, but by lunchtime, the house was looking a lot better. Most of the rooms were painted, and the kitchen was nearly finished.

"I think the house is feeling a lot better," Rafe said as we stood on the front yard and stared at it, each of us eating our midday sandwiches.

"I agree. It hasn't popped a floorboard at me all morning."

"And it hasn't slammed a door on my arse."

I grinned, so pleased that I could feel the warmth filling my chest. It had been a hassle to have a house with personality, but now that it was happier, I had the strongest sense of satisfaction.

There was still way too much work for us to do on our own, however, even with my magic giving us extra speed and strength. For one thing, the electric and roofing were outside of both our skillsets. Rafe was managing with the plumbing, but just barely. Anyway, there was probably too much for him to finish in addition to the doing all the cabinets and trim work.

But the house was happier now, which changed things. "I think I'm going to call the coven and see if they can come over and give it a seal of approval that the town contractors will respect. We need help with the rest of it."

"We do," he said. "Even if we could learn how to fix electricity in an old house, there isn't time. And that roof probably needs to be replaced. Even some of the beams might need attention."

"I'll make the call."

"I'm going to work on the upstairs master bath." He popped the last of his sandwich in his mouth and went inside.

I called Emma, who picked up on the second ring. "Isobel? Hi!"

"Hi, Emma." I relayed my request.

"Hmmm. We don't really have a process for that, though we could possibly come up with something." There was a frown in her voice. "But I'm not sure that's what you need."

"Really?"

"Really. The town has been afraid of that house for decades. And they respect the Aurora Coven, but us giving it our stamp of approval might not be enough. After all, that's just a piece of paper. I think they need to see it for themselves."

She had a point. We needed people soon, and there wasn't time to wait for the town's opinion to change. "What are you thinking? An open house?"

"I'm thinking that we throw a barbecue tomorrow afternoon. Let people come by and have some fun, walk through the house and see the progress that's been made."

"That's a genius idea, but there's no way I can throw a barbecue on such short notice."

"That's where I come in. Or rather, that's where Vivienne and Madeline come in. My grandmother-in-law and aunt-in-law are expert party planners, and they have the connections to pull one off quickly."

"But will people be able to attend?"

"For free beer, food, and a live band at one of the most

talked-about places in town? Absolutely. You're just lucky tomorrow is Sunday."

"Good point. Are you sure this isn't too much?"

"Of course not. Vivienne and Madeline love a challenge, and so do I. I can make up invitations today and get them out. I know everyone to invite."

"Oh, my gosh, thank you so much."

"That's what friends are for," she replied.

"Thank you." I smiled, so incredibly grateful that I'd found my way to Charming Cove. "Can you send an invitation to Judith, who lives on the hill next to Lavender House?"

"Who?"

"The older woman who lives next door."

"Hmm, sure. I'm not sure I know her, but I'll get it done."

"Thank you." I wanted to include her because I liked her, but also because I needed to ask her about the enchantment that had given the house a personality. I was sure that the woman in the vision had reminded me of her.

And with that, I went to tell Rafe the news.

CHAPTER
TWENTY-THREE

Isobel

THE MORNING of the barbecue dawned bright and clear, for which I was immensely grateful. To successfully throw the party, we really needed good weather. I didn't want to have to shove everyone into the house at once if it was raining. Far better to have them congregating outside and go into the house in smaller groups, just to let the building get used to their presence.

Rafe and I had spent the rest of the day and night making sure the house and garden looked their best. We moved all the rubbish to a giant skip that he'd had delivered, then cleared away the rest of the weeds and debris. Then we tidied up the tools and work spaces in the house, and it really was thrilling to see it all coming together.

But now that it was the morning of the party, the nerves were setting in. Were we really going to pull this off?

Yes. We'd convince the local contractors to work on Lavender House, and then we'd have time to address Rafe's curse. I was so hopeful that I'd already called the Welsh coven geographically closest to the stone circle where Rafe's miserable ex had cursed him. They were the ones most likely to know her, and it was also polite to check in with them before visiting a sacred space so close to their coven. We set up a tentative meeting, and if all went well, Rafe and I would be one step closer to breaking his curse by tomorrow evening.

I just hadn't told him that yet.

"I think someone's here!" Rafe called up the stairs.

I dragged on a jumper to repel the worst of the morning chill and hurried down to the main level. A massive old car was pulling up the drive, and it screamed sophisticated elegance from a previous era. I'd never even seen a car like that outside of old films. Two women sat behind the windscreen, and I didn't recognize either of them. The driver was older, however, and she had to be Vivienne.

I waved as they parked, then walked out to greet them.

Vivienne climbed out of the driver's seat, her gleaming white hair pulled up in a perfect chignon. Her wool suit looked like it had been handmade in London, and her pearls gleamed in the morning light. She looked like the dowager duchess that she was.

The woman at her side wore a flowing, colorful dress and an enormous hat to keep the sun off her perfect complexion. Massive sunglasses covered her eyes, and she looked as sophisticated as the older woman, but in a more bohemian way.

Both of these women came from money, it was clear, and I couldn't help but feel the faintest bit awkward in my over-large jumper and jeans.

The younger woman, who was probably in her fifties, grinned widely and held out her arms. "You must be Isobel!"

Before I could respond, she hurried toward me and gave me a hug. Behind her, the older woman's eyelids flicked in what I assumed was a titled person's version of an eye roll. "You really must ask a person's permission before you embrace them, Madeline."

"Oh, Mother." Madeline pulled back and waved her hand at Vivienne. "So old-fashioned."

The dowager duchess sighed and approached, holding out an elegant hand to shake mine. I had to tell myself to shake her hand like a normal person and not like an awkward weirdo.

"We are very glad you're here, darling." The dowager duchess's tone was warm and genuine when she spoke, and I relaxed. She might have a different style than her daughter's, but she was just as kind and lovely. "Emma has said only the best things about you, and we can always use more good witches in this town."

She and her daughter were vampires like the duke, but I was glad to see they liked witches. Unlike the vampires of human myth, they had no need to shy away from the sun.

Both women turned to gaze up the hill at Lavender House.

"Why, it's already looking better," Vivienne said. "It will be stunning when you're finished."

"Thank you, Your Grace."

"Call me Vivienne."

"And me, Madeline," said the younger woman. "Have you spoken to Aria at the Enchanted Garden about landscaping? Surely she can get you set up quite nicely."

"I'll do that." I'd hardly started thinking about the garden, but it was an excellent suggestion.

"We've got the caterers arriving at ten to start setting up," Vivienne said. "Do you mind if we go up and have a look to see where things should be placed?"

"Of course. Let me show you around."

"I'll drive," Vivienne said, gesturing to her short heels. "These aren't suited for a walk up the hill."

"Of course not." I smiled and climbed into the back of her massive car. It was upholstered in the softest, smoothest leather I'd ever felt, and I was pretty sure the dash was inlaid with mother-of-pearl. It was the perfect car for a dowager duchess.

At the house, I showed them around, grateful that it was on its best behavior. All the same, we all agreed that the main festivities should be set up outside. The rest of the morning passed in a whirlwind as the caterers and band arrived and set up. Meg, from The Sea Shanty, came with a portable bar and two of her best kegs. Emma, Holly, Aria, and Tabitha arrived to help, and excitement was in the air. Even the weather was great, with a cool breeze and bright sky.

By the time the guests started to arrive, I was buzzing with anticipation, praying this would work out. The band played on the side lawn, right next to a portable dance floor. How Vivienne had got one of those at short notice, I had no idea. The air smelled delicious with the grilling sausages and vegetables, and a long table was set up with salads and desserts.

By two, the yard was full of people. I recognized Charlie the plumber and his friends, Carlos the electrician and Lee the roofer.

Emma sidled up to me and pointed them out. "Perfect, right? They're just what you need."

"The dream team," I said, remembering what I'd called them back at the pub when we'd met. "I've never been so excited to see a roofer in my whole life. And don't get me started on the electrician."

Emma grinned. "I doubt you've ever spent so much time thinking about one."

"True." I looked around, searching for Judith's familiar white hair, but I couldn't see her anywhere. I was pretty sure she'd arrived, though, since I'd caught sight of her floral dress as she'd walked toward the bar. "I'm going to go look for someone. Thank you again for helping me with this."

"Oh, I love loaning out Vivienne and Madeline. They're like a tactical party-planning team, ready to be deployed at any moment. They'll be in a good mood for a week after this."

"They strike me as frequently being in a good mood."

"They really are. I'm lucky they're my in-laws."

We said goodbye, and I went to find Judith. She was nowhere to be seen in the garden, so I checked the house. There were a few people inside, though most were still too shy—or worried—to enter. I hoped that would change as time passed.

I found Judith standing in the room where the heart of

the house was hidden. We'd covered over the wall where the crystal resided, but it still pulsed with power from its hiding place. There was nothing on the exterior to indicate what was inside, though.

"Do you sense something there?" I asked as I walked in.

"I do." She sounded confused but intrigued, and turned to me. "Do you know why?"

"I do." I smiled. "I was able to see more about the spell that gave the house a personality. The heart of that spell is in a crystal within the wall. I cleaned out the space where it sits, and I think it really improved the house's mood."

"It definitely did." She looked around, a broad smile on her face. "You've really brought this place back to life. It looks beautiful."

"Thank you. There's a lot of work left to be done, but I'm hopeful." I searched her face, unable to stop thinking about the woman I'd seen in the vision. "You remind me of the person who cast the spell, actually."

"Really?" She gave a small laugh. "Do I look like her?"

"Not exactly, no. I don't know why you remind me of her." I gave my voice a prodding tone, hoping she might fill in some of the blanks.

"Perhaps she was an old woman like me."

She was trying to distract me. "No, she wasn't. I think there's a connection between you two, though."

"Surely not." She shrugged. "Perhaps it's just that I live next door."

That made absolutely no sense, but I couldn't say it to her face. "Maybe just a coincidence."

"That's probably it." She agreed readily, and I knew there

was more to this story than she was telling me. But I couldn't exactly call her a liar to her face.

"I think there are some people here to see you, dear." She pointed to the space behind me, and I turned.

Charlie stood in the doorway, along with Lee and Carlos.

"Hi, guys!" I turned back to Judith. "I'll see you later. Thank you for coming."

She waved me away. "Go on, dear. Talk to your friends."

I left her where she was, staring at the wall that hid the crystal, and walked over the men who had just stepped inside the room. They wore the heavy work boots and worn jeans that were the uniform of contractors everywhere, though it was clear they'd put on their good jumpers for the party.

I smiled at them. "Thank you for coming. Charlie, Lee, and Carlos, wasn't it?"

"It was." Charlie grinned at me. "Thank you for having us. You've really done a lot with this place."

I gestured to the room behind me. "I've got it all fixed up and ready for some professionals to come in and work their magic." I winked, making it extra obvious and even a little cheesy. "Like you guys."

"Oooh, was that what this was all about?" he said, his tone distinctly flirty. "You just wanted to lure me and the guys here?"

"Guilty." I raised a hand. "Truly, though, I was hoping to show you that the house is safe to work in."

"It seems good." He looked around. "The beer and sausages were a nice touch. And the band is excellent."

"I thought I'd grease the wheels a little." I shrugged.

"Anyway, I want to meet the town, and this is a great opportunity."

"So, you're on a deadline with this house?" Lee asked.

"I am. It needs to be finished by the middle of the week after next for me to inherit it. Otherwise, it goes to my miserable uncle."

"That's a strange requirement of a will," Charlie said.

"I know. I've got no idea why my grandmother wrote it that way, but I've got a little less than two weeks to keep my new home. I was hoping you guys might be able to help me." I considered batting my lashes, but that would be laying it on too thick. "I'll pay you overtime, of course. A rush fee, even. Are you free to do some work?"

"We could be." Charlie smiled. "It would be a shame for you to lose this house, especially after putting so much work in. And you're definitely an asset to the community."

"An asset to the community?" I grinned.

"Oh, most definitely." He was flirting up a storm with me, which I was so not used to.

"So, that means you're in?" I asked. "There's quite a bit of electric, roofing, and plumbing that needs to be done."

"We can start tomorrow," he said.

"Oh, my gosh. That's what I was hoping you would say." I was so excited, I wanted to clap.

"It's because he likes you," Carlos said. "Ever since we played darts at The Sea Shanty, he's been hemming and hawing about how to contact you without seeming like a creep."

Charlie turned to him. "Really, mate? You're going to spill my business like that?"

Carlos shrugged. "Women like honesty."

"That is true," I said. "And I do really appreciate you guys finding time to help. This is a huge deal for me."

"It's not a problem," Charlie said. "We'll be here around lunchtime."

"Excellent. I'll leave the house unlocked, if that's all right. I've got a meeting tomorrow and I might not be here, but I'll be back the next day. You just get started, if that's all right."

"Perfect. We'll be here." He winked. "And maybe afterward, you and I could get a drink?"

Oh, damn.

I should have expected this when he started flirting, but stupidly, I hadn't. And I should say yes. He was just the right kind of guy for me to go out with: fun and easy, not intense at all. I would have a good time, but I wouldn't get totally wrapped up in him. That was exactly what I needed. The opposite of Rafe, basically.

And yet, I couldn't say yes.

Nothing would happen between Rafe and me because he would leave. And even if he didn't, I couldn't get into a relationship that would end up becoming intense. Because with Rafe, it definitely would.

So why was the thought of him stopping me from saying yes to Charlie?

With horror, I realized that I'd waited too long to respond. Fortunately, Charlie took it in stride. "You think on it," he said. "I'll ask again after the job is done."

His tone was so easygoing that relief surged through me. He really was perfect for me.

And yet...

The guys turned to go, and I spotted Rafe in the other room. Had he heard any of that? It was impossible to tell. But it shouldn't matter if he heard Charlie flirting with me.

I headed toward him, unable to read his expression. Awkwardness made me barrel into the words I wanted to say next. "I've got good news. There are contractors lined up to work on the house starting tomorrow, and I've got us an appointment with the coven in Wales that's closest to the stone circle where your miserable ex cursed you."

"Wait, you *what*?" He sounded grumpy, but I ignored it.

"I've got us a meeting tomorrow. We'll go meet them and ask about her, then check out the stone circle. I'm sure I'll be able to read more about the curse if I'm in the place where it was cast."

"You passed out last time you tried. You can't possibly plan to try again."

"Of course I'm going to. I wasn't even hurt after passing out. I felt great, actually. It was the amount of magic on the island that I couldn't handle. It had nothing to do with the curse."

"Are you sure?"

"I'm sure of it. Anyway, it's my decision. I *need* to use my magic."

He shook his head. "We have less than a fortnight to fix up the house. You're mad."

I gestured at the beautiful room in which we stood. It was freshly painted, with the trim fixed and the floor refinished. I'd done that last bit, and it wasn't impressive, but it was done. "Look around. We're making great progress. And now that we have help, we're in the home stretch."

"There's still a lot to do," he grumped.

"And the professionals will do it. It's not like either of us can rewire the house or replace the roof. There will still be plenty of time for you to finish the cabinets and windows and for me to do the bits and bobs."

"But *now*?"

"You've been miserable for a decade, Rafe, and that's killing me. Also, you've helped me enormously. It's time for me to help you."

"You don't owe me anything."

I decided to ignore that bit, but I wondered why his tone was so short. "Tomorrow morning is the only time the coven is available to meet this week, so we've got to go. We'll leave tonight and be back by tomorrow evening. So quick you'll hardly know we've done it."

He gave me an incredulous look. "Now isn't the time."

I frowned, a thought popping into my mind. "Are you scared of what you might find?"

He glared at me. "No. I'm—" He raked a hand through his hair. "Maybe, all right?"

It sure was something, to see such a big and powerful werewolf admit to being scared. It made my heart hurt for him. "Whatever we find, won't it be better to know?"

"Definitely." He said it without hesitation. "I just didn't expect an answer so soon."

"It's been a decade, Rafe."

"Yeah, a decade full of failure. I'd given up."

"Well, I'm here now. And we're going to get to the bottom of this. I'll give you one day of trying to fix your curse in exchange for your help with the house. I owe you that much. And now that we've got professionals here to help us, we have the day to spare."

"You just won't give up on this, will you?" Annoyance echoed in his voice, but I ignored it.

"Nope. So you'd better accept it."

CHAPTER
TWENTY-FOUR

Isobel

We left the party when it ended at four and immediately got in the car to begin our drive. The coven and stone circle were located in southern Wales, near Brecon Beacons, a gorgeous natural area known for its magic.

I'd packed a small bag and arranged for two rooms at a B&B close to the coven headquarters, and Rafe offered to drive. As we set out, I started chatting about the party. Soon enough, I realized that Rafe wasn't responding as easily or as quickly as he normally would.

We were about an hour into the five-hour trip when I shot him a sidelong glance. His jaw was tight, and I frowned.

Rafe the grump was back, but why?

This was genuine grumpiness, too, not just the fake grumpiness he put on when he didn't want me paying attention to him. He'd been grumpy while I'd been convincing him to go on this trip.

"Are you all right?" I asked.

"Fine. Just thinking about everything to do at your house."

That might be true, but that wasn't all there was to it. He'd thought about the house plenty in front of me and never looked like that.

"Are you annoyed we're going to Wales?"

"No, it's fine."

Huh. That was a seriously short tone of voice. Something was up with him.

I debated trying to prod it out of him, but we were trapped in the car for another four hours. What if I made a total mess of things? It would be awkward as hell—even more awkward than it was now.

And he was the one driving. He could turn the car around and take us back to Cornwall.

Yeah, it was a bad idea to poke him. I'd let him stew for a while, then maybe ask when we arrived.

"I'm going to take a nap." I curled toward the window. "Thank you for driving."

He just grunted, and I rolled my eyes.

I woke up when we were deep into Wales. According to the clock, we only had about thirty minutes left. The headlights cut through the darkness. I squinted out the window but was unable to see anything.

"We're close, right?" I asked.

"We are. Nearly to the B&B."

"Great." I pulled a sandwich out of the bag I'd packed and passed it to him, then took one for myself.

We ate in silence, then polished off our meal with an apple each. By the time we arrived at the pretty white B&B on the outskirts of the village of Llanmarthen, I was beyond ready to get out of the car. Rafe still hadn't spoken.

He pulled the car to a stop in the pebble drive in front of the rambling old house, and I climbed out. The innkeeper came to the porch as I carried my small bag up, a smile on her round face.

"Hello, there! I assume you're the Whitwells? You're my last guests for the night."

"Yes." I nodded. "Thank you for having us on such short notice."

"Well, of course! A full B&B is a happy B&B, and I was glad to give away the last room."

Last *room*?

Had that been singular?

I shot a glance at Rafe, who had also clearly clocked the tense.

"Let me show you inside." She gestured for us to follow her into the prettily decorated entryway. Pale pink wallpaper covered the walls, and the dark wood floor gleamed. "This way, up the stairs."

She chattered away about the breakfast schedule and options while leading us down the hall to a room at the end. When we arrived, she pushed open the door to reveal a small room with one double bed. "And here it is!"

"Thank you," I said, craning my neck to see if there was

perhaps another door to a separate room. "Where is the second room?"

"Second room?" She frowned. "You booked one, dear."

"I booked two, I think." I smiled, not wanting to annoy her. This was a tiny town, and her B&B had been the only one with a vacancy.

"Sorry, love. One is all I have."

"Oh, okay." My mind scrambled. We couldn't sleep in the car, and it was too late to go anywhere else.

"Remember, breakfast starts at seven," she said before leaving and shutting the door behind her.

I looked at Rafe, who stared at me with an incredulous expression on his face. "One room?"

"Seems that way." I walked in and put my bag on the chair by the little hearth.

"I'll sleep in the car," he said.

"Don't be ridiculous." I turned to see that he hadn't entered the room yet. He still stood in the doorway, looking awkward as hell.

"There's only one bed, Isobel."

"And?"

"It's one bed." He said the words like I should understand what he meant.

"I know."

"You can't possibly expect me to put up with that?"

Offended, I gasped. "Are you seriously saying you can't bear to sleep next to me? That it would be torture?"

"Yes. That's exactly what I'm saying."

"Ugh." I crossed my arms. "I thought we were getting along."

"We are."

"Then why?" I gestured to the bed. "It's just one night. We'll put a wall of pillows between us."

"That's not going to cut it."

I rolled my eyes. "I can't believe you're so prudish."

"Prudish?" He frowned. "What do you mean?"

"You won't share a bed with a friend who's a woman. I call that the definition of prudish."

Something unrecognizable flashed on his face, and he stalked toward me, dropping his bag at his feet and looming over me. The heat in his gaze made me draw in a breath. "You think it's prudishness that's keeping me from that bed?"

"Or the fact that you've been in a miserable mood all night, yes."

A low growl escaped him. "I watched those damned builders flirt with you all afternoon, and I watched you flirt back. Which is your right, of course. But Isobel, I'm not made of steel."

The breath rushed out of me. "You were *jealous*?"

The air around him vibrated. "I've wanted you since the moment I laid eyes on you, Isobel. You're perfection. So yes, I was jealous."

I just blinked at him, shocked.

"How can you possibly be surprised?" he asked, his voice softer.

"I—" I just *was*. But I didn't care about that right now.

What I cared about was the way he looked at me, his gaze fathomless. Suddenly, we were the only two people in the world. We'd been dancing around this for what felt like forever. Would it be so bad to just go for it?

"Isobel." His tone was heavy with desire. Tortured, almost. "You can't look at me like that."

"Like what?" I stepped forward, so close to him that I had to crane my neck to meet his gaze.

"Like you want me."

"I *do* want you." The words were out before I could stop them. Any thought of maintaining my distance was away with the wind. "Don't you want me?"

He groaned, low and soft, then reached up and cupped my cheek. "More than I've ever wanted anyone or anything in my life."

"Then kiss me." I didn't care about the future or consequences or the heartbreak that was inevitably down the line. All I cared about was him. This moment. This opportunity to have something that I'd never had before.

And he seemed to care about the same, because he leaned down and kissed me with a passion that made my head spin. He cupped my head in his large hands, holding me still for the delicious onslaught.

I wrapped my arms around his neck, kissing him back like it was the last time I'd ever kiss him.

It might be, because this was probably a mistake.

But I wouldn't think of that because I couldn't stop myself.

Instead, I pulled him toward the bed, dragging him down on top of me. His weight was divine. I parted my thighs, and his hips settled into place, the hard length of him making my breath catch.

LINSEY HALL

I moved against him, desperate for more of the delicious friction. A low groan tore from his throat. Sparks of pleasure exploded behind my closed eyelids.

I fumbled between us, trying to pull his shirt up. He reared back and yanked it over his head, revealing the broad expanse of muscle that I'd been admiring for the last fortnight.

"You are so hot," I said.

He laughed, a low, sexy sound, and said, "Coming from you, that's a compliment."

"Coming from me?" I quirked a brow.

"The sexiest, smartest woman I've ever known."

A smile tugged at the corner of my mouth, and I reached down to pull my shirt over my head. Any shyness was banished by the desire in his eyes.

He wanted me.

Badly.

I loved it.

Quickly, I tugged my bra off. His gaze followed my every move, and a low groan escaped him. He bent low to press kisses against my neck, trailing his mouth down to my breasts. I arched up against him, wanting more. The heat of his tongue dragged against my nipple as his strong hands gripped my waist.

"You're incredible," he murmured, pressing kisses against my stomach.

Happiness bubbled within me, followed by a streak of pleasure when he ran his tongue along the expanse of skin right above the waistband of my jeans.

He looked up at me, his fingertips at the buttons.

"May I?"

My breath grew short as I nodded.

He had me naked in what felt like seconds. When he pressed his mouth to my center, hot and wet, I gasped. Pleasure exploded through me, and he was relentless, as if he couldn't get enough of it. As if he couldn't get enough of me.

I reveled in the feel of his strong hands gripping my hips as his tongue made me see starlight.

When I could take no more, I tugged on his shoulders, trying to drag him up along my body. He did as I requested, propping himself up on his arms over me. I reached between us, gripping his hardness through his jeans.

He groaned, pleasure rich in the sound, and I met his gaze. My voice trembled when I spoke, but I meant every word. "I don't want anything between us. No clothes. Nothing but your skin against mine."

Desire darkened his gaze, and his voice was rough when he asked, "Are you sure?"

I nodded. "I'm on birth control, and Tommy and I...well, it's been a long time, actually. A very long time. So I think I'm good there."

"Me, too."

"Good." I kissed him, my heart hammering with anticipation, my skin hot with desire. "Now hurry."

He did as I commanded, and I watched, breath held, as he stripped out of the rest of his clothes. Fully nude, he was glorious. Every inch of him was perfect, and when he settled himself on top of me, I moaned, unable to bite back the sound of pleasure.

His body fit perfectly to mine, and when he filled me, it

was the most glorious thing I'd ever felt. He moved, all heat and hardness and strength, and the pleasure nearly blinded me. I'd had so many orgasms already, and yet it seemed there was one more waiting to follow. It built and built, a delicious pressure that bound us together.

Rafe pressed his lips to my neck, his breathing quick and harsh as he drove me wild with the perfection of his body. Magic seemed to spark in the air as the waves of pleasure crashed over us, and I thought that I could follow him to the ends of the earth.`

CHAPTER
TWENTY-FIVE

ISOBEL

I AWOKE ALONE in the bed the next morning. For the briefest moment, I thought it had been a dream. It had certainly been that incredible. Out of this world, even. Nothing in my past life had prepared me for what Rafe could do.

I groaned and stared at the ceiling.

There was no way that had been a good idea. If I wasn't obsessed with him before, I certainly would be now. It was too soon after Tommy, and I couldn't trust myself to put my own interests first. I had to find myself, damn it.

There was a fire under my butt as I climbed out of bed and dressed. As expected, I found Rafe in the breakfast room, sitting at one of the six small tables. No one else was in the room, thank fates.

He looked up at me, his expression guarded. It caught me slightly by surprise, but I barreled forward.

"Last night—"

"Was amazing," he said. "But a mistake."

"Yes. Exactly." I sat across from him, trying to keep the blush from my cheeks. "I can't be involved with anyone right now, so let's pretend it never happened."

"Agreed." His tone was stiff, and I couldn't read it, but I shouldn't even be trying. Attempting to get a better understanding of his feelings and motivations was exactly the opposite of the easy, lighthearted friendship we were supposed to have.

Fortunately, the B&B host came out of the kitchen at that moment, two large plates in her hands.

"I ordered for you," Rafe said. "I figured you'd want to get out of here quickly."

"You were right, thanks."

"Two full breakfasts," the host said as she set the plates on the table in front of us. We thanked her, and she headed back to the kitchen.

I looked down at my plate. Eggs, sausage, bacon, tomatoes, toast, and a little square of something I couldn't identify.

Rafe saw me looking at it and said, "Laverbread. Not bread, but a seaweed cake. A Welsh delicacy."

As if we'd called her name, Poa appeared on the floor next to me. I looked down at her. "Really?"

Of course. Her nose twitched. *I'll have the sausage, please, and the laverbread.*

"You're familiar with it?"

I'm a world traveler, unlike some people. She gave me a look that made it clear I was the subject of her disdain.

I rolled my eyes but put the sausage and laverbread on the tiny plate that sat to my right, then lowered it to the ground for her. "You're lucky it's a big breakfast."

No, you're *lucky.*

I laughed, unable to help myself.

We ate in silence, and I'd be lying if I said it wasn't awkward. Every time I looked at Rafe, I thought of last night. It had been incredible. So incredible that it proved it was a bad idea to get too close.

By the time we were finished, I was ready to get the heck out of there. I needed some space to breathe and a distraction so I wouldn't think about the night before. We collected our bags and said goodbye to the innkeeper, then piled into Rafe's car. Poa insisted on sitting on my lap, and she dug her claws in every time he took a turn.

We reached the coven headquarters right before our meeting was meant to start, and I gasped with delight. Unlike the Aurora Coven, which kept their headquarters on Charming Cove's busiest street, the Ceridwen Coven was situated deep in the woods. The small stone cottage sat in a clearing in a tangle of rosebushes. A pretty creek burbled by to the right, and a fawn leapt over it.

"How beautiful," I said as I climbed out of the car.

Rafe followed. "I want to be skeptical, but this place feels fine."

"Skeptical?"

"It's too perfect."

A dog waddled around the side of the house toward the front yard. He was the sort of creature that was so ugly he was cute, with a lolling tongue, heavy jowls, and a tuft of fur

241

on his head that looked like a toupee. As soon as he saw us, he stopped and farted. Quite loudly.

I laughed. "See? Not too perfect."

A reluctant chuckled escaped Rafe.

I headed toward the main door, raising my hand to knock. It opened before I could make contact, and a witch with brilliant red curls grinned at me. "Isobel?"

"Yes." I was pretty sure I recognized her voice from the phone. "Laurie?"

"The one and only. Come in, we'll have tea in the back garden. Verona and Marvela are waiting. They're two of the other coven members."

We followed her into the house. The dog toddled in behind us and clambered up onto the couch by the fire. Laurie led us through to the back garden, where a long wooden table had been set up under a huge oak. Fairy lights glittered around the oak's branches, and flowers were piled in the middle of the table, growing from an inset trough. What a clever idea.

Two witches sat at the end of the table, a tea service between them.

"Have a seat." Laurie gestured for us to sit in the chairs that had been decorated with colorful floral cushions, and we joined the other witches.

Laurie poured the tea while Verona and Marvela handled introductions. When everyone was acquainted and had tea in front of them, Laurie leaned toward us. "Now, tell us why you wanted to see us. And you would like to visit the stone circle as well, I presume."

"Yes. We're here because of a curse." I gestured to Rafe. "Perhaps it's better that he explain."

He drew in a deep breath, obviously wishing he were anywhere else. I gave him a nudge, and he gave me a glare. I just grinned.

"A little over a decade ago, I was cursed." He told them everything he knew about the witch who had cursed him, which wasn't much, sadly. But recognition flashed in Marvela's eyes.

"I think you're talking about Coraline."

"Coraline." He said the name slowly, as if testing it out.

"Don't worry if you don't remember it," Marvela said. "She erased it from your mind. It won't feel familiar."

"It doesn't. But do you know where she is?"

"Dead. Vindictive, that one. Mean-spirited. And it got the better of her when she went up against a meaner, more vindictive sorceress."

I blew out a breath. That was a bad end. And it was bad for us. I hadn't wanted to meet her, but if I couldn't break the curse, she would have been the only one capable.

That left one option. "Is it all right if we go to the stone circle?"

"Of course," Laurie said. "You'll need one of us to accompany you so that the protection spell doesn't repel you. Would you like to go now?"

"That would be fantastic, thank you." I rose, and Rafe followed.

Laurie led us from the cottage. "I'll drive my car and you can follow, okay? Then you can have as much time as you like."

Rafe and I drove in silence as we followed her to the stone circle. Fortunately, it was only twenty minutes away via a single-track road. She pulled over into a small, unmarked lay-by, and Rafe squeezed his large car in behind her. She climbed out of her vehicle and gestured for us to follow her. "This way."

We climbed up a hill and through some trees, which were turning with the season, red, orange, and yellow leaves falling like brilliantly colored confetti. A family of curious red squirrels followed us, chittering away as we walked on the crunchy leaves.

After about fifteen minutes, we reached a clearing at the top of the hill. The sun peeked out from behind heavy clouds, shining a single beam of light onto a massive stone circle in the middle of the clearing. Twenty-one tall granite spires reached toward the sky, each slender yet strong and decorated with beautiful carvings.

"Well, that's quite a sight, isn't it?" Laurie said. "The sun rarely cooperates like that. Your visit must be fated."

I hoped so. I wanted success so badly that I thought I could taste it.

"Let me walk you in." She started across the soft green grass toward the circle.

The air prickled with protective magic as we walked, but Laurie murmured a quiet incantation. The air shimmered around her, and the prickling sensation calmed. When we stepped inside the stone circle, it died completely. A sense of welcome enveloped me, and I smiled.

"This place is wonderful," I said.

"Isn't it?" Laurie smiled and spun in a circle. "I just love the energy here."

She said her goodbyes and left us in the circle.

I turned to Rafe. "Ready?"

"You're sure you're not going to pass out?" Worry creased his brow.

"I'm *sure*. That had everything to do with Avalona Island and nothing to do with your curse, I promise."

He sighed and reached for the bottom of his shirt. "Same as last time, then?"

"Afraid so." I smiled, but it was a weak gesture.

It would be impossible not to think of last night while touching him. But it was the best way to read the curse, and I was determined to succeed.

I tried to keep my eyes averted from his pecs as he stripped off his shirt. The cool autumn air blew past us, but he didn't so much as shiver. A family of birds piped up as if singing a glorious chorus to his nudity. I wanted to hiss at them to chill out, but that was an entirely outsized reaction.

"All right." I rubbed my hands together like a magician preparing for a trick, and he stepped toward me. "Same as before."

He nodded and closed his eyes as if unable to bear my touch. Or perhaps it was too much for him. He'd certainly liked it last night.

I shoved the thought away. There was no point in trying to guess at his feelings. Instead, I put my energy toward reading the curse. A deep breath steadied me, and I pressed my hand to his chest, feeling a shiver run up my arm at the contact.

I called upon my magic, opening myself to the enchantment all around me. It felt familiar now that I was touching him, as if his body had stored some of the magic of this place. It probably had. Visions flowed easily though my mind, and I watched as a dark-haired woman stood in front of a young Rafe, chanting words that I could now recognize. They seared themselves into my mind.

At her feet, flowers sprung up, orange, yellow, and red. I was annoyed that something so beautiful had been used for such a horrible curse.

When it was over, the younger Rafe in my visions collapsed. Coraline stalked away without another glance, and I scowled. I shook it away and blinked, my vision returning to the present day.

"Are you all right?" Rafe asked. "You're pale."

"But not unconscious." I grinned, thinking how far I'd come since last time. "It was much easier to read the spell here. I think I've got it all."

"Really?"

"Don't sound so surprised. I'll have this curse broken in no time."

A smile tugged at his lips. "I shouldn't have doubted you."

I shrugged. "So many people have failed before me. Heck, I doubted myself. But coming here was the right call." I stepped away from him, moving toward another part of the circle, and bent over to inspect the grass.

He pulled on his shirt and followed me. "What are you looking for?"

"This is where she performed the spell." I pointed to the ground. "Can you see the way it glows pale white?"

"It just looks like grass to me."

I shook my head and knelt. The glowing ring was the spot where the flowers had bloomed around her. I needed some of those seeds. They probably still lay dormant in the ground, having been dropped by the blooms as they faded.

I pressed my hand to the grass and closed my eyes, asking permission from the towering stones that stood sentinel around me. It was a wordless process, my soul speaking with the ancient magic inside the granite pillars, and a faint buzz of approval shot up through the dirt and into my palm.

I pulled up the grass, digging into the cool earth and retrieving some of the seeds. Once I'd collected a variety, I held my palm out to show Rafe. "These are the key. They were an integral part of the spell, and they'll help me break it. I just need to get them to sprout first."

"You're incredible," he said, his voice soft with wonder.

I laughed awkwardly, then stood. "Save that until I actually succeed. Now let's go home."

CHAPTER
TWENTY-SIX

Isobel

THE RIDE HOME passed in silence, and I would have fiddled around with my phone to pass the time, but the battery had died that morning. Of course, I'd forgot my charger.

It was dark by the time we arrived, and the contractors must have finished up at the house, because it was empty.

"I'm going to go check the progress," Rafe said as soon as he parked.

"That desperate to get me out of your house, huh?"

He just gave me a long look, then climbed out of the car.

I groaned and flopped my head back against the seat. Why had I said that? At some point in the last few days, that joke had clearly worn out its welcome.

Desperate for a distraction from my own idiocy, I headed up to my flat for a shower. On the way, I plugged in my phone to let it charge.

Once I was clean and dressed, I returned to my phone and turned it on. Immediately, it began to buzz with messages and missed calls. What the heck had happened while we were gone?

I pulled up the missed calls and noticed that they were all from Charlie, with whom I'd exchanged numbers before he'd left the barbecue. I called him back, and he immediately picked up.

"Your house is ornery again," he said without preamble.

"What?" Disappointment surged through me. "What do you mean?"

"I mean that it booted us right out. Popped the floor-boards under our feet until we left."

"Oh, no," I cried. "I swear, I didn't know that would happen."

"I know, I know. It's not your fault. But the house was moody. Too moody to work in, especially for Lee and Carlos. Worst-case scenario for me is getting drenched. For them..."

He let the sentence trail off because it was easy enough for me to fill in the blanks with how the house could seriously injure the guys fiddling with the electricity and climbing around on the roof.

I pinched the bridge of my nose and squeezed my eyes shut. Damn it. Everything had been fine the day of the barbecue. Plenty of people had walked through and told me how lovely it was. So what was different?

"I'll try to figure out what's going on with the house," I said. "But will you please, *please* come back tomorrow? I'll go in first to make sure it's safe."

He sighed. "I'll see what I can do about the guys. It'll take some convincing, but I think I can have them there at nine."

"I'll have pastries and coffee from Margot's. Anything they like. Just text me. It'll be the spread of the century."

"Better than that barbecue?" He laughed.

"Yes. Even better."

He chuckled. "We'll be there."

"Thank you *so* much." I rang off, then went downstairs to see Rafe.

He was just letting himself back in. "The guys didn't do any work that I could tell."

"I know. I just got off the phone with Charlie. Apparently, the house made them very unwelcome."

He frowned. "It was fine when I was up there. A bit moodier than the other day, but not terrible. No popping floorboards."

"That's not what the guys said." Worry tugged at my heart. What if I couldn't get them back in tomorrow? We couldn't afford this setback.

"Ah." His expression cleared as he thought of something. "The house probably wants you there when strangers are around. You were there the whole party, and everything was fine."

"You think so?"

"I know so. You make everything better, and the house knows it."

You make everything better. The words rang in my head. Had he really just said that?

From the faint color on his cheekbones and the way he

was looking away—yes. And he hadn't just been talking about the house.

"Ah, I'm going to get to bed," he said, rubbing the back of his neck. "Early morning tomorrow."

"Sure. Thanks for the help."

He nodded and headed off, then turned back to me. "Actually, I should be thanking you. Today was...unexpected."

I grinned. "Tomorrow will be even better."

"Don't be focusing on the curse, now," he said. "We need to finish that house."

"I know, I know." And he was right.

As I went up to bed, I typed out a text to Aria. Now that I had the seeds and some dirt from the stone circle, I had almost everything I needed to break the curse. I just needed a bit of her help. We sorted out a plan, and I was asleep almost before my head hit the pillow.

THE NEXT MORNING, I was out of the house before dawn. I dropped the dirt and seeds by Aria's house, an adorable little cottage right on the coast within walking distance of town. Her familiar, Boris the badger, lay asleep in the bushes, a half-finished donut by his paw.

Someone had a big night. Poa sniffed disdainfully.

"As if you haven't done the same."

I always finish my donuts.

I laughed, then knocked. Aria opened the door, a cup of coffee in her hand and a man's large T-shirt acting as her dressing gown. Her hair was pulled up in a messy knot, and she had a happy glow on her face. Behind her, a shirtless man was flipping pancakes on the stove. He waved at me, and I waved back, then looked at Aria with raised eyebrows. "No wonder you look like you're in such a good mood."

"Callan makes the absolute best pumpkin pancakes in the world. Want to come in and have some?"

"Wish I could, but no time." I nodded down to Boris, whose little feet stuck out from underneath the bush. "I'm sure he'd be interested, though."

Aria scowled down at him. "Absolutely not. That little heathen stole the entire box of donuts that was meant for this morning."

Ah, that explains the unfinished donut. I could hear the respect in Poa's voice.

I shook my head and looked back at Aria. "Pumpkin pancakes sound like a better deal, anyway."

"You're right about that." She grinned. "Coffee to go?"

"No, thanks. I'm headed into town to get bribery coffee and pastries from Margot's. I want to be the contractors' favorite client."

"Uh-oh, did something go wrong?" I explained what had happened, and she nodded. "I agree with Rafe. It'll be better if you're there."

"Here's hoping." I turned to go, then watched in shock as Poa sauntered into the cottage and straight up to the man with the spatula. "And what do you think you're doing?"

She looked back at me. *Getting breakfast. Will you tell him I like a lot of milk in my coffee?*

"You weren't invited."

Aria grinned. "It's fine. The invitation was for both of you."

Poa stuck out her tongue at me, and I glared. "She likes her coffee black."

Poa hissed.

"It's all right, cat," Callan said. "I know you take a lot of cream."

"How can you possibly know that?" I asked.

"She's a cat."

"Okay, good point. I'm out of here before this goes further off the rails."

Aria took the bag of dirt and seeds from me. "I'll see what I can do about getting these to bloom ASAP. Check back with me tonight."

"Thank you. Lifesaver."

We said our goodbyes, and I headed into town. My first stop was the Aurora Coven headquarters, where I tested my ability to open the locked door without a key. It worked, which still shocked me. I texted Emma to let her know, then went up to the workshop to consult one of the curse-breaking books I'd seen before. I already had an idea about how I would do it, but I wanted to confirm something.

I got lucky and found the info on the first try, along with some supplies that would come in handy. I texted Emma to ask permission before taking the vial of fire suppression powder, and once I had it, I was on my way to Margot's. The whole stop at the coven took less than twenty minutes, and I was out of Margot's even quicker, loaded down with goodies for the guys.

By the time I made it back to Lavender House, it was

right before nine. I parked at the house and carried my treats to the front door. I was nearly there when a truck pulled in behind me.

Charlie, Lee, and Carlos climbed out, wary looks on all their faces.

I gave them my most charming smile and held up the box of pastries and the tray of coffees. "I got your favorites."

There were some grumbles and smiles, and I took that to be a success.

"I'm not sure I want to go in there with a hot cup of coffee in my hand," Lee said, and I hated to admit that he had a point.

"Why don't we leave them out here?" I set everything on one of the chairs we sat in during lunch, then headed into the house.

They followed me, footsteps slow and a bit wary.

Nothing was wrong with the house, as far as I could tell —no stench, no groaning, no popping floorboards—and I looked back at the guys with hope on my face. "Well?"

"It's certainly better than it was yesterday," Charlie said. He'd made it about two meters into the foyer. "House? Are you cool that we're here?"

The house said nothing, of course, but I decided to go the extra mile and say, "I'll be here all day with the guys. They're going to make you feel better."

I felt the house's pleasure, though I couldn't describe the actual sensation. I was sure it was okay, though.

"I'll go get the coffees," I said.

I brought them back in and handed them around, then

explained, "We think the house wanted me to be here since it doesn't know you well."

Charlie gave a shrug that suggested he could see the house's point. "You know, I never thought of it that way, but if the house has a personality, it makes sense."

"So you'll be here while we work?" Lee asked, and I couldn't help but appreciate his practical nature. He was the roofer, after all, and he probably didn't want to be chucked off the roof.

I couldn't blame him. "I will. The whole time, I promise."

"All right, then," Charlie said. "We'll get to work."

Rafe appeared from the back of the house, his tool belt strapped around his waist. He gave the guys a friendly nod, and I appreciated that he didn't do that silly rooster thing Tommy always did when he was around other men. He always tried to seem bigger, sometimes even breaking out a horrendous strut.

How had I stayed with him for so long?

I shook away the intrusive though and said, "I'll be upstairs, painting one of the spare bedrooms. Call if you need me."

"Will do." Charlie gave a friendly salute, then headed back out to his truck, presumably to get supplies.

The day passed quickly, and I was struck with the strongest sense of satisfaction every time I saw one of the contractors repairing something I could never hope to repair myself. As for Rafe, I did my best to avoid him. Whenever I was near him, my heart raced, and my tongue felt completely useless—like if I tried to talk, I would just make a ridiculous noise.

But that didn't stop me from seeing him everywhere in the house. He didn't even need to be in a room for me to see him. If I went into the kitchen, his presence was everywhere in the stunning cabinetry that he'd built. He was truly an artist, and he was leaving his mark all over the building. I'd never be able to forget him at this rate, and that would make recovering from his loss even harder.

And I *would* lose him because I was going to break that damned curse. He would be free of it, and then he would inevitably return to his pack, wherever they lived.

I slammed the paintbrush down into the tray in frustration, then gave an angry little squawk when I saw how the droplets splattered against the wall.

I really needed to get my act together. Losing it over a guy was so not in my plans.

As carefully as I could, I smoothed the paint back into the wall so that the color and texture were perfect, then cleaned up my supplies and headed downstairs. The contractors had left for the night, and so had Rafe. When I reached the boathouse, I found it empty as well. There was dinner on the table for me, though, a hearty sandwich and salad next to a note with my name on it.

A band tightened around my heart.

How was he so perfect?

I shook the thought away, then sat at the table and texted Aria to check on the progress with the plants. I ate the sandwich as I waited for her response. It came a few minutes later.

. . .

256

THEY'LL BE full size tomorrow afternoon. And I think your cat lives here now.

I ROLLED MY EYES. Of course Poa did. She'd probably found their snack cabinet or recruited Boris to join her in petty crimes. Although, given his recent donut heist, he was probably already involved in plenty of his own.

CHAPTER
TWENTY-SEVEN

Isobel

Rafe and I worked alongside the contractors the next day, relying on my magic to increase our speed. With every hour that passed, I grew more hopeful about finishing the house in time.

At five, when the contractors left, I went to the Enchanted Garden to pick up the plants that Aria had sprouted for me. Colorful butterflies escorted me down the path through the garden as I walked toward her office. This little cottage that she'd turned into the garden headquarters was cute as could be, with roses climbing the walls and smoke billowing from the chimney. It was brisk today, and I was sure the fire would feel divine.

I'd just raised my hand to knock when she opened the door, a broad smile on her face. "Wait until you see your plants."

"They look good?"

"They look fantastic. Let me get them from the back." She went to the rear door of the cottage and disappeared outside for a moment. When she came back, she carried a big tray of orange, yellow, and red flowers—exactly the same as I'd seen in the vision. I could feel the power and potential in them, and I drew in a deep breath. "They're perfect."

"You'll break his curse with these?" she asked, handing them over.

"Yes, I'm sure of it." I leaned down and smelled the flowers, then winced and reared back. "They stink."

"I know. They have since they sprouted."

"Makes sense. They were used for a terrible purpose the first time."

"You're going to undo that."

"I am." I grinned, loving her faith in me. "Thank you again."

"Anytime. And don't forget girls' night this Thursday."

"I won't, though I'm not sure I'll make it. The house needs so much work."

"We can move it to your place, if necessary. Just give us some tasks with no power tools, and it'll be fine."

I laughed, then said my thanks and left.

By the time I got back to the boathouse, it was fully dark. The lights were on at Lavender House, brilliant against the black sky. Carlos had managed to wire most of the rooms, so we were no longer relying on lanterns at night.

Since Rafe was still hard at work, I decided to get a quick dinner started. It was just frozen pizza in the oven, along with a salad kit from a bag, but when it was done, it smelled amazing. Once I popped a bottle of red wine, we had a proper meal.

Rafe entered as soon as I'd set the glasses on the table, and I turned to smile at him. "Do you have a radar for food?"

"I must, because I suddenly felt the strongest desire to come down here."

I gestured to the spread I'd laid out on the table. "Only the finest cuisine for you, good sir."

He grinned. "Looks amazing."

We sat and helped ourselves. The food ended up being better than I'd expected, and we were nearly finished by the time I blurted out my exciting news. I just couldn't wait any longer. "I can break the curse. Tonight."

He blinked at me, stunned. The last slice of pizza, which was currently on its way to his mouth, stilled. "Really?"

I nodded. "Really. The biggest part was finding out exactly what the curse was. Once I knew that and Aria sprouted the flower seeds I brought back, I had everything I needed."

He blew out a breath and set the pizza down. "Do we need to go somewhere special to do it, like the island?"

I shook my head. "We can try here. I think it'll work. If it doesn't, we'll go to Avalona."

"All right, then." He stood, the food abandoned. "Let's do it."

I hopped up, excitement and nerves making me jittery. "Let's go up onto the hill. It's the perfect place."

"Do I need to bring anything?"

"Just yourself."

On the way out of the house, I collected the pallet of

small plants Aria had sprouted for me, along with the bag of supplies I'd collected from the Aurora Coven headquarters. Rafe took them from me and carried them up the hill toward Lavender House. I passed the quiet building and kept climbing, wanting to get closer to the top.

Once I'd found a good patch of grass that was relatively flat, I said. "You can lay the pallet down there."

Rafe did as I asked, and I knelt and gently removed a root ball from the plastic container, careful to keep the dirt intact around the delicate roots. I held the orange blossom in one hand and pressed my other to the dirt, murmuring, "*Foramen*." A small hole appeared in the dirt, and I placed the root ball inside, letting the flower stand tall above the grass.

I repeated the process with the remaining flowers, creating a circle of blooms similar to the one I'd seen in the vision. When I was done, I pulled the bottle of gray powder out of the bag I'd brought. I poured a thin line of the fire-repressing powder on either side of the ring of blooms, surrounding with the dust. Then I pulled the matches from my bag and looked up at Rafe, who watched quietly in the moonlight. "Do you recognize the flowers?"

"No." He shook his head. "Were they part of the curse?"

"They were, but I'm going to use them differently." I stood and gestured for him to enter the circle. "Come on. We're ready."

He nodded and joined me, his jaw tight.

"Are you worried?" I asked.

"This really feels like the last chance," he said. "Before, with the Jade Sorceress, I was convinced it was the last time. But this is somehow so much more final."

"Well, the good news is I'm going to succeed."

"I love your confidence."

I could tell from his tone that he meant it, and pleasure flushed through me. *I* loved having confidence in myself. It was a new feeling, and it never would have happened if I'd stayed in my old life. I had so many reasons to love Charming Cove, and this was one of them.

"All right, time to light this baby up," I said.

"Light it up?" He frowned.

"Yep. I've got the ring planted, and now it's time for them to burn. That's what the gray powder is—it's a fire repellent to keep the blaze from spreading. But the flowers themselves will burn." I pulled the matches from my pocket and bent to an orange bloom. I dragged the match across the rough strip of paper on the bottom of the box. It flamed purple, and I held it to one of the small petals.

The orange flower ignited, burning purple and pink thanks to the magic imbued in the match. The flames began to lick at the next blossom, then the next. As the fire traveled around the circle, I stood and returned to Rafe, stopping in front of him. Soon, we were surrounded by a ring of burning flowers. Sparkling smoke filled the air, and I began to chant.

I'd memorized the curse when I'd heard it, and now I recited it backward. I'd practiced several times, thank fates, and I didn't stumble over the words. Rafe's gaze burned into me as I pressed my hands to his shoulders. Since I wasn't trying to read a curse, he didn't need to take his shirt off. A good thing, too, since I couldn't afford any distraction.

Around us, magic filled the air as the flowers burned. The seeds had contained the remnants of the magic that had kept

Rafe's curse strong, but as they were consumed, I could feel it weakening. Exhaustion and excitement fought within me, and I kept the words flowing, my gaze on Rafe. Tension filled the air as I neared the end of the spell. It felt like the curse was fighting back, but I was stronger.

The fire died abruptly, and with it, the curse finally broke. It felt like a champagne cork popping inside me, and I gasped.

Rafe stumbled backward, shock on his face. He blinked rapidly, his gaze going blurry. His breathing stilled.

"Rafe?"

"I—remember." He shook his head, dragging a hand over his face. "I have family. Parents. Friends. A home."

I smiled, tears pricking my eyes. Tears of joy for him, tears of sadness for me. "I'm so glad."

He nodded, his gaze a million miles away.

It had all happened so much faster than I'd expected it to. One minute, he'd had no memory. He'd essentially been all mine, though I knew that was an absolutely ridiculous thought. Also selfish.

But now he had a whole life that he remembered.

"You should go to them," I said. Did he have a girlfriend back there? Worse, a wife? No, it had been over ten years. He would have been too young to have a wife, and any girlfriend would have moved on.

"They might not even remember me," he said.

"I'm sure they do now. If the curse broke on you, it broke on them. They'll be searching for you."

"I can't even imagine."

I knew what he meant by the words. He couldn't imagine

anyone caring about him. He'd been alone so long that the idea was entirely foreign.

I care about you! I wanted to cry.

Instead, I pinched my lips closed.

"We're going to finish your house first," he said.

"You can't keep putting me first."

"You've been putting me first. Insisting we go away to Avalona, to Wales, all while you're on a deadline to finish this house if you want to keep it."

He was right. It had been my fear that I'd put a man's interests before my own. But it was different with Rafe because he also put me first.

We'd been putting each other first all along.

The enormity of it made my throat tighten.

This felt real—real in a way it had never felt before.

"Isobel." He stepped closer, his voice rough. He reached out to cup my cheek, and I leaned into him. "I'm not leaving you until you don't need me anymore."

I drew in an unsteady breath. "Rafe."

He leaned down and held his lips over mine, waiting for something. For permission, I realized.

We'd agreed to not do this, and yet, I couldn't remember why. Whether or not this could last forever, I wanted it right now.

I leaned up and pressed my lips to his. The cool wind whipped past us as he picked me up. I wrapped my legs around his waist and kissed him, feeling the starlight on my skin.

He spun me in a circle, and joy filled me.

"I want you," I breathed against his mouth. "Now. Tonight."

He nipped at my lip, then carried me down the hill. We made it as far as the chairs in front of Lavender House. With the moon high above, we made love against the backdrop of the sea and stars.

The feeling of Rafe beneath me, inside of me, was so glorious, so overpowering, that I could feel it imprint on me. Pleasure like I'd never known flushed through me, and I kissed him with all the passion in my soul. More than anything, I didn't want this to end.

But it would, a thought that I tried to drive from my mind as I desperately chased the pleasure that he promised. No matter what happened, we would have tonight. And for now, that would have to be enough.

CHAPTER
TWENTY-EIGHT

Isobel

THE NEXT WEEK passed in a blur of work and happiness. Rafe and I had taken it to the next level, and even though I knew we shouldn't have, I couldn't help but love every second of it.

We spent the most glorious week together, working on the house and then living our lives in the evening. They were short evenings due to the long hours at Lavender House, but we always ate dinner together, then shared his bed. It was magical.

He hadn't yet contacted his family, and I had a feeling he needed a bit of time to process the changes that were about to come. But they had to know he was alive now, so at least they had the hope of seeing him soon. That made me feel a bit less guilty about keeping him to myself for the last week.

By my twenty-eighth day in Charming Cove, Lavender House was complete. The contractors had put the finishing touches on their work, I'd repainted any areas of the wall that had been disturbed by the electrical and plumbing repairs. Rafe had put the finishing touches on all the gorgeous woodwork, and I'd even got some furniture from Vivienne. She was redecorating Blackthorn Hall, the ducal estate where she lived on the outskirts of town, and she'd had loads of gorgeous old furniture that needed a new home. With Vivienne and Madeline's help, we'd arranged it all into a quirky, eclectic house with character.

I *loved* it.

Even Poa liked it, despite the lack of figurines to watch her every move.

Rafe and I stood on the lawn, looking at the beautiful stone house with its new roof. Aria had planted some bushes and autumn flowers, and the exterior of the house looked perfect.

"It's gorgeous." I leaned against Rafe, staring up at the house.

"It really is."

"And now it's time to go see your pack."

He frowned down at me. "The solicitor will be here the day after tomorrow to check on the house—"

"I know. But the house is finished. I can come back in time to meet the solicitor, but your family has waited long enough."

"You're right." Guilt flashed on his face. "They know I'm alive. A pack can feel when it loses a member. But all the same, I should go see them. I *want* to go see them."

"Definitely." I grinned at him.

"Come with me."

I drew in a shuddery breath. I'd been hoping he would ask. I'd even spoken like I planned to go. But I loved hearing that he wanted me there. "I'll get packed for the night. Shall we meet in an hour and go? We'll make it there by evening if there isn't too much traffic."

"Okay." He reached for my hands and squeezed them. "Thank you, Isobel."

"It was nothing." I stepped back, about to go.

He tightened his grip, his gaze intense. "It was everything."

I drew in a shuddery breath and nodded. There was nothing I could say to that.

He released my hands, and I hurried upstairs to pack a bag. On my way back down, I heard a car in the drive. When I went outside, I saw that Emma, Holly, Aria, and Tabitha had arrived. They climbed out of Aria's car.

"Hello!" Emma waved a bunch of flowers at me.

Tabitha hurried around the side of the car, a big white bakery box clutched in her hands. I spotted Margot's logo on the side.

"What are you guys doing here?" I asked, smiling as they approached.

"We came to see the house!" Emma shoved the bouquet at me. "I heard from Vivienne that the furniture is all in and the place is done!"

"It is." I grinned. I still had about twenty minutes before we were meant to go to Wales. "I can show you really quickly. Come on."

I led them up the hill to the house, letting them in through the beautiful blue front door. We'd painted it a glossy navy, and it looked gorgeous with the fall wreath hanging on the front.

The main foyer gleamed—everything from the newly varnished wooden floors to the shining light fixtures. Vivienne's beautiful old side table sat against the wall, an antique lamp on the top. I would put the bouquet on that table as soon as I had a vase.

"It's gorgeous," Emma breathed.

"Let me show you the rest." I led them on a tour of the house, and my soul lit up with happiness as we walked into each room. Every window had a view of the sea or the green hills, and I couldn't believe how lucky I was.

As for the house? It was clearly happy with its new paint and varnished floors and properly sealed roof. The beautiful kitchen and baths suited the traditional style of the house, but they now had all the amenities that had been lacking before.

I could have stayed here all night, looking at every new feature, but the hour was nearly up, and I needed to meet Rafe.

I turned to my friends. "I've got to go, but you guys stay here as long as you like. There's even milk in the fridge for tea."

"Where are you going?" Tabitha asked.

"Rafe and I are headed to Wales to meet his family."

Aria gasped. "He agreed to go?"

"Yep." I'd told them about our progress when they'd come over last Thursday for a girls' night of wine and painting the last guest bedroom. "I think I'll meet his parents."

269

Holly blew out a breath. "That's a big deal."

"I know." I shook my head. "But it's not like it's going to work out, so I'm just thinking of it as a friends thing."

"Not going to work out?" Emma sounded appalled. "I've seen how he looks at you."

"Yeah, but he's going to move back to Wales to be with his family. He already told me. And I'm not leaving Charming Cove." I looked around the gorgeous blue living room in which we stood. "This is my home. And anyway, he hasn't asked me to go with him." Not that I would. I just couldn't give up the life I was meant to have—not for a man. Not again. "It's okay, though. I'm getting my life together. I'm happy."

"You definitely have your life together." Aria gestured to the house around us. "And Hazel wants you to formally join the coven once your house is approved and you're an official resident of Charming Cove."

I smiled, pleasure rushing through me. It was just one more reason I couldn't leave. I had a life here. Friends, a house, a job. It was more than I'd ever had before.

Everything was working out...except for the one thing that mattered the most.

CHAPTER
TWENTY-NINE

ISOBEL

RAFE'S PACK lived in a seaside village about fifty miles from the stone circle where Coraline had cursed him. The drive was just as long as it had been the first time we'd gone to Wales, but the vibe was very different. There was silence, but it was heavy with anticipation.

By the time we pulled into the village where his family lived, I was nearly shaking with anxiety. The village itself was lovely, with a row of small cottages along the rocky coast and a village shop that had a pub on one side. It was far smaller than Charming Cove, but it was just as beautiful in its own way.

No wonder he'd ended up in Charming Cove—he was drawn to the sea.

"It's wonderful," I said, looking at the crashing dark waves on the rocky shore.

"It's familiar." There was awe in his voice. "Nothing has been familiar in a decade."

I reached over and squeezed his hand. He squeezed back, then pulled into the parking spot in front of a little cottage with glass fishing floats decorating the front yard beneath the main window.

"Your family's house?" I asked.

He nodded but didn't move to leave the car.

"Come on. They've waited long enough. And if you wait any longer, you might wimp out."

"Wimp out?" He turned and smiled at me. "Did you just say I might wimp out?"

"Prove me wrong." I grinned, poking him in the arm.

"All right." He climbed out and headed up the path to the front door. There was a small sign over the door that read *Harrington.* That had to be his last name. I followed, heart pounding. But no matter how nervous I was, Rafe had to be twice as on edge.

He knocked, and I held my breath.

The door swung open almost immediately, and a woman in her mid-fifties stared at us in shock. Then she burst into tears.

"Mum—"

"Rafe!" She launched herself at him, wrapping him in her arms. She gripped him hard, her delicate floral blouse and slender hands contrasting with the dark T-shirt that stretched across the broad plane of his back.

I couldn't help it—tears burned my eyes, spilling onto my cheeks.

"Honey!" A man's voice sounded from farther back in the

house, and I saw him enter the foyer behind the woman. He was staring down at his phone. "Honey, Terrence says they have a lead on him. Some village in Cornwall."

I gave a shuddery little gasp.

They were looking for him.

"Randall, he's here!" the woman cried, her voice thick with tears and muffled against Rafe's shirt.

Randall looked up, his face going white with shock. Then his face crumpled, and tears filled his eyes. He strode toward his wife and son, enveloping them in his embrace.

More tears spilled.

This was, without a doubt, the best thing I'd ever witnessed.

I cannot handle this.

Poa's voice made me look down. She was staring at the group, her little face scrunched into a weird expression. I hadn't realized she was there, but the intensity of my emotion must have drawn her.

"Are you crying?" The words were hard to squeeze out of my tight throat, and I wiped the tears from my eyes.

If it were physiologically possible, I would be. She glared up at me. *I don't like it.*

I gave her a watery smile. "You don't like that he found his family?"

Of course I like that. I just don't like strong feelings about anything other than sausage rolls and lattes. It's uncomfortable.

"But in a good way."

There was movement from the little crowd in front of me, and I looked up to see them pulling apart.

~

Rafe

I turned to Isobel, my throat tight with emotion. Seeing my parents' faces...

I hadn't thought about them during the last week. I hadn't allowed myself. I knew they'd feel that I was alive and healthy—werewolf magic allowed for that. But I'd owed it to Isobel to finish her house. She loved that place, and I wouldn't be the reason she lost it. Not when she'd spent so much time helping me.

But I'd felt guilty about not going to my parents immediately, and I hadn't been able to make myself pick up a phone. After ten years away, it felt too...insubstantial.

So I'd packed away thoughts of them and focused on helping Isobel, knowing that I'd see them soon.

But now that I was here, part of me wished I'd come sooner, that I hadn't made them wait.

"Who's this?" My mother wiped the tears from her eyes and gave Isobel a smile.

"My friend Isobel. She's the witch who broke the curse. Isobel, this is Kay. And my father is Randall."

My mother gave another loud sob and threw herself at Isobel, who put out her arms just in time to catch her.

"Thank you," my mother said. "Thank you, thank you, *thank you*."

"Come on, honey." My father pulled her back, as if to give Isobel space. Then he clearly thought better of it and hugged her himself. She gave me a wide-eyed look over his shoulder but didn't seem too bothered.

"Randall, let the girl go. We need to have tea. And cake!" My mother turned to me. "Ever since the curse broke and we remembered you existed, I've been baking your favorites while the whole town looks for you." She shook her head, a disgusted expression crossing her face. "I can't believe I forgot my only son!"

"You didn't forget me, Mum. You were cursed."

"I'm going to find whoever did it, and I'm going to wring their skinny neck."

"She's dead."

"Good." Her voice was firm. "Did you kill her?"

"No, Mum. Of course not."

"I would've." She sniffed, then turned toward the kitchen. "Come in, now. We need to eat cake."

"Come on, son." My father beckoned us along.

I smiled and followed them, making sure that Isobel and Poa made it inside before I shut the door. I didn't know when the cat had shown up, but she didn't seem bothered that she was walking into a house full of werewolves. My parents liked cats, at least.

The house had been decorated since I'd been there last, redone in shades of cream and muted green, but the bones were familiar. My father led us into the living room while my mother went into the kitchen. Within seconds, she was back with a platter full of cake and small plates.

"The kettle is on, tea bags already in the cups," she said. "Randall, you can get the tea when the kettle goes off."

"That was quick," Isobel said.

"Well, we had a town meeting as soon as everyone remembered Rafe." She set down the tray on the coffee table, then took a seat next to my father. "We all agreed that the town would search while we waited here."

My father shook his head. "I wanted to go out and look, of course, but your mother insisted we be here if you turned up. Now I'm glad we were."

"The whole town is looking?" I asked, stunned.

"Every last one of them." My father shook his head. "Even that Wiley boy that you beat in pool after your A-level results day."

I grinned. Calvin Wiley had been furious.

It was so strange to think of the past and have memories to go along with it.

The kettle went off in the kitchen, and my father hopped up.

"What's happened in the last decade?" I asked.

"Well, not much," my mother said. "The pack is still doing well. Your father and I have been out of sorts, obviously, unable to understand why there was such a hole in our life." She gave a weary, almost bitter laugh. "Turns out we had a son."

"And you just remembered me?"

"At eight p.m. last Tuesday." She shook her head and blew out a breath. "Just sat up in bed and burst into tears."

"Oh, Mum. I'm sorry I didn't find you sooner."

"We're going to discuss that, young man. You should have come home right away. Or at least called."

Guilt struck. "But you knew I was alive."

"We did, yes. In your defense, I could feel that you were

still alive and well. I would have known if my only son were gone."

"So no harm done." I didn't look at Isobel. The last thing I needed was my mother to blame her for my absence, when it was really about me and wanting to do what was right by her, as well as getting my head on straight.

My father returned with the tea, and my mother began to serve the marmalade cake that had been my favorite since I was a child. I looked at Isobel, feeling something in my chest tighten at the sight of her with my family.

My mate.

I still hadn't told her. It wasn't something that non-shifters understood, and I didn't want to scare her off.

"So, we'll be having a party tonight," my mother said. "I've already told everyone in town that you're back, and they're coming over for a big celebration."

"When did you have time to do that?" I asked.

"I texted Barb while I was in the kitchen. She took care of the rest."

"Barb. Of course." She'd been my mother's best friend since childhood, and she could definitely get the word out to the whole town.

"I just can't wait until you move back!" she said. "Obviously, you can stay with us. But there's also a new cottage for sale just down the road. It's lovely."

I nodded, uncertain of what to say.

"Lay off him, honey," my father said. "The boy just got back."

"Fine, fine. The party starts in a few hours, anyway. I

need to get ready." She looked at me. "You're helping me. In fact, you're not leaving my sight the whole night."

It was clingy, but I couldn't blame her. I'd disappeared on her for ten years. I owed her some serious time. "I'd love to."

"Isobel, dear, do you want to rest?" my mother asked her.

"No, I can help with whatever you need."

"Excellent." My mother stood up and clapped. "Let's get ready for the party!"

CHAPTER

THIRTY

ISOBEL

RAFE'S FAMILY was absolutely wonderful. As a kid, I'd often dreamt about what the perfect family might be like. There were a dozen different iterations of the fantasy, but now I knew that I'd found the perfect one.

For one, they adored Rafe. Both of his parents clearly thought he was the most perfect person in the world, and I could tell that he adored them right back.

We spent a lovely afternoon preparing for the party that would happen down on the rocky beach later that night. My heart ached every time I saw Rafe looking perfect in this environment, because I knew he'd come back here to live. But it was a selfish ache. I was happy for him. Genuinely.

Still, sad for me.

But I did my best to ignore it as I stood at the drinks table that night, filling plastic cups of wine for the first guests. I didn't know who to mingle with, and I liked having some-thing to do with my hands.

This afternoon, I'd helped Rafe's father set up tables and chairs on the beach. Most people were mingling while standing up, though they would probably sit to eat later. A barbecue was smoking away at the edge of the beach, and the table where I stood was covered in bottles of wine and buckets filled with ice and chilled lager.

About ten meters away, Rafe stood with a group of four other men his age. From the smiles on their faces, they were clearly friends from long ago.

Rafe, with *friends*.

It was wild.

The grump I'd met a month ago was far less grumpy now, and he had friends.

I sighed, pouring the wine until something cold and wet dripped onto my hand.

"Crap." I stopped pouring and looked at the overfilling cup, then shrugged. "Might as well." I took a big sip, then another. It probably wouldn't make me feel better, but I could try.

It was just a no-win scenario because I *wanted* him to live here, to be happy with his family and friends. He was clearly meant to be among his pack. There was just such a good energy here, and they clearly all got along well. They were puzzle pieces that fit into one perfect picture. Rafe had been the missing piece, and now that he was back, I imagined that the town was complete.

I sighed.

A pretty woman a few years older than me stepped up to

the table. She wore a russet orange jumper dress and tall leather boots, her blond hair perfectly curled.

"Wine?" I asked, gesturing to the bottles on the table. "There's white and red of just about every variety you can imagine."

"Any, please." She grinned. "It's just such a fabulous day. Rafe has returned."

"It really is."

She took a plastic cup of red. "You're the witch who broke the curse?"

I nodded.

"Thank you." The genuine sincerity in her voice made me smile. "It's amazing to have him back. There's been a loss in the village, and no one quite knew why. Then we all remembered him, and it made sense."

"It was no problem, truly. I was glad to do it."

"You gave us back more than just Rafe, though. You gave us back part of ourselves. Every memory we had with him was gone. Empty." She laughed. "It was so weird. There were photo albums around town with blank spaces that didn't make sense. In fact, no one could figure out how we'd won the regional football championship in secondary school when we'd played with one less player than the other team, and none of our team could score worth a damn!"

I smiled. "He played football?"

"He was the best on the team. And as we all realized last week, he was the reason we won that mysterious game."

"Wow, that curse was awful, wasn't it?"

She nodded. "It really was. We all sensed something was

wrong but couldn't quite understand. Not until you broke the curse."

I blew out a breath. This was all so much more than I'd expected.

"Anyway, thank you. We're all just so happy to have him back. The town will be better now."

She spoke like he would be returning for good, and of course he would. His mother had talked about him buying the house down the street, and he'd agreed. He'd introduced me as a friend, which had hurt but was true. We'd never agreed that we were anything more.

After we'd finished eating the burgers his father had grilled, Rafe turned to me. "Do you mind if I go for a run with some of my mates from school?"

"Go for it," I said.

He smiled and stood, then walked over to join them at the edge of the beach. A swirl of dark blue magic obscured him from my vision. When it faded, a massive black wolf stood where he'd been.

I'd never seen him in wolf form before, and he was beautiful—strong and powerful, with the same brilliant green eyes. His friends shifted in swirls of their own magic, and then the group ran off toward the woods that were further inland.

I sipped my wine and watched them go.

I DIDN'T TELL Rafe when I left the next morning. We'd slept in his childhood room, both of us too exhausted to do anything more than collapse into each other's arms and go to sleep.

When we'd woken, the house already smelled of cinnamon buns and coffee. Rafe stared at the ceiling, his arm over his eyes. "I'd forgot that smell."

"It's amazing," I said, inhaling deeply. "Forgetting that might be the greatest tragedy in this whole situation."

He laughed and sat upright. "Come on. Big day ahead of us."

"Yeah?" I rose.

"Yes. My parents will boss us around all day as we help with the house. I guarantee it."

He turned out to be right. After a delicious breakfast of cinnamon rolls, coffee, and fresh orange juice, we were put to work. Rafe went off to help his father with the garden, and I stayed in with his mother.

She stood at the counter, staring out the kitchen window at her husband and son. I joined her, watching them repair the wooden fence at the back of the garden.

"Randall taught him to use those tools," she said. "And now he builds boats. Incredible, isn't it?"

"It is."

"Have you seen them? The boats, I mean."

"Yes, and they're gorgeous."

She chuckled. "I'm not surprised. I offered him the day off to lounge around here, but he insisted on helping. Said he had a decade of chores to make up for."

"That sounds like Rafe." I smiled.

His mother turned to me, her expression sincere. "Thank you again. We'll never be able to repay you."

I shook my head. "There's nothing to repay. I would have done it, no matter what."

"Well, we're just so grateful you brought him back to us."

Suddenly, I couldn't bear it anymore. It was just too painful. Rafe was going to leave, just like my parents had. Just like Tommy had, although he'd done it in a very different way. And even though Rafe was leaving me for something much more real and wholesome—and I genuinely wanted him to be happy—it still hurt like hell.

I needed to leave first.

My phone buzzed in my pocket, and I looked down to read the text. It was just Emma, checking in to see how we were doing. But an idea formed.

I made my face crease, and it wasn't necessary to fake disappointment. That was right under the surface. "Oh, no. I need to get back to Charming Cove." I'd see Rafe when he came back to pack up his things, and it would be good for him to have this time alone with his family. Mostly, I just needed some time to be sad in private. I couldn't ruin this special time with my selfish moping. "There's a work thing I need to deal with. Will you please tell Rafe I'll see him when he comes back to pack up the boathouse?"

"Sure, darling. Can I give you a ride to the train station?"

"That would be wonderful, thank you."

"Do you want to say goodbye to Rafe?" She gestured out the window.

"No, they look busy. And anyway, I don't want to miss

the next train." I scrolled through the ticket website on my phone. "It looks like it leaves soon."

"Of course, let's get going."

It took me only five minutes to grab my things out of the room upstairs, and I was in Kay's car a moment later. Within fifteen minutes, I was on the next train out of town. I spent the ride back in a daze, so out of it that it was a lucky thing I managed to make my connections.

I love him.

There was no other explanation for how I felt. It was like an asteroid had just hit my life. This was *way* worse than when Tommy had cheated on me.

Emma picked me up at the train station, her face creased in concern as I climbed into her car.

"Okay, why am I picking you up here?" she asked. "I know for a fact you left town with Rafe in his car, and you should be coming back the same way."

I tilted my head against the seat and closed my eyes. "His family is wonderful. The nicest people I've ever met."

"That's a good thing!"

"He's moving home. He even talked about which house to buy with his mother."

"Oh."

"Exactly."

"I'm sorry." She squeezed my thigh. "Let's get you home and open a bottle of wine, shall we?"

"Yeah." It was hard to muster any enthusiasm, but I loved her for trying.

"Do you want to come back to my place, maybe? I can get

Alaric to go stay with his grandmother so we can have a girls' night." Alaric was her fiancé...and the Duke of Blackthorn.

"No, I want to see my place. It's my home. Half the reason I'm staying." I reached for her hand and squeezed. "Besides you and our friends and the coven, of course. I've got a life here." I'd never even dreamed of something like what I'd had with Rafe—it was too good to be true and too good to last.

"It's going to be amazing," Emma said. "Let's go to yours and have a girls' night there. I've got a boot full of goodies we need to eat *and* drink. I picked them up, just in case."

"You're the best."

She grinned and pulled away from the train station, heading toward Charming Cove.

We pulled up to Lavender House thirty minutes later, and I frowned. Lights blazed throughout the house, their golden glow lighting up the night. "I don't think the lights were on when I left. It was a bright afternoon."

"They weren't," Emma said. "We made sure of it when we left."

"Could the solicitor be here early?" Even as I said it, I knew it absolutely wasn't true. He was the sort of man to make an appointment and stick to it. "Something's wrong."

"Come on." Emma got out of the car, her face set in a scowl.

I followed, stalking toward the house. I didn't know what was going on, but I had a bad feeling. Poa joined us near the door, worry on her face.

Something bad is in there. She stuck close to my side, a little bodyguard.

When I opened the front door, I gasped. Paint was splattered all over the gleaming wooden floor, and the beautiful side table was smashed. The flowers that my friends had brought me were scattered on the ground among shards of sparkling glass.

I ran into the next room, finding a scene of similar damage. The window overlooking the side garden was smashed, and the fireplace mantel had been torn away from the wall. The couch was torn up, and great gouges marred the freshly painted walls.

I raced to the secret spot in the wall where the enchanted crystal was hidden. If the intruder had taken it or destroyed it...

The idea of the house losing its personality—its *life* —made me cold with fear.

Thankfully, I found it untouched, the wall not even marred. But the rest of the ground floor was ruined, every room the victim of horrible destruction. I didn't even realize I was crying until Emma grabbed my arm and whispered. "Shh. Do you hear something?"

I gulped back a sob and listened. A crashing noise sounded from upstairs, something obviously breaking.

Rage shot through me, hot and fierce. I scrubbed the tears away and raced up the stairs, jumping over pieces of broken banister. When I reached the main bedroom and saw Tommy with a baseball bat, his hands glowing with destructive magic, I shrieked. "You bastard!"

He turned to me, a glare twisting his features. "Finally back, are you?"

Once upon a time, I might have been scared of him. I never had been before because he'd never been violent. But

I'd been powerless before I'd embraced my magic. It would have been smart to be scared in this kind of circumstance.

But I wasn't.

I had my power. I had Emma. And Poa.

He had a silly little baseball bat and some weak magic, most of which he'd probably spent to keep my beautiful house from evicting him while he'd destroyed it with a bat.

I looked around at the destruction, shocked. "What is *wrong* with you?"

"Wrong with *me*?" He frowned as if I were an idiot. "You left. You wouldn't even *speak* to me."

"Of course I wouldn't." Anger bubbled within me. "You cheated on me."

"But you didn't give me a chance to explain."

"Explain?" I laughed. "Explain *what*?"

"That I care about you. That she didn't mean anything."

I frowned. "Didn't mean anything? You'd never taken me on a date that nice."

"Because you didn't care about those things."

Anger bubbled. "Of course I did! Any woman would want her boyfriend to treat her like that! It's just that you never did, and I was too young and stupid to know that I deserved better than being the housemaid you sometimes got to have sex with."

"Come on, we had a good time." He dropped the bat, and his hands stopped glowing with magic as he gestured widely. "We were happy. I don't understand."

"No, Tommy. *You* were happy. And now you're here, making my life miserable again." I looked around. "Why? You've never been violent before."

He scratched his head as he looked around, wincing. Suddenly, he looked more like the Tommy I remembered. Boring. Bland. Then his face hardened. "You just left me without explanation. And then you blocked me. *Blocked* me. It made me angry."

"Yeah, I blocked you for being a creep who wouldn't stop bothering me. And now you've stalked me here and ruined my house."

"Exactly. You'll have to come home now."

I laughed, and it sounded slightly insane. "So you figured out the contents of my grandmother's will, huh? How did you do that?"

He bristled. "I have friends."

"Of course. Friends with magic who helped you when you couldn't do it yourself. And I presume these friends helped you find me, even though my coven hid me and Lavender House from you?"

"Yes, as a matter of fact." He frowned. "Your coven? I thought you didn't like to use your magic."

"No, Tommy. *You* didn't want me to use my magic because you're a weak sorcerer who can hardly light a match. You didn't want me to use my magic because it made you feel worse about yourself." Fates, it felt good to say these things. "I blame myself for falling for your manipulation, but no more. I'm free of you, and my life is freaking amazing."

He looked around at the room he'd destroyed. "Doesn't look that amazing anymore."

I shrieked with rage. I was so done with that bastard. My soul was alight with righteous indignation as I called upon my magic, remembered a curse that Catrina had taught me.

She'd taught me several, in fact, and they were all perfect for Tommy.

First, I gave him a tail.

The magic whooshed from my fingertips as I recited the words, and he yelped as a great furry tail sprouted from his backside. I didn't even know what animal it was from—I'd just wanted to make it too big to hide in his trousers, and I'd succeeded.

"That's nothing," I said, grinning widely. "You're about to quack like a duck every time you try to be a jerk—that includes lying *and* manipulating." Catrina had been particularly fond of this curse because it had been her final salvo against the bully she hated. Her mother hadn't been able to complain about it, either.

I'd laughed so hard at her story, then made her teach me when she'd come over with her mother to see the house. I recited the words now, hurling my magic at Tommy. Glee shot through me as he started to quack. The noise was jarring and so obviously coming from his mouth that a delighted laugh escaped me.

I looked over at Emma. "What do you think?"

"Is he lying or just practicing his quacking?"

"I don't know, and I'm not sure I care." I turned back to him. "Tommy? Can you speak like a regular person?"

"I can." He glared at me. "Now undo this spell."

"No." I grinned and crossed my arms. "Tell me you're not afraid of cats." From the way he'd always acted around Poa whenever he saw her, I'd suspected he was. But I'd never got him to fess up."

"I'm—" He quacked, and it was the loudest, most ridiculous sound I'd ever heard. Even louder than before. I howled with laughter.

Poa hissed at him, back arched, and he eyed her wildly as he shouted, "You're a miserable bitch, Isobel, you know that?"

I grinned. "No, I'm a *happy* bitch. Happy and powerful."

"You're going to be alone forever," he snapped.

The words stung, but only because they made me think of Rafe. I decided to turn that anger into action. I looked at Emma. "Can I get a little help, please?"

"Anything." She said it with a vehemence that made me smile, and walked toward me.

I held out my hand for hers. "We're going to make the quacking spell permanent."

"Oh, I like it."

Tommy looked between the two of us, terror on his face. He might be a failed sorcerer, but he knew as well as I did that making a spell permanent required a lot of magic. I couldn't do it on my own—almost no witch could—but with Emma's help...

We began to chant the spell for permanency, our voices rising as wind whipped around us. Broken pieces of wood flew through the air, the remnants of the beautiful furniture that Vivienne had given me.

Tommy screamed and darted for the door, but we turned to follow him, chanting as we walked. I felt powerful—like, *really* powerful. And it felt good.

He quacked as he ran down the stairs, the spell starting to take hold. Poa followed him, tail held high. By the time he made it to the ground floor, he was almost flying, he was running so fast. From the top of the stairs, we could see all the way to the front door. On the way out, the house slapped him on the butt with a floorboard.

Good. He deserved it.

Exhaustion pulled at me as we finished the spell. The magic followed him out the door, and I could hear his quacks as he ran away. Poa stopped chasing him, clearly deciding he wasn't worth the trouble.

When I was finally out of power, I sat down heavily on the stairs.

"Well, I'm beat." Emma leaned her shoulder against mine.

"Me, too, but thanks."

She grinned. "It was a good one. You can't get in trouble if you make a liar stop lying by embarrassing him." She laughed. "Can you imagine him going to the police and saying he's mad because his ex-girlfriend cursed him to quack if he lied?"

I grinned. It was the reason Catrina had chosen the spell for her nemesis, and it made it perfect for my purposes as well. He'd be able to get another witch to spell the tail away pretty easily and cheaply, but the quacking was an entirely different matter.

But the effort required to create a spell like that had drained me. I was unsteady as I looked around at the destruction. Tears pricked my eyes when Poa started to rub against my leg. "The solicitor comes tomorrow."

"Surely he'll give you an extension," she said. "If you tell him how this all happened."

"No extensions. He made that clear." A hiccupy little sob escaped me. "And I'm so tired. I can't even try to clean up."

"After the spell we just did, of course you're tired. We'll be lucky to get down the stairs. But what you need is a good night's sleep. It'll look better tomorrow."

A bitter laugh escaped me as I looked around. There was no way in hell this could look better tomorrow. Lavender House was destroyed.

CHAPTER
THIRTY-ONE

ISOBEL

I woke to the sound of shouting, my head pounding like a toddler had crawled in there with a mallet. I blinked up at the ceiling, realizing that I was in my bed in the boathouse.

Memories of last night returned. I'd used so much power that I was essentially hungover, and it *sucked*. Emma had helped me to bed, then Alaric had come to pick her up. She'd been too tired to drive home after joining her magic with mine.

But what was all that shouting about?

The solicitor.

Surely it wasn't him, but he was supposed to arrive today —just in time to see my dreams go up in flames. Or down in pieces, considering the fact that Tommy had shattered everything in the house, including but not limited to the furniture and many structural elements.

Even the idea that he was now quacking his way back to London couldn't make me feel better. We'd created such a beautiful place, and now it was gone.

My heart ached for the house, too. It must be so confused. I'd been so exhausted and hurt last night that I'd made sure the crystal was still there, but I hadn't stopped to think about how the house must be feeling.

I needed to go check on it. Make sure it was okay. A bitter little laugh escaped me. It wouldn't be okay. I just prayed it wasn't traumatized. Tommy must have used all his miserable strength to create that destruction before the house could stop him.

Aching, I dragged myself out of bed and took two paracetamol, then dragged on some clothes and headed downstairs. I wanted a coffee, but I needed to go apologize to the house for not taking better care of it.

As I stepped outside into the early-morning light, I realized that the shouting I'd heard was coming from Lavender House. I stared up the hill, shock pinning me in place.

There were people *everywhere*. I could see them behind every window, moving around the rooms like busy bees. A line of folks carried rubbish out of the house and fresh supplies in.

I could barely breathe.

They were fixing Lavender House.

As far as I could tell, it was the entire town. And then I saw Rafe's mother. And father. And that beautiful blond woman from the barbecue. His entire pack was here.

My head spun. They'd all come to help.

How could this be happening?

"It's amazing," a woman said from my left.

I turned to see Judith, who looked at the house, tears in her eyes.

"Judith."

"You might as well call me Gran, if you don't mind."

I blinked at her, so confused and shocked and over-whelmed that I could barely string two thoughts together. "Gran?"

She nodded, then turned to me. Magic shimmered in front of her face, and the glamour fell away. In front of me stood my gran, about twenty years older than when I'd seen her last, but it was definitely her.

"I think I need to sit down."

"You probably do." She went to a bench by the wall of the boathouse and sat, then patted the place next to her. "I think this is a good spot. You can see your friends helping you. The house is fine, by the way. It likes all these people and knows they're here to help."

I couldn't stop looking between her and the house as I walked toward her.

Gran is here. The town is fixing Lavender House. Rafe is here.

The words repeated themselves as a mantra inside my head, but I still couldn't understand.

"Explain. Please." The words came out as a croak.

"I'm not dead, for one."

"I can see that." And I was happy about it. Joyfully so. But I was also really confused.

"The terms of the will still stand, though. If you can fix up the house, it's yours. And it looks like you're going to manage it." She grinned. "I've already been inside, and they're almost finished. It's incredible what people can do when they come together."

I gave a little sob, unable to help myself. She reached a hand toward mine, then pulled back, clearly thinking better of it.

I reached out and grabbed her hand, squeezing tightly.

She smiled. "I wasn't sure if you'd want to." She gave an awkward laugh. "Hold hands, at least. I haven't been the best grandmother."

"That's past us now," I said. "The first thing I thought when I heard you'd died was that I wished I'd tried harder to know you. I still have no idea what's going on, but that stays the same."

"Oh, dear." Her eyes filled with tears. "I don't deserve you."

"I'm not worried about that. But what the heck *is* going on? I really need to start understanding things, and fast."

"Well, it's all a bit convoluted, but I think my plan might have worked out quite nicely." She smiled at me.

"Spit it out already, Gran."

She nodded. "You know I wasn't always the best grand-mother. Quite distant, I know. I was obsessed with my own life—always trying to improve my magic, you see. I've never been much of a witch, but I wanted to be. And that made me too self-centered."

Story of my life. But unlike Tommy, she seemed to be on a different track. "It sounds like you've had some real reve-lations."

She laughed. "Age will do that," she said, and sighed. "About five years ago, I realized that I wouldn't live forever."

She tapped the wrinkles at the sides of her eyes. "It was when these started appearing, you see. A reminder every day in the mirror that I was mortal."

I supposed it made sense.

"Anyway, I did the thing that many people do when they age. They think about their life and wonder if they did it right. For me, the immediate answer was no. First, I was distant with your mother. You've seen how she turned out, though I have a feeling that, too, might change as she ages. But you were never as cold and distant as we were."

"No, I wasted my life on a miserable man instead."

"Yes, he was awful. When I started checking up on you about a year ago and saw how terrible he was, I knew I needed to act. Then that lovely young man enquired about the boathouse, and the idea came to me."

"You mean Rafe?"

"Yes, Rafe. I've kept tabs on Charming Cove since I still own Lavender House, even though I was never able to fix it up myself. That's always bothered me, but that's life. Then your uncle sold the boathouse to that handsome werewolf a year ago, and as soon as I saw him, I knew he was perfect for you."

"I thought you owned the boathouse."

"No, dear. I just told the solicitor to lie to you."

I felt my jaw slacken. "Malcolm *lied*?"

"I know he doesn't seem like the type. But when I described your situation and my plan, he agreed it was a worthy cause."

"What *was* your plan?"

"Isn't it obvious? I knew you had the power to fix up

Lavender House in a way I never could. So I set you and the boatbuilder up and forced you to spend time together, fixing up the house under a deadline."

Oh, that *was* clever. "But how could you possibly have known he would help me?"

"Psh, of course I could tell. I'm not great at magic, but I can read people. And I'm quite good at plotting and scheming." She gave a pleased smile. "Though this all worked out much better than I'd hoped." She gestured to Lavender House, which was still bustling with activity. "The whole town has come out to help you! Why, this could make an excellent TV movie. Even the big screen!"

I laughed. "So, what next?"

"You live in Lavender House, happily ever after. The money is yours, too. I still have a bit, enough to keep me in the cottage next door, if you don't mind your gran being your neighbor."

"I can't imagine anything better." I wrapped my arms around her and hugged her. "Thank you so much. You gave me a whole new life."

"No, darling. *You* built a new life. I just gave you some building blocks to get started. What you did with them is more than I could have ever imagined. You're an incredible witch and an incredible woman."

My eyes pricked with tears, and I smiled. "Thank you."

"No, thank you. I love you, Isobel."

"I love you, too, Gran." I sighed as I looked back up at the house, searching for Rafe. "Although I'm not sure I'll get the happily ever after with the boat builder. Do you think Uncle

Albert might want to move into the boathouse instead? We can have weird family game nights."

She laughed. "He would *never*." She gestured up the hill. "As for the boat builder, I wouldn't be so sure. Here he comes."

My heart stuttered as I spotted him. He looked perfect, of course, with his tool belt around his waist and his close-fitting jumper pushed up to his elbows.

"Go on, now." My grandmother gave me a little shove.

I got to my feet and went to him, unable to slow my racing heart. I stopped in front of him, gesturing to the construction chaos behind him, and asked, "How?"

"Emma. She called to tell me what happened."

"She must have called everyone else in town, too."

"I think that was Aria, but yes." He smiled as he looked back at the scene. "I do think this is everyone in Charming Cove."

I blew out a breath. "Incredible."

He moved to stand by my side, gripping my hand. "I'm going to miss the boathouse." He looked down at me. "That is, if you'll have me."

I blinked up at him. "What?"

"I'm inviting myself to move in."

My jaw slackened. "You're not."

"Ouch." He winced. "Not moving in?"

"Not staying in Charming Cove."

"I most definitely am." He frowned. "Why would you think otherwise?"

"Because you've found your pack. You told your mother you would buy that house."

"I believe I just grunted when she mentioned that."

"Um." I couldn't think of what to say. "Are you serious?"

"Yes. I love my family. I'll visit them often. But not every werewolf stays with their pack. Most do, but not everyone."

I gave an incredulous laugh. "So you're saying you want to stay with me."

"I love you, Isabel." The corner of his mouth quirked up. "I want to stay with you always."

The air rushed out of me. I couldn't believe what I was hearing.

"And, not to freak you out, but you're my mate."

"Your mate?"

"The one fate has decreed is perfect for me, yes. I can feel it. And I agree with fate. You're perfect."

This could not be my life. I was going to wake up from this incredible dream and find myself...somewhere else. Somewhere definitely not as good.

"It would be really great if you would say something." He smiled. "I'm getting a bit worried."

"I love you, too!" I threw my arms around his neck and kissed him. "I love you, too."

He spun me in a circle, and I laughed, so joyful that I couldn't hold it in. The sun was shining, and the sea breeze blew my hair back from my face. When he finally put me down, I grinned up at him. "I can't believe this is happening."

"Believe it, because there's no going back."

"Perfect." I looked around for my friends. I needed to thank them. "Do you know if Emma's here?"

"I haven't seen her, but Aria's over there." He pointed to

the east side of the house, where Aria was replanting some bushes that had been pulled up.

"Come on, let's go talk to her." Now that he'd said he was staying, I didn't want to let him out of my sight.

I hurried up to Aria, never once letting go of Rafe's hand. "Aria!" I called when I neared her.

She hopped up, a big smile on her face. "Do you love it?"

"Love it?" I threw my arms around her. "It's amazing. I haven't even seen the inside, but I know it's amazing. Thank you so much."

"Thank Emma. She's the one who called everyone."

"Where is she?"

"Probably just waking up, if you've just woken. She was pretty knackered, too."

"Of course." We'd both drained our magic. I looked around at all the people, some of whom were still wearing pajama bottoms. "When did you get here? It's still early in the morning."

"I know." She grinned. "Most of us arrived shortly after midnight."

"*Midnight*? You did all this in the dark? While I *slept*?"

"Well, that bastard wasn't able to ruin your electricity, at least. And it took a little while to convince the house to let us in, but eventually, it agreed. Then the shifters showed up around three."

"It took us a while to make the drive," Rafe said.

"Everyone worked overnight," Aria said.

"You were on a deadline." Aria pulled her phone out of her pocket to look at the time. "When does the solicitor arrive?"

"I'm not sure he's going to." I looked back down the hill at my grandmother, who still sat on the bench, a cup of tea now in her hand as she watched the activity. "Judith, my neighbor, is a lot more than she let on. She's my gran, and she says the house is mine."

"Um." Aria's brows rose. "You'll have to tell me all of this. ASAP."

"I will, as soon as I've seen the house."

"Then let's go see it! I think everyone is almost done." She grinned and pointed to the driveway. "And Emma just arrived."

I turned to see a removal van. Emma sat in the passenger seat, and Vivienne, of all people, sat behind the wheel.

"This cannot be real." I watched as Vivienne hopped down from the cab, landing perfectly on her pale pink kitten heels. She straightened the coat of her perfectly tailored pink wool suit, then walked toward the house, clearly on a mission.

"It's real," Aria said. "And the dowager duchess just showed up with a van full of furniture for you."

"Isobel!" Emma waved wildly, a huge grin on her face. "Come see what we've brought you! Vivienne decided she needed to redecorate a few more rooms!"

I laughed and hurried toward her, looking back to make sure that Rafe stuck with me. He did, and I reached for his hand, delighted when he squeezed mine tightly.

We stopped in front of Emma. Vivienne had already disappeared inside the house, and I was pretty sure I'd seen a tape measure gripped in her perfectly manicured hand.

I threw my arms around Emma. "This is incredible. Thank you."

She pulled back and looked at Rafe. "I don't think we would have finished in time without the wolves."

"Well, however it happened, I'm just so grateful." I pulled her in for a hug.

"Let's go check out the house," she said. "I'm dying to see what they've done. I wish I could have been here, but I was out cold."

"Same," I said, grinning at the memory of the magic we'd used together to set Tommy straight.

"Let's go." She turned and headed into the house.

I gripped Rafe's hand and smiled up at him. He leaned down and kissed me, then whispered, "Ready to see your future?"

"So ready." I beamed up at him, then followed Emma into the house.

It was exactly as it had been before, but better. In every repaired wall and timber, I could see the love of everyone who had worked on it, and it made my heart swell.

As for the house, it was happy. Deliriously so. I could feel it in my soul.

~~~

If you'd like a sneak peek into Rafe and Isobel's future, Click here to sign up to my newsletter to get a bonus short story set on Christmas morning.

ACKNOWLEDGMENTS

Thank you, Ben, for everything. There would be no books without you.

Thank you to Jena O'Connor and Ash Fitzsimmons for your excellent editing. The book is immensely better because of you!

ABOUT LINSEY

Before becoming a writer, Linsey Hall was a nautical archaeologist who studied shipwrecks from Hawaii and the Yukon to the UK and the Mediterranean. She credits fantasy and historical romances with her love of history and her career as an archaeologist. After a decade of tromping around the globe in search of old bits of stuff that people left lying about, she settled down and started penning her own romance novels. Her Dragon's Gift series draws upon her love of history and the paranormal elements that she can't help but include.

®

BONNIE DOON PRESS

Linsey@LinseyHall.com

Printed in the USA
CPSIA information can be obtained
at www.ICGtesting.com
LVHW082009021123
762905LV00003B/263

9 781648 820359